THE INVENTORY

THE INVENTORY

A NOVEL

GILA LUSTIGER

TRANSLATED FROM THE GERMAN
BY REBECCA MORRISON

ARCADE PUBLISHING • NEW YORK

FIRST ENGLISH-LANGUAGE EDITION

Originally published in Germany under the title *Die Bestandsaufnahme* in 1995 by
Aufbau-Verlag GmbH, Berlin

Library of Congress Cataloging-in-Publication Data

Lustiger, Gila, 1963–
  [Bestandsaufnahme. English]
  The inventory : a novel / by Gila Lustiger ; translated from the German by
  Rebecca Morrison.
            p. cm.
  ISBN 1-55970-549-3
  I. Morrison, Rebecca. II. Title.

  PT2672.U823 B4713 2001
  833'.92—dc21   00–58274

Published in the United States by Arcade Publishing, Inc., New York
Distributed by Time Warner Trade Publishing

Visit our Web site at www.arcadepub.com
EB
10 9 8 7 6 5 4 3 2 1
Designed by API

PRINTED IN THE UNITED STATES OF AMERICA

All events described are based on historical fact. Many characters are freely invented, but their fate resembles that of thousands of others. Biographical details of some of the protagonists correspond to reality, while individual sequences of events, thoughts, and motives are fictitious.

—G. L.

"Truth is created in the same way as is the lie."

—*Odysseas Elytis*

Contents

Where there is no love,
utter not the word.

Johannes Bobrowski

THE INVENTORY

A Romantic Start in Eight Scenes

(A Rose-Shaped Brooch)

DORA WELLNER WAS A HEADSTRONG WOMAN. Despite the Slavic influence in her family tree, she had not relinquished a shred of her infamous Galician stubbornness. One morning, in spite of her mother's protestations, she took from the attic the suitcase her father had bought some twenty years before when he had been planning to emigrate from Krakow to America, a trip he ultimately didn't make because of a pair of chestnut braids belonging to the daughter of a distant relative.

Dora took the mutinous suitcase, shook off the dust, and filled it with the clothes she had freshly washed and neatly folded on her bed. She carried the bag two flights down — dragged and heaved it, rather, to the accompaniment of quiet curses — and around noon stood on the edge of the sidewalk, second-class train ticket in hand. There she was, waiting for the cab and looking around at her hometown.

To the right were the orchard and the church, to the left the terraced houses with red-tiled roofs, and far back, at the end of the street, the cemetery, the path through the meadows, and the forest.

The blacksmith was still hammering away. He had taken off his shirt and opened the door wide. Three men came from the fishmarket and piled empty crates onto a van parked in front of her home. A cloud floated by the church tower. The blacksmith's wife called her husband in. The hands of the church clock pressed relentlessly forward toward one o'clock. Dora sighed. At least she had her mother's blessing, if not her father's. While her family was back there sitting at the kitchen table, Dora was traveling where her happiness beckoned, as it beckoned to so many young people — to Berlin.

Scene two: Dora sat next to a woman who was knitting away at something red and stared out of the window. She had left the solitary farmhouse and the brick factory behind her a good hour earlier. The countryside was the same; only the place names sounded unfamiliar. The conductor came through and nodded cheerfully at the young woman. Next stop Stettin.

Dora opened her lunch bag. The promises made at home could not be kept of course. What on earth was she supposed to do with a childless widow, a cousin of her mother's, when she had only just broken free from home? She laid her sandwich aside and took her purse out of the suitcase. Not enough for a hotel, but perhaps sufficient for the small family-run pension near the Ku'Damm, with geraniums at the windows — she had seen the postcard, advertising the pension, on her piano teacher's kitchen table. Dora nodded and contentedly finished off her sandwich. Then in spite of her excitement, she fell asleep, missed both the River Oder and the River Spree, and arrived at last after a wearisome day of travel.

Not a soul knew where she had gone. Her mother's cousin did not know, although she definitely had a notion, which she kept to herself. She remembered a mustachioed man, with whom she had almost eloped to Leipzig thirty years before, because, well, she had not always been a woman of virtue. Would she now have to give up on the idea of the silver fox-fur stole, she wondered? She had wanted to buy it with the first month's rent, and it was ready and waiting for her in the back room of the furrier's. As soon as Dora's mother had announced her daughter's impending arrival and they had sorted out the finances, she had had it put aside for her.

Nor did the mother know where her daughter was. Terrified, she checked the Friday paper and focused on the wrongdoings of the thieves and swindlers, who were up to their usual nasty tricks, particularly in the vicinity of train stations.

The father did not know. He was busy amassing a stockpile of reproaches that he intended to fire at his wife, and therefore had no time to dwell on his daughter.

Dora's sister did not know either, but she dreamed of following suit a few years later. She imagined herself in a pretty frock, sitting in a café, gorging herself on cakes and cream. She was the closest to the truth.

And all the while, Dora was sitting on the edge of her bed, looking by the light of a lamp hanging from the ceiling at a hat, complete with a feather, and a shawl that she had found at rock-bottom prices. A week later, by the light of a different lamp, she was staring at a black dress and starched apron. She had learned her first life lesson: if a person with no income declines to repress his or her tendencies, believing that earning money will progress at the same pace as his or her needs, that person is living an illusion. In short, she was broke. And when she realized that a penniless person does not go far, Dora, now without means but perfectly healthy, was hired by Helene Hirsch as a full-time maid and joined the working masses.

The days went by. Dora stood with her arms on the windowsill of the kitchen window, and that takes us up to scene three.

So this, then, was Berlin she was looking at: the No. 68 streetcar; the advertisement on the wall across the way for the original Luta dolls and baby carriages, impossible to break and easy to clean; the flowery curtains of the third floor were part of it, as were the words of wisdom in the magazines on the coffee table, which explained to Dora how one offers one's ungloved hand upon meeting and upon taking one's leave, and how a lady of breeding even takes her glove off in the street and, furthermore, while paying a hospital visit. Dora read this avidly and stored the information away for later — after all, one could never tell what fate might have in store.

Such tidbits weren't particularly helpful for the here and now, however. For the here and now it would have been more useful to learn how to get rid of butter or margarine stains on the sofa, or to know whether the painting in the drawing room could be dusted.

Dora had declared war on all dust, as well as water stains on the floor. Their life span had always been fleeting in Mrs. Hirsch's home: this was one of the most difficult trials of the cleaning lady, and the one that often led to her downfall.

But why did she do it? Why did she work so hard? Because she had to? Because she had no choice?

Because, secretly, she already had regrets. She carried out every imaginable domestic task to prevent her from having any time to mull things over. For she did not want to face up to what she was ashamed of: she knew not a soul in Berlin; the capital city she had dreamed of so long did not appeal to her at all; she still did not have a boyfriend, and could not have one, since, distressed by the nonexistence of this boyfriend, she never left the house.

She neither slept well nor ate well, and was, in a word, depressed. For a long time she had felt the pangs of despair, which her little game of forgivable self-delusion could not dispel.

She longed to be home. There she had never swept a floor, let alone scrubbed one. But she could not simply go back.

Berlin, you beautiful city. You beautiful city, Berlin. Dora felt sorry for herself. Well, she had gotten what she had asked for. But what a sad, miserable lot for a girl, brimming with impatient youth, and with voluptuous curves.

Reinhard was in a good mood, nestled between two cobalt blue cushions that had made their way all the way over from China to his Aunt Helene's drawing room with the briefest of stopovers in the O.B. department store. His eyes flitted back and forth from the racing results to the maid, who was pouring the afternoon tea.

And this is what he saw (scene four): a powerful back, a curvaceous bust, legs a little on the short side, light brown hair tied back in a ponytail, a suppressed laugh, and delicate fingers which impishly caressed his smooth-shaven cheeks while Mrs. Hirsch was bent over the sugar bowl.

Contrary to all expectations, Dora had delivered herself into Reinhard's hands, and had thus preempted his desires before he himself was even aware of them. Certainly Reinhard was sometimes bemused by his great success, but not for long. He was not a man given to pondering, not one of those painstaking types who immerse themselves in deep reflection; he merely accepted gratefully such fortunate turns of fate without digging for their meaning.

Thus he found himself in an agreeable, relaxing situation. Relaxing for both sides, naturally, thought Reinhard, believing that if he felt at ease surely everyone else did too.

If only his sluggish nature had allowed him a trifle more awareness, he would surely have realized that while he was sipping sweet mocha with Uncle Leo and Aunt Helene, Dora was washing up. That while he was reading the newspaper in the living room, she was folding the laundry. That while his hand hovered languidly over the cookie jar, she was scrubbing the floor. That while he was listening for the soft creaking of the door leading to the upstairs quarters, a quiet sound but one fraught with meaning for him — it was customary for maids to live in the room off the kitchen, but her womanly figure and the complacent smile lighting the face of the master of the house had necessitated other arrangements — she was setting the table for breakfast. Nor were her chores at an end there because, once in her room, she still had to wash, comb her hair, and beautify herself for him. And had he only admitted to himself that Dora was endangering her position through this liaison — that far from being a relationship of comfort, her nerves were frayed and she was horribly tense, in a state of hypersensitivity — the fact is, he would not have acted any differently.

He was experienced, intelligent too, but he simply was not interested in opening his eyes. His lethargic contentment smothered any scruples.

Scene five: Already during their third nocturnal coupling, as he lay next to a sleeping Dora, tracing the sweeping curves of her back with his eyes, Reinhard couldn't help thinking of the end. It was not that he was wearied by it all, he simply had a nagging doubt. However he looked at it, staying with her would mean renouncing other things. It also irritated him that he could do whatever he wanted with her. Did he not deserve something better than a girl he could twist around his little finger whenever he chose?

She certainly had her uses — Reinhard made the most of them — but the more she gave him the less he appreciated her. The same old story.

If demand had risen momentarily, supply remaining constant or declining a tad — had, for example, a rival entered the scene — Reinhard's desire would doubtless have quickened. But Dora, who had not the slightest idea about the interdependency of commodities, who had never heard of production control, who could not hope to realize that some commodities, in spite of their high practical value, have low exchange value . . . well, Dora had no time for games.

We cannot deny that Reinhard tried his hardest. He relished the good things in life, and was not ungrateful. And certainly he wanted to be seen in a favorable light. But if that meant, for example, giving up a chess evening at the neighbor's, not to mention several other pleasant pastimes, he would have been very sorry indeed.

What good are pangs of conscience in such a case? It was all decided. The relationship had to be brought to a halt, quickly and painlessly. Reinhard went into town and found a brooch in the shape of a rose, set with splinters of garnet. That should do the trick, he thought. A pretty farewell present that he would pop into Dora's white apron when she was not looking — and cheap to boot.

He can drop dead, thought Dora, reading Reinhard's note that evening. He had attached it to the brooch, and in it he explained to Dora the profound symbolism of the gift. In simple terms — the letter being addressed to a maid, after all — he pointed out that this brooch was not only beautiful and precious, but also a symbol of attachment, as it encapsulated, as everyone knew, something that in this case could only be a memory of evenings spent together, which he would look back on for the rest of his life.

He can drop dead, thought Dora, after reading the lines, complete with melancholic kisses. She undressed, washed, got dressed again, and rang the doorbell of the neighbor on the first floor. He opened the door, smiled at the furious young woman, and, although he had intended to go out, invited her into his bachelor's pad for a nightcap. Scene six: no explanation required.

When Reinhard was back home, busy unpacking his bag, he came across the brooch. Bemused, he turned it around in his hand — it was beyond him. Honestly, what more could one expect of him? Oh, well, he thought. Then he placed the brooch on the bathroom shelf as a souvenir.

And so it came about that every morning when Reinhard reached for his razor blade, his face smothered with lather, he was reminded of the obliging maid. And soon something was ignited in him: if not love, at least wistfulness.

In scene seven, we see Reinhard in a train. He is standing in the corridor smoking a little comforter, ten pfennigs apiece. He is on his way to Berlin. His suitcase is on the overhead shelf. Thoughts whiz through his mind. Briefly, he reflects upon freedom, bowling, beer, family tree, dowry, and culture. And to top it all off, she was a maid. Love is surely no ground for marriage.

Reinhard got out the brooch and held it in his hands, smiling. There he stood, a smiling fool. And the train chugged leisurely onward through Altmark.

In spite of Reinhard's flattering speech, Dora did not let the young man in through her door. She also indignantly refused the brooch that he had brought to make up. From his former sweetheart's coarse behavior Reinhard deduced that he had been replaced — Dora did nothing to contradict him. Frenzied, he demanded a rendezvous, which was not granted, and had to go off to bed having achieved nothing.

Was it the first-floor neighbor, or some other man? Another day went by. Love was no ground for marriage. Had Dora become an obsession for him? He shook his head. He could fight his desire for her. After all, he had managed to give up smoking, apart from the occasional comforter, 10 pfennigs apiece. But not right now, because he did not know whether it was the neighbor on the first floor or some other man.

Scene eight: to clear up this question once and for all, he climbed up to the top floor. It was dusk. Outside, the street lamps were going on. Next door someone was listening to music, and there was the sound of flushing. A neighbor shuffled through the corridor. Reinhard knocked, knocked again, and ran his fingers through his hair. After she had asked what he wanted this time, he delivered, in an embarrassed way, the proposal that she had been waiting for all day.

So there it is, wretched youth in a dark corridor: she is sobbing, he is laughing. They stand there with no ill intentions — there is kissing too — and they do not realize that they have fallen into the trap that life has set for them, using a rose-shaped brooch for bait.

Black Chronology

In the spring of 1924, in spite of vehement protest by the teaching staff, the College of Arts and Crafts at 8 Prinz-Albrecht Straße merged with the Academy of Fine Arts and relocated to Charlottenburg. This decision was generally approved of, although it brought a bitter end to the dream, not yet fifty years old, of the independent position of applied arts. Through the merger and the move to another area, considerable sums of money were saved.

When the tangible assets and the furniture had been transported to the new location, the path was clear for generating profit. As neither the Academy nor the Ministry of Culture wanted to bear the operating costs of the empty rooms, a large advertisement was placed in a widely read newspaper, announcing that part of the building was for rent. This would not eliminate the holes torn in the budget of the various ministries by the war; it is a well-known fact that in critical times even such limited cuts in culture have a calming influence.

Before long, several parties voiced interest in the property. To entice them, they were given a linen-bound book extolling the beauty and the historical importance of the area. In fact, the building stood next to the most distinguished Berlin example of the Schinkel school of architecture, and something of its aura rubbed off on the college, or at least so the authors of the book hoped. Whether due to their edifying words or the central location of the building, six months later a proper lease was drawn up between the Prussian Board of Construction and Finance and a private holding company.

On July 1, 1925, the company, Richard Kahn, Inc., took over the free floors. The College of Arts and Crafts held on to the attic and the library. Although Mr. Kahn brought no further fame to the building — nor did he otherwise achieve anything noteworthy for the history books (not even the local ones) — his name should be mentioned briefly. The reason lies with an essay he wrote in his leisure time. Subject: the history of the building rented by Richard Kahn, Inc., and its neighborhood.

What induced him to embark on such a project, Richard Kahn himself could not say. He was a young man in his early thirties, who had managed to keep his sense of humor in the face of several trying situations. Perhaps the facade of the building reminded him of his high school in Bukowina. Perhaps he involved himself in research to take his mind off an unsuccessful love story. But we are not here to analyze his actions from every possible psychological angle. We simply want to copy down some important passages from his notebooks, written with the silver fountain pen he had bought for this purpose:

> The glorious history of the southern part of Friedrichstadt began in 1737 with the erection of the palace contracted by Baron Vernezobre de Laurieux, which served as his summer residence. Shortly after its completion, the palace played host to many important cultural events in Berlin. Every year, amateur theater productions were performed under the direction of the Baron, and translations of works by Italian writers were commissioned as well.
>
> In 1751 the Baron was briefly suspected of having been part of the brutal and apparently ritualistic murder of a seamstress. His name was soon cleared, yet the Baron could never entirely convince the general populace of his innocence. It was the Baron's hospitality that gave grounds for gossip. For a number of weeks

the Baron entertained four black Africans, and other people of foreign extraction were often seen with him.

After ownership had passed through several hands, including those of a banker, a Turkish ambassador, a Prussian minister, a margrave, a princess, a soup kitchen for the poor, and a benevolent foundation, the palace was acquired by Prince Albrecht, for whom it was named, and remained his residence until his death in 1872. He hired Karl Friedrich Schinkel to modify it, and Schinkel brought a simple elegance to the castle. In the left wing, he had the convoluted boudoirs, writing and music chambers of the former mistress of the house torn down and transformed into a lofty hall. In similar fashion, Schinkel had a riding school and stables built that were quintessentially modern as regards dressage and breeding.

In 1877 the foundation stone of the Museum of Arts and Crafts was laid not far from the palace. Three years later, construction of the Museum of Ethnology started on the same side of the street. Unique treasures could be viewed there, among them the largest collection of national and popular costumes in Europe.

In 1887 the Four Seasons Hotel, later named The Prinz Albrecht, came into being, which is ranked as one of the most distinguished hotels in the city. The Persian carpets in the lobby belong to the first owner of the building, and are hand-knotted. Singers, politicians, and even some actors have graced the hotel with their presence.

Campaigned for by artists and craftsmen, the College of Arts and Crafts was built in 1905, based on a design by the Ministry of Public Works. The College helped considerably to heighten the interest in German arts and crafts on an international level. Its annual exhibition "Wood, Ceramic, Steel" met with wide approval. Many high school students could familiarize themselves with these rather unprepossessing materials.

Since 1925, 8 Prinz-Albrecht Straße has been under the administration of a holding company. It has turned the classrooms of the first, second, and third floors, together with the sculpture workshops of the south wing, into office space. Forty-two workshops in the attic were made available to artists.

Contrary to the widely held belief in the acumen of Jewish businessmen, Richard Kahn had to file for bankruptcy on October 31, 1932, after a failed attempt to stay afloat. For obvious reasons, his lease, which expired on March 31, 1933, was not renewed.

After this shameful episode, Kahn's interest in the building and its neighborhood waned too. The jottings he continued to write out of habit are incomplete, erroneous, and dry up completely in April 1933.

Thus, it transpires that the most important protagonists of our novel have no place in the notebooks of Richard Kahn. He does indeed record, although he saw it as a fleeting intermezzo in German history, that in 1918, at 5 Prinz-Albrecht Straße, the Communist Party of Germany came into being, and that on April 1, 1932, the publishing quarters of their official gazette *Der Angriff* * moved to 106 Wilhelmsstraße. What Kahn did not know was who was to move into 8–9 Prinz-Albrecht Straße and 100–104 Wilhelmsstraße[†] in the spring of '33. At that time, incidentally, he had other worries, being a Jew converted to Christianity.

---

*"The Attack."

†Prinz-Albrecht Straße 8: Gestapo Headquarters.
Prinz-Albrecht Straße 9 (Hotel Prinz Albrecht): Reichsführung of the SS.
Wilhelmsstraße 100: principal seat of the SS.
Wilhelmsstraße 101–104: Security Service, headed by Heydrich, and the Inquiry and Control Section for Jewish Affairs, headed by Adolf Eichmann.

The Iron Cross

THE IRON CROSS WAS BLACK AND MADE OF CAST IRON. The shrapnel they pulled from his leg, and his besieged lung, were proof that it was truly deserved, so much so that a general had felt prompted to pin the Cross with a military salute to his chest — sweet compensation indeed. While the Cross could not soothe his lung, condemned to incessant coughing, it did warm the cockles of his heart.

It hung now on a background of red velvet on his living-room wall, and was dusted by the cleaning lady twice a week. The red velvet made the Cross stand out, and reminded him of his own blood shed on the field.

The cleaning lady was oblivious to the fact the Cross was a first-class Cross. All she saw were corners that collected dust, and she considered taking it down every so often to give the material a good wash, for she could not abide half-done jobs.

The dog did not take any notice of the Cross either. It never tired of the wooden walking stick taken on walks, though — some stubborn pieces of shrapnel were loath to leave his master's leg. The dog sank its teeth into the wood and was smacked. The hurt dog got its revenge by mauling the stick, so a new one had to be bought each year. The Cross, on the other hand, looked brand new. Quite simply, the walking stick was made of wood, and the Cross of cast iron.

The gentleman's brother, Leo, who sometimes took the dog out to the country to let it run free, fully appreciated the Cross's value, however. He knew that the Cross had been endowed in 1813; anyone, regardless of position, rank, or file, could receive it for merit displayed during war; and he knew that in 1918, thirty-five thousand Jews had received this award for their bravery, some together with cannon fire over their graves.

One of these valiant men, albeit one who had not absolutely sacrificed himself to the Fatherland — it was more heroic and economical to expire at the front than to come back mutilated — one of these valiant men was his brother, Ernst, who now limped and coughed.

Leo felt a close tie to the Fatherland, too. Oh, how he wanted a beautiful uniform of his own! He raced to sign up. But while Ernst joined the infantry and went off to the front with flowers and applause, Leo was assigned to the communication unit. He sat there, dreaming of stripes, marching, and the raw companionship born of common dangers survived. He sat there and was miserable, for he was no less patriotic than his brother, now dug into enemy territory as commanded. He could not help it that his legs were two inches too short; had they been wanted, they would have found a way to shake off their disadvantage. But it was a lost cause. So he settled down at his desk in the orderly room, thereby strengthening, through no fault of his own, the widespread belief during wartime: Jews avoided the front.

This idea was extremely hurtful to Leo, and the more perilous the war climate became and the more acute the economic decline, the more deeply it was embedded in the minds of his German companions.

He might not be able to change the outcome of the war, thought Leo, but at least he could alter the views of his fellow citizens. For knowledge is illuminating, and prejudices should be countered by gentle sobriety. He published numerous articles in which his brother Ernst's damaged lung and walking stick cropped up, although Ernst was unaware of these tributes. He also brought up the Iron Cross. Surely, Leo thought, the Iron Cross inspires respect and reverence, even among pacifists. It was the highest distinction bestowed by the Fatherland, after all. And his brother had honestly deserved his: not because he had wriggled out of sight in the army, as enemies of the Jews would have it, laying the blame of loss at their feet, but because he had wriggled in trenches on a field, trying to hold onto a hillside torn from the enemy at the cost of many a sacrifice, represented now by a small red dot on the general's map.

Yes, Leo strongly believed that the reasoning so apparent to the German citizens of the Jewish faith would be equally convincing to German citizens of Christian faith.

Yes, Leo strongly believed the chemical makeup of cerebral matter in both groups of citizens did not essentially differ; nor did the blood that seeped into the earth when a citizen was hit by an enemy bullet in the heart, in the stomach, in the lung, or indeed in the muddled brain. The blood that nourished the earth and its delightful hills, rivers, and forests, the suffering and the tears, increased fecundity. Yes, the agony his brother went through also canonized the earth for him.

Hence, he concluded that the red fluid that had been pressed from the bodies of 12,000 Jewish soldiers until they grew stiff meant he could lay claim to the country he had defended from the communication unit, his legs being on the short side.

He wrote about the many Jews displaying first- and second-class Iron Crosses on their chests, for he was aware that blood could neither talk nor back up what he knew and wanted to spell out in his pamphlets. He pointed out the Jewish fencer, too, who had a legendary reputation in the fraternity; as well as Professor Sternfeld, the Wagner expert; Laband, the master in the field of German constitutional law; and Dernburg, the Jew who had converted to Christianity. Also mentioned, of course, were strict discipline, the focus on family, and good business sense, without which one cannot advance at all.

No, it was not popularity he sought. Quarrels are common

in the closest of families. He just wanted to be accepted — oh, how he longed to be part of it all.

Therefore, he got stuck into the vitally important question of religion. The modern-day Jew does not adhere to ritualistic practices, he explained. You could come to his house unexpectedly anytime, night or day, just to check — you could even ask the neighbors. Like everyone else, he ate smoked ham, sausages, chops, and pork meatballs, freshly prepared by the butcher every other day.

"Really," he said, "you can shake it off at any time," referring to his religion, the religion of a people of slaves. "And not simply to become a reserve officer, as the countless baptisms prove."

The Jew was indistinguishable socially and economically, culturally, and ethically from the Teutonic. The unity of the nation was not based on skull shape and hair color. Incidentally, he, just like his brother, who received the Iron Cross and now coughed, and his father, whose son received the Iron Cross and now coughed, and his uncle and aunt, whose nephew received the Iron Cross and now coughed, were blond. The unity of the nation was not created by hair, but by will and determination, and by the blood that flowed from Jews, who wanted to be, and felt, German.

He explained and proved, and argued and preached and analyzed and pointed out and reiterated, his arguments indisputable, clear, and compelling — but convince he did not.

Dora Lipmann, formerly Wellner, had her opinion about her new uncle's leaflets. She felt it would be better for him to look after his wife: while he was dreaming of the mingling of German and Jewish blood, she was doing just that with Mr. Schellenberg, the young neighbor from the first floor (he had whispered this in her ear on his sofa). She also told her husband what she thought, and all this in impeccable German:

She did not use the negative to express the positive; she did not answer a question with a question, as is often the case with certain Jews — ask a Jew, even an assimilated one, "How are you?" you'll usually get in response, "How should I be?"; she did not whine; she did not say "Oh, God above!" or "Woe is me, where on earth shall I get flowers from?"; she did not use rhetorical questions (a Jewish malady); she did not gesticulate or make faces; she did not fall into singsong, did not mumble, did not speak loudly as though in Torah school, or softly like Jewish conspirators; did not speak with her hands and did not use any unpronounceable slang apart from "Goimnaches." This word seemed to her to best capture and define her new uncle's obsession with convincing.

The Printing Press

On DECEMBER 26, 1928, AT ABOUT 6:00 A.M., Constable Erich Hagel came to his precinct and confessed to having stabbed a person to death in cold blood. The person in question was Miss Ella Feigenbaum, with whom he had been socializing for over two months. Of course, no one believed him, Hagel being viewed by all as a trustworthy colleague. Only after he had demanded several times, insistently, to be put in a cell, did a colleague draft the report:

> I got to know Miss Feigenbaum at Hilde Andacht's tavern in Schillerstraße. She was a regular there and, apparently, very popular. To begin with she did not pay me any attention. I always sat up at the bar reading my newspaper, whereas Miss Feigenbaum would be in the back room, playing the piano and singing. A good time was had, it seemed.
>
> One time I wanted to relieve myself, and had to make my way through the back room. I waited at the door, as they were in the middle of a dance. That is when she noticed me. She smiled at me, and whispered something in the ear of the man next to her. They both laughed. I turned around and beat a swift retreat to the bar. I was ordering another beer when she approached me, and asked me to dance. Taken aback, I declined at first with the excuse that I did not know how and besides I was still in uniform. But then, to avoid attracting further attention, I yielded. After that I also met up with her in the afternoons. We went walking together, and to

the movies sometimes. I told her about my father, my mother, and my friends in the force. She was very interested, and wanted to know everything. She said I was introducing her to an unknown world. Politics never entered the discussion. She gave me books to read — *Don Carlos, Elective Affinities, Danton's Death* — where she had already underlined the important passages. She often referred to me teasingly as her Prussian Pygmalion. I did not consider that an insult and saw no reason to break our ties.

We always parted at her front door. Only once did I enter her apartment and I waited in the lobby while she was looking for her hat in her bedroom.

The night of the crime, we met as usual in Mrs. Andacht's tavern. Miss Feigenbaum was sad and asked me to drink with her. She said that she had lost a friend. She cursed womankind. She said all women were underhand and base whores. She talked in a very confused manner. When we were long past the police curfew, and the proprietress wanted to close, I paid the tab, and we left the bar together. Close to home, she asked me if I had plenty of cigarettes on me. I answered in the negative and therefore we went into another bar. I did not want to go in just for cigarettes, so I bought us each another beer, which we quickly drank. After that I had to more or less carry her home. I opened the front door with difficulty, dropping the keys several times. I could think clearly, but looking back on it I must have been very inebriated by this stage. In the hallway Miss Feigenbaum fell down, so I had to lift her up and carry her to bed. I took off her coat, removed her hat, and slipped the shoes from her feet. Then, I suddenly did not know what to do with myself, so I went to the kitchen and smoked a cigarette.

I must have been on my second or third cigarette when she asked me what I had forgotten at her house. I had not heard her coming in and got a fright. She was leaning against the doorframe, and started swearing at me. She should have been grateful to me — she certainly would not have gotten home without me — but instead she called me a fraud. That irritated me greatly, and I decided to head homeward. As I was about to go past her, by mistake I grazed her body. She smelled of sweat and alcohol, and she repelled me. Although nothing in her behavior suggested it, I was convinced that she would try the next second to kiss me. A prospect that filled me with disgust. To prevent her from doing so, I pushed her against the wall. I must have handled her fairly roughly for her face twisted with pain. I do not know if she intended to scream, but I feared so. I reached for her throat with both hands, and squeezed. At first she defended herself, then she collapsed. I kneeled next to her on the floor, my hands still on her throat.

While strangling her, I had gotten a slight erection. Although the erection subsided immediately, desire had been awakened in me to attempt intercourse with the body lying on the floor. Assuming that she had only fainted, believing I could still feel a pulse, I tore the clothing from her body, whipping off her stockings, too. Hoping to reach a state of sexual arousal, I pushed her right leg up so that I could see her naked genitalia. Still no reaction. An indescribable rage took hold of me. It grew still worse when the woman started to cough.

What happened thereafter, I cannot report in any chronological order. I snatched the kitchen knife that was on the table and thrust it into her left breast, perhaps I pulled it out and stabbed her again, because she was moaning. I dealt her several blows with my fists, very probably before stabbing her, and in between the two acts of stabbing and beating — or perhaps it was even before stabbing, but in any case, before seeing all the blood — I busied myself with her sexually. Then I fell asleep. I am not sure how long I lay there next to her, nor am I sure what else I did. I have the vaguest memory of washing myself and using a brush to remove the blood from my body. I also tried washing my shirt, but gave up on that. In the morning, I covered the corpse with a sheet, switched off the light, and left the apartment. Then I took the first train to the police station, and having demanded to be put under arrest, I handed in my revolver and belt.

Looking back on that night's proceedings, Erich Hagel could attest in the positive to the act of strangulation. When asked "What did you do next?" or "Did you also stab and beat her?" he described the moments of stabbing and beating in the order above. He could not recall any instances of biting. Only dimly could he remember feeling some resistance in his mouth. At the end of his report, when asked at what point he had attempted sexual intercourse, he stated that the precise memory of that moment eluded him.

The mortal shell of Ella Feigenbaum was released one week later, and put to rest quietly. Miss Feigenbaum's mother saw to the funeral costs. Three weeks later she received a box by registered post. In it were her daughter's diary, address book, three bundles of letters, and some photos. Scandalized by the police procedure — no one had informed her that her daughter's intimate writings had been confiscated — Mrs. Feigenbaum demanded a detailed report on the course of the investigation. She learned that the discovery of a printing press in the bedroom had prompted a larger scale investigation of her daughter's activities and circle of friends — an investigation that soon proved fruitful.

In a cellar Miss Feigenbaum rented, brochures and leaflets of subversive content were seized. Mrs. Feigenbaum was also informed of the constant stream of male visitors received by her daughter. In the case of such loose-living women, Detective Mehring took the liberty of adding, one could hardly be surprised by a violent form of death.

As far as the personal motive of her daughter's murderer, Mrs. Feigenbaum reached no satisfactory conclusion. According to the doctor's autopsy report at court, Ella Feigenbaum died from internal bleeding caused by stab wounds to the heart and lungs. The bruises on the neck, and the bite wounds on the breasts, calves, and thighs, along with the damage to the external genitalia — scratches, most likely — were of a superficial nature, and did not lead to death.

In spite of his memory lapses, Erich Hagel was declared accountable, and was sentenced to life imprisonment. In May 1929, he was placed in solitary confinement, and was due to be transferred to a temporary institution. In August 1931, he was pardoned thanks to the persistent intervention of a member of the Reichstag from the Deutschnationalen Volkspartei.

The diaries and notebooks of the murdered woman led to the arrest of several communist agitators and the deportation of a Polish man. They were returned only in part to her mother.

The printing press was auctioned at a charity ball held by the police in 1934. It went, after a special permit had been obtained in writing from the Gestapo, to the local group leader, Dieter Walter, who had immediate plans for it.

The "mysterious murder" was written about in fifteen articles by the national press. Journalists reported the details of Ella Feigenbaum's murder during the first week of the trial, but the story was dropped a few days later, just before Hagel's sentence. Only one editor of a culture magazine, a certain Dr. Justus Bernstein, Ph.D., picked up the case again; a much-shortened version of his article appeared in the special spring edition.

All in all, two files were filled with the "Feigenbaum Case." The files were forwarded to the attention of the State Court, the Court of Appeal, and to the High Command. The collected information was to prove most useful even years later.

Dry Earth

(Five Grams of Clock Parts)

A SHORT PASSAGE OF NO REAL PURPOSE, other than general relaxation.

Were the Fates feeling benevolent? Or was it the couple's carelessness that allowed the door to yield with a soft sigh? The children darted, one after the other, into the barn with its aroma of hay and wood, and drew to a halt, listening out for a noise from the enemy ranks.

But nothing stirred. No "Who's there?" no angry shout, not even a rustling disturbed the silence. Only their own quick breathing echoed off the walls. Cautiously they took another step, and another, another. And then they heard it, quiet, suppressed, but escaping nonetheless, oozing thickly down from the hay: the throaty laugh of a woman, exotic to their ears. Neither their mother nor their father, even during his evenings with his friend Bernstein in the study, laughed like that. Yes, the children had a feeling that this laughter hanging in the air over their heads, uncanny, was not meant for them. It was the sort of laughter that means one wants to be alone.

But now they simply had to know. One after the other, they clambered up the ladder to the hayloft. As always, curiosity won out over fear, for the children were determined not only to hear, but also to see what the tavern owner's son was doing in the barn with the waitress, while outside the band hired for the evening struck up a cheerful polka.

One ought to visualize the scene as follows: The waitress and the owner's son, not suspecting a thing, are up there — in what state will be revealed — in the hay. The waitress is laughing the aforementioned laugh, strange to the children's ears. As to whether the owner's son is also emitting noises, let us leave that one open for now. Meanwhile the children, about two meters below, are advising one another with hand signals or perhaps through whispers what they should do next. Then they climb up the ladder.

So, we have three children standing on the ladder, jostling one another, for they do not want to miss a thing, and two adults in the hay. So, we have three pairs of children's eyes, perhaps also a nose or two, but certainly no mouths as they are keeping themselves hidden as far as possible. They strain forward, a couple of inches above the floor, intending to watch from this unusual angle, from below, a reclining couple. But what they see — just to mention it briefly before introducing the characters — is something quite different.

Let's not do it by age, or alphabetically, but rather by pecking order.

That would make Vera Lipmann first: a contrary girl with pale freckled skin. Her brother Hermann, older by two years: top of the class, gentle, a Karl May expert. Oswald Blatt: he is beaten into submission once a week, wears checked shirts, and is expected to follow in his father's (the village schoolteacher) footsteps. Franzi Zink, the tavern owner's son: an only child, he will inherit the bar one day. The waitress, Berti: chubby, good-hearted, and lazy.

We should refrain from adding any further defining features here. For this example of childlike curiosity is not supposed to explain or prove anything. Nor do we want to claim any right to investigate the personal motives in detail. The reader can breathe a sigh of relief. He or she will be spared the economic, political, psychological, biological, legal, and ideological specifics.

So what do the children see? They see a kneeling man and a woman standing with legs wide apart like a goddess, her head bent back as though challenging the invisible stars. A woman, then, and the outline of a man, who, judging by his checked bottom half facing the spectators, is none other than the owner's son: only he sports pants of such tasteless material.

The children see his bottom half, then — red and white checks with dark stripes running through — they also see his arms, stretched upward, and his sizable torso, but not his head. In other words, they see a headless man, and this prompts an interesting philosophical question: whether reality is what our senses take in, or rather recognition based on experience and knowledge.

Yes, the children did not realize immediately, only after their initial shock (they had expected something, but not this), that his head had not come off, that the owner's son had not been beheaded by a waitress consumed by madness. Instead, quite simply, his head was nestled into the cozy hollow between the waitress's enormous breasts, as though he were taking a rest.

But no peace reigns supreme for long. The waitress, feeling her neck start to stiffen, turned her head to the left then to the right, and, when her gaze wandered over the hay and landed on the heads of the three children, she almost toppled over with astonishment.

"There, look there, there," she stammered, pushing the owner's son aside, and drawing her blouse over her breasts, trembling. She pointed to the ladder, and tried to explain with these clumsy words what had disturbed her.

"What's wrong?" asked the owner's son, getting up heavily.

Thinking of saving their skin and of the powerful fists of the owner's son, the children took flight, and climbed helter-skelter down the ladder. And since despite their urgency they could only use the ladder one after the other — the man was now standing threateningly above them — Hermann, who had dared go highest, simply jumped the last few rungs and sprained his

25

foot. Limping to the door, he was the only one to catch an earful of angry words from the owner's son.

The owner's son could avenge himself only with words, for any physical punishment to the children would have necessitated his confessing that he had been in the barn with Berti, and under no circumstances did he want that. And as he should not have been in the barn, certainly not with Berti and certainly not at this time of day, he had therefore not been in the barn, and thus he could not have seen children trespassing on someone else's property, who in their turn could not have seen him, because he, as already mentioned, had never been there.

Therefore, and not through lack of wanting it on the part of the owner's son — oh, how he would have loved to have beaten up just one of the children — the adventure came to its dramatic end with the chaotic retreat and, as a result thereof, Hermann's sprained ankle.

After four or five days the swelling went down, and with it the fear of retaliation, for no one knew about the owner's son's domineering mother, his Achilles' heel, whose connection to his feet was the fact that he still did not stand on his own. Yes, when not a bruise or scratch remained as proof of the incident, it became a memory. Memory as fragmentary as dry earth in the heat of summer. Soon, no trace survived other than as entries in Vera's diary and a geometrical drawing completed the very next day. It was of a dark-colored circle hemmed in by two long flesh-colored ellipses, and seemed to rest on a bulging rectangle, a checked cube. To make it three-dimensional, Vera had stuck on a winding coil and some cogs that had come out of an old broken watch of her mother's. For our heroine simply did not have words for such an experience.

The Story of Little Löwy

(A Single Postage Stamp)

I WILL NOT INTRODUCE MYSELF. You may call me W. or E., as you wish. I am a child of my time. No better or worse than many others. Men of my stamp inhabit this world rather successfully. We eat too much meat, smoke too much tobacco, and lend too much importance to the female physique. Every fifty years or so we engage in war in the name of some interchangeable truth, so that our world, overpopulated in some places, thins out a bit. In between, we pour our energy into creating families. We are herd animals, cannot live alone, and look for a suitable partner early on.

I was born in 1918. I had my first erection when I was ten years old, and the first hint of downy male hair at twelve. The first time I looked at a naked woman, with an, as yet, untrained eye, I was six. My smooth upper lip opened to a wide "Ah" (nothing down below moved yet). It was, by the way, one of those harmless little pictures, which were enormously popular back in my youth, a picture of a busty siren stretching her pink buttocks toward the beholder.

Later, I collected a whole album of those pictures. I got them with my pocket money from a dealer on the run, and sold them at double the price at school. From an early age I understood the laws of the market. I offered my schoolmates the old, tatty ones, ones that had already served their purpose for me, in order to stock up on new, more daring positions.

My mother discovered my collection in a box under my bed during her big annual cleanup. With a great hue and cry she confiscated them. My father did not let this opportunity slip through his fingers, and gave me one of my last spankings, turning my bottom a rosy red color. I saw the pictures again one day while carrying out some research in my parent's living-room cupboard. The liquor was kept next to the playing cards, and, as I was taking out the good brandy tucked away behind the crystal glasses in a corner, I saw them. They were in the same bashed-up shoe box and belonged now, it appeared, to my father. I felt hurt, and wanted to ask my mother why what was considered dirty in one place was allowed in another, but following a gut feeling I let it go.

I would have had to explain what I was looking for in the liquor closet, and would probably have been awarded a smart slap on the ear. That is when I understood that there are different levels of justice: one for the strong, and a more diluted version for the weak. But my formative years are not the subject at hand. By the time I am going to talk about now, I had moved on from still life to living models and had taken to bending over and squinting through various keyholes. Those little pictures had lost all charm for me. By the way, a few years after rediscovering them I sold the pictures to the younger brother of a school friend. I had got him hooked on this hobby by giving him his first picture free. Neither my mother nor father ever asked for them back.

But let us skip this interesting chapter of my biography. Following the strict rules of selection, we ought to leave the erection and all the rest of it behind. For, although I could not answer "how," or "why," I do know "when" it all began. And now I will tell the story of Little Löwy.

I am fifteen and have been given a hunting knife on which two words are engraved, which could leave no young boy cold: *blood* and *honor*. I think of the words as I proudly polish the blade until it shines. Blood and honor, and I believe I know the meaning of them: honor I know, or think I know, and blood belongs to knife, as salt does to bread.

And what of Little Löwy at this time? He must have been fourteen or fifteen years old, not so little, I admit, but he was stuck with the name as he was smaller than his father the watchmaker. So he was always called Little Löwy, even when he was fourteen or fifteen, except when he was taught a lesson — but that belongs to the next chapter — when he was known simply as Jewish Pig.

He will have done what all boys of our age did. He will have compared airplanes and racing cars, stolen something in the shop next door, smoked his first cigarette in the school toilets or in the playground, collected little pictures — he was not one of my clients, but there were several sources, for where demand is high, business flourishes. Some scratches and grazes, wet dreams, torn trousers, faded shirts, maybe a broken leg: just the normal bill of fare.

But let us begin at the beginning and indeed, as in every novel that considers itself as such, with the description of a building:

Our house was a modern building. I do not say that to brag in any way, rather to set the scene properly. We had a front garden, complete with a lilac bush, lawn, and a paved path. The lilac bush had not blossomed properly for quite a few years, but had managed to retain the respect of the tenants in spite of its feeble old age, and that says something about its former splendor. There were double-glazed windows on the second floor; a balcony with decorative railings for each apartment; a backyard; a rod for beating the carpets; a shed; gray detachable shutters chosen, after a long and hard search, from the firm Hinkel and Sons (my mother was very conscientious about such things); and, coming to the point, a central hot water heater down in the basement, which was operated solely by me.

So one day I'm down there again, shoveling in more coke. I've taken off the sweater that my mother knitted me for Christmas, and pushed up my shirtsleeves. It is Friday, and I'm sweating. My mother does the washing for the house, and earns a little extra that way. I help her like the good son I am, and shovel so that she has enough hot water.

I heap in a hefty shovelful, and because it's tiring work, but not intellectually challenging, I decide to take a look out of the basement window to see what's going on up there in the yard. Of course, I do not expect to see anything other than the carpet rod and the washing line, attached to it: various items of clothing belonging to the tenants are on display already, including, far be it from me to hide anything, a battalion of flesh-colored bras.

So I open the hatch, more out of boredom than real interest, raise my head in anticipation of those blown-up upper raiments, and instead see two short legs which I recognize immediately. No one other than Löwy has legs like those. I ask myself what he's doing there in our yard, thinking that he is really asking for it, when his two trotters start trampling on the ground so fast it almost makes me dizzy. Then I hear one of our tenants giggling. Her name is Vera and she is three years younger than me.

Now I am intrigued. What on earth can the second-floor tenant want with that lardball? I gather from the giggling and the wiggling of legs that something important is afoot.

I interrupt my Friday afternoon role of water-heater-upper for a moment and go upstairs, but not directly to the yard: he will get his face smashed in later, I think to myself, but first I just want to take a look, to size up where best to step in. I go to a strategic post, one I have often used because of its wide view of the whole yard almost — our kitchen. The window there is useful for a second reason, too: from here you can see everything while not being seen.

Many sales representatives have sung the praises of high-quality German net curtains. I wonder why, rather than referring to their durability, they never once point out this aspect: the fact, I mean, that behind them you are invisible. I think they would attract a whole other kind of customer with this argument.

Since I am preparing for a longish wait, and my knees have always been sensitive, I fetch a cushion from the sofa and kneel down on it comfortably. My mother is in the washroom, and will not disturb me. I'm just going to get something to drink when I see Löwy kissing Vera, or Vera kissing the fatty — who is kissing whom is hard to tell from this distance — and he is slobbering and drooling as though he were eating one of those chocolate cream éclairs that he swiftly rams down his throat walking down the street.

Just like on the banks of the river Jordan in the Bible, I think, just as revolting, wah, yuk. He can keep the girl as far as I'm concerned if she can't tell wheat from corn, or however it goes. What a bitch, I think to myself, to be with that dark-skinned Jewish bastard, who kisses her so underhandedly in the yard. He has no gumption, has to hide away from the world, in the yard, just like at the river Jordan in the Bible. Then my mother comes and slaps me because I'm dreaming at the window rather than heating up water. Of course I can't tell her why I'm there. Nor why this little domestic scene with the tenant from the second floor, whose body was still not quite developed that summer, affects me so. I suffer everything in silence, therefore, to let my mother go on believing that we have a decent backyard. I go back down to the basement, fierce fury tugging at my heart, to where the rumbling boiler and my blue and red striped sweater await.

I will give them what they deserve, twofold, threefold, I think to myself, and open the oven door. I grab the poker, prod around in the heat, stoke the fire, push the ashes to the wall of the oven with the poker, take the shovel, plunge it into the sack, and heap the coke into the hole. Because today is Friday, and Friday is wash day, that is how it is at home, that is how it has always been, come what may. *Officium servare, officium facere, officium explere, officio fungi,* not to be confused with *fundi, fundo, fusus.* In German: to defeat, to demolish, to destroy the enemy. For, as I already said, *diligens officii,* and I am after all the building's Friday-afternoon-water-heater-upper.

Monday morning, nine o'clock. Second period: current affairs. The events of the month are divided into:
Deaths of the month:
>First, Fürstenberg, Carl, well-known German banker, Head of the Berlin Trading Company.
>Secondly,
>*Composure, it all has to do with composure*
>Becker, Helmut, Former Prussian Minister of Culture
>*people will swallow the biggest red herring if told with composure*
>famous reformer of the German school system
>*for example, you should always sit up straight, strong straight spine*

Catastrophes of the month:
>*Sitting up straight shows straight character*
>First, the burning of the Reichstag, February twenty-seventh. Due to insidious arson
>*look into the eyes, eyes are the windows of the soul*
>undertaken by the world Jewry and the Communist Conspiracy
>*interested, but not too interested*
>the German Reichstag goes up
>*not greedy, he who stares is greedy, he who looks downward has something to hide, he who squints is stupid*
>in flames.
>*A calm look, serious and direct*
>Secondly, sixty-two people were killed
>*On to the profile, things are looking up, straight nose, German profile, blond hair, Grecian,*
>in a gasometer explosion in Neunkirchen on the Saar River.
>*heroic.*

Anniversaries of the month:

First, the German fieldmarshal Alfred, Count Schlieffen, inventor of the Schlieffen Plan, was born one hundred years ago.

Secondly,

Secondly, secondly . . .

It is fifty years

Cleanliness, of paramount importance; of paramount importance, cleanliness,

since the death of

are my nails clean, good, shirt, good, cuffs, good, trousers, good, shoes, damn, damn it, damn them . . .

Richard Wagner (1813–1883)

shit, shit, shit . . .

Saying of the month:

I'll just have to, I'll have to go to the john afterward . . .

If the farmer's purse is healthy, the world is wealthy,

If the farmer's in the red, the world will not be fed.

And finally please note down the latest agricultural news. On to today's subject: the fruit tree, double underline.

According to the most recent count of fruit trees . . .

Count-fruit treeing, tree-count fruiting, count-fruit shitting, shit-count treeing,

in the Reich there are 155 million fruit trees:

70 million apple trees,

36 million plum trees (versus 57 million in 1913),

versus seventy-five million in nineteen thirteen,

25 million pear trees

18 million cherry

2 million peach

1.4 million walnut and

0.3 million apricot trees — new paragraph.

Teacher, could I have a quick word with you? No, no, cooler,

The majority of apple trees are in Württemberg (around eleven million) *cool, calm, confident, Teacher, it's to do with, no, no, no,*

as well as the majority of pear trees (four million), whereas most cherry trees are in the province of Saxony — full stop, new paragraph.

I'll go up to him, and clear my throat, unfortunately I have to . . . , I have to unfortunately . . .

In nineteen thirteen there were still one hundred and seventy-five million fruit trees in the Reich — comma — that is a disturbing decrease of twenty million fruit trees — comma — which comes about through — no   comma — a lack of space and neglecting the farming traditions — full stop, new paragraph.

These dwindling numbers refer to — colon, new paragraph:

plums,

Yes, plum cake

Damsons,

Damson cake

Yellow plums,

Yellow plum cake

Reineclaudes,

Reineclaude, I don't know that one,

Morellos,

Sweet cherries and . . .

Dring dring dring goes the school bell, high-pitched, followed by a drawn-out bing-bong. Pause. Everyone rushes out of the classroom to the playground. I stay behind, fiddle around in my trouser pockets, pick my nose, and loiter. Then I approach the teacher's table. Not directly. First I pass by another bench. I draw my finger over the desk's wooden surface, just as my mother does when she wants to see whether the German housewife's most hated enemy has made itself at home on the sideboard. No dust has left its gray traces on my classmate's desk. Only some writing tablets, a pencil case, and a crumpled ball of paper, whose days of glory, as Guardian of the Sandwich, are behind it now.

The shortest distance between two points is a straight line, I think to myself, but crooked lines can also serve a geographic function. Eventually I arrive at the teacher's desk. Brackmann is putting his books away in his bag. I clear my throat. A skeptical pair of glasses look over the desk at me.

"Teacher?"

"What do you want, Eckstein?"

It is now or never, I think, opening my mouth and running my dry tongue over my lips. I even take a deep breath, to lend my voice the power that comes from breathing from the stomach. I want to be taken seriously.

I am ready now, and firmly stand my ground. I have wet my lips with my tongue, emptied my lungs, and am feeling calm and collected. As the first word is already forming in my mind, is bubbling up from the depths, I see a black bristly hair protruding from the teacher's nose. It robs me of speech.

"Yes," says Brackmann, tapping his pencil on the desk several times, "What is it, Eckstein?"

What is it, Eckstein, I think, my eyes drawn again to the glistening nose hair peering maliciously out at me. Come on, say it, come on, say it now, I tell myself. I stare at Brackmann's hands, having wrenched my gaze free, and hang my head as though in shame. For goodness sake, open your silly mouth and speak now.

But I can't do it. I simply can't. Not a squeak passes my lips, because I'm forced, as though drawn by a magnet, to look up again and to take in the landscape of the nose, complete with hair. I'm under the spell of the teacher's nose hair. I've seen noses before, and hair, and don't know what is wrong with me. So I stand there blankly, like a mute dope, like a staring carp that has got caught in a net and is gasping for air, in front of the teacher, who in turn begins to stare at me.

My hands are damp now. My upper lip breaks out in sweat, too. I know that all is lost, and wipe the palms of my hands on my trousers. And as I'm standing there, staring at Brackmann as though he were a statue — the unknown soldier in front of the Military Museum, for example, whom I ought to admire devoutly in the hope that some of its powerful, decisive strength may find its way into my heart — I hear the clasp on his bag snap shut. He turns his back on me, shrugs his shoulders, mutters something about the idiocy of youth today, and leaves the classroom.

I stay behind, silent and sweating. And then it comes, the liberating word, out it comes in a torrent:

"Shit, shitty, shit, shitty, shit, shit."

I'm not particularly creative at the moment, and limit my speech to two reliable old friends. As I'm kicking the teacher's chair, for I've finally managed to shake off my paralyzed condition and am filled with fury, I hear a guffawing behind me. Then, as though that weren't enough, a sickly sweet: "Teacher, Teacher." The guffawing starts up again and goes on in a bleating tone that pierces me straight to the heart.

What should I do, how can I save my temporarily lost honor? There's no time for complicated strategies. The braying laughter is behind me, the door is in front of me. What on earth should I do? I do the only sensible thing. It seems obvious. I don't react at all. I walk out of the classroom, looking very relaxed, whistling a tune, aiming a kick with my right leg as I go, as though flicking a book out of my path. I don't look back. Nor do I look sideways at the blackboard, nor at the desks that are set up in two rows behind me: you know what happened to Lot's wife. I make a beeline for the wide open door, for the shortest distance between two points is, as already mentioned, a straight line.

Had the person, whose voice I recognized and who seemed so highly amused by me, followed me out of the classroom, through the corridor to the reading room, he would certainly have thought of the well-known and reliable saying about the order in which different laughs come and the subsequent quality of the laughter. But the person stayed put, and therefore didn't see me pick up the German encyclopedia. A machiavellian idea had taken root in my mind. In my best handwriting, I wrote down something I had come across the day before while looking up some phenomenon in the animal kingdom. It was to do with alcohol intoxication and the devastating effect it has on the human organism. I was interested in this somewhat dry text for two reasons. First, it included words — impotence and idiocy — which filled any boy of my age with respectful horror. Then I had learned from my mother (who can be believed, since she knew all there was to know about the goings-on in our neighborhood) that the whole Uhland clan enjoyed the bottle: the grandfather, the uncle, and the father of one of my classmates had become slaves to alcohol. A sad state of affairs, some people might be saying now, but what does the Uhland clan have to do with it?

I will answer you, and won't be sidetracked, although I don't want to detract from the tension. I wanted to use Uhland's anger. I had chosen him as my instrument of revenge, a privilege he knew nothing about, nor should he. Uhland, who was powerfully built, would execute the sentence without realizing that he was acting on my behalf. He reacted angrily to any comment regarding his family's heavy consumption of alcohol. Now you're getting the drift. My plan was to pass him a message from Little Löwy. Then I would step aside and watch how he paid him back for the humiliation written by me.

I went stealthily into the playground. Ten minutes to go. Plenty of time. I approached the small group. They were talking about ghost ships that made seas dangerous. There were thousands of them and Lloyd's, the English insurance company, had just decided to have them sunk for security reasons. The boys, huddling in a half-circle, were making bets on how long it would take a ship to sink. I couldn't get excited by such things, but I suggested that I write down all the bets and volunteered to be in charge of the money. My offer was turned down, and I got out my sandwich. Meat loaf. I wasn't hungry, but munched away out of habit.

Very slowly, I slipped my hand in my pocket. The note was still there. I bit into my bread, then I got it out.

They were talking about ships that had been missing since '27.

"I'm supposed to give you this from Löwy." I stretched my arm up high. True enough, I could have found a smarter opening gambit, I could have introduced the subject with some observation or joke. I waved the note in the air.

"So what?" said one of them, turning to me. The bet had reached one mark already.

"It's from Löwy."

Now all the boys were looking at me silently.

"It's nothing to do with me." I held it under Uhland's nose.

He opened his hand. I took a step up to him, and handed him the note without a word. Uhland smoothed out the ball of paper, grown damp in my pocket, with a disgusted expression.

"You better pray that I care about this, or else . . ."

He narrowed his eyes as he always did when concentrating on something, tapped the paper with his index finger, then put his finger on my chest. I tried to grin.

"You read it."

I felt a tight knot in the region of my stomach, surely I couldn't . . . I hadn't . . . I . . . I started to read.

I can't remember who spotted Löwy first. He was standing with one leg against the wall that separated our yard from that of the liquor wholesaler — courtesy of whom our secretary had the privilege of typing letters of complaint on her new typewriter. He did not run away as we approached. He just watched us with interest, as though this were a tricky math problem to be solved.

After the first punch, delivered with expert precision by Uhland to the middle of his face, his nose and lip started to bleed.

His blood smelled sweet and dripped onto his bright green linen shirt. It left big dark stains there that looked like sweat.

Löwy still didn't react after this hit. He simply stood there and looked disbelievingly at his hands, at his shirt, and at Uhland. Someone tripped him. As he was falling, he covered his face to protect it. I saw his brown hair sticking out from between his crossed arms, his wide open red mouth, and his white teeth shining like bones in an open wound, but I didn't see the look in his eyes. I started to kick him. Cautiously at first, testingly, then harder and harder. Uhland and the others joined me. We formed a circle around him, and kicked. Then, at one point — the bell must have gone — I was left alone with Löwy. He lay curled up in the dust, moaning. I kneeled down to his level and looked at him. His shirt was torn. His nose was bleeding. He had shut his eyes. I put my mouth to his ear, and whispered to him what I had to say. He should know his sentence. I took out my hunting knife — I always had it with me — and looked at the blade. It reflected the few rays of sunlight in the yard. I raised his right hand.

With a quick stroke I cut open Löwy's thumb. He showed no resistance. Some blood stayed on the blade. I wiped it off on his trousers. Then I did the same to myself. I pressed our thumbs together.

"Blood and honor," I said, "Blood and honor," and licked the bitter blood of my peculiar new brother.

I got out all my belongings and looked for a suitable gift. I had some coins, my knife, some string, a pair of dice, and, in my shirtpocket, a postcard that I had taken because the postman hadn't pushed it completely through the first-floor tenant's letter box. I looked at the foreign stamp — you hardly ever got anything from abroad in those days. I folded the card in two, creasing the young woman who was smiling stupidly in front of a glacier, and stuffed it into Löwy's trousers. Then I quickly went back to the building, hurriedly wiping the dust off my clothes.

I don't know whether I felt pity for Löwy, though I did. I

only remember one observation I made while standing over him, a strange one considering the situation:

After every kick, Löwy's body gave a jerk, as though my feet and his rump were harmonious, meant for each other, part of the same strange machine. Yes, it seemed to me that there was only him and me at that moment, joined in punishment, unnoticed, helpless, forgotten by the world, just the two of us, and nothing else.

Spring Bulletin

1. Restructuring

Dear Dr. Heillein,

At the meeting of the thirteenth day of the month, held in the presence of the signatory president, to which you were invited (agenda: resolution on matters of vital importance affecting the department), the following conclusion was reached:

In view of the present circumstances, immediate decisions must be made by the department. The department will endeavor to restructure itself from within; it is therefore obliged to supply each member with the enclosed questionnaire, and ask for an immediate response of yes or no, and your signature. Your response must be received by the Academy by the twenty-first day of March.

2. Yes or No

Dear Dr. Heillein,

In recognition of the change in the historical situation, are you willing to continue dedicating your person to the Prussian Academy of Arts? An affirmative response to this question bars all public political antigovernment activity, and binds you to loyal cooperation with the national cultural duties accorded the Academy as defined by the changed historical situation.

Yes   No

(Please strike whichever is inapplicable.)

3. Classification

Dear Mr. Bernstein,

We are currently updating our members' personal records, and require information about your religious denomination. I would be grateful if you would let us know your denomination as soon as possible.

4. Membership

Dear Mr. Bernstein,

Due to the information gathered by the responsible authorities, I unfortunately have to inform you that, in line with the requirements of the restructuring of the Prussian state cultural institutes, you are no longer considered a member.

5. Declaration

Dear Colleagues,

I, Bertolt Heillein, hereby declare: after careful investigation, there is to my knowledge, no reason to doubt that I am of Aryan parentage nor that my grandparents were Aryan; most specifically there is no cause to believe that my parents or grandparents at any time followed the Jewish religion. I am aware that disciplinary action may be taken in case of any false information in this declaration.

The Sculptor's Workshop

1.

He was awakened. There was some confusion about handing over the summons (stamped in a rush, the seal could not be read properly), then Volker Tilling, a high school student, was led to the car. It was to take him to his interrogation at 8 Prinz-Albrecht Straße. The inmates had been told that first thing after being awakened they should stand ready and waiting against the wall of the cell, but when the door next opened, Tilling was squatting on the stone floor, his hands in his lap. Brute force was required to drag him out to the courtyard. He had an obstinate look about him in the car, too, so he was handcuffed for safety's sake.

Tilling, together with five other high school students, stood accused of having painted antagonistic slogans on the wall of 112 Kurfürstendamm at two in the morning. Spotted by a neighbor, who immediately notified the police, three of the young men were caught and arrested after a ten-minute chase through the deserted streets. Although it was a minor offense, and none of the youths had been charged before, one of the students was to be taken to the infamous Gestapo prison in Prinz-Albrecht Straße to be interrogated with all the usual forms of intimidation, to nip any other protests in the bud. Whether because he confessed to the deed without hesitation, or because of random selection, seventeen-year-old Volker Tilling drew the lot.

Tilling had a funny feeling that he knew the guard, who took his tie, belt, shoelaces, and wallet. He advised him in a paternal manner to cough up the names of those sons-of-bitches right away. By that he meant the young man's friends at the Young Socialist Workers, disbanded a year ago, this being 1934.

There were no cross-examiners at this early hour, so he was taken to a cell. He continued in vain to try and remember where those dark brown, short-sighted eyes had looked at him before. It was only when the guard brought him a cup of coffee, that it came to him suddenly. Intimidated by the unbearable silence of the cell, in stark contrast to his inner turmoil, he found no comfort in the thought that the enemy bore a human face: the eyes were the same sad eyes of his father.

2.

Tilling waited impatiently for his interrogation to begin. It was not pain that was eroding his courageous decision to say nothing; rather, it was despair. Punches would be preferable to this fevered waiting. He had laughed proudly in the face of the policeman who had handcuffed him. Where was this pride now, that pride that stemmed from his youth, and youth's claim to immortality?

He had already been told at the police station that he could expect something really special from the in-house prison. But what? Although he normally denounced the outpourings of swastika-sporting men as lies, he took the policeman at his word. Only, his usually fertile imagination was letting him down pitifully. When he heard the words *special treatment* nothing came to mind apart from a black, threatening Something: he saw its amorphous outline in the distance, creeping closer to him every expiring minute.

He watched the door with an anxious heart. He heard the sound of steps approaching several times. Yet it seemed to him on that interminable morning that they would never stop in front of his door.

Let us leave Tilling to talk briefly about the cell, not unaptly nicknamed the Purgatory by a well-read guard. What is so special about it that we give it priority over a description of our hero's frame of mind? A dark cell, three meters long, two meters wide, and lit by a single bulb.

Several years ago it had been part of a sculptor's workshop. It was there the sculptor had made a plaster of paris model of a member of Parliament, fallen from grace in the meantime. Now industrious workmen had constructed walls and divided the room into nineteen cells. In these cells, nineteen men, among them Tilling, await their fate, embodied by an SS man, smoking three floors up.

Perhaps the prisoners could still smell it, that bitter scent of metal, stone, wood, and paint that once pervaded this workshop. Perhaps they could sense something of the solemnity of the occasion when the father of German democracy, whom they all admired and looked up to, was sketched there. No, that is hard to imagine. They were in a state of extreme agitation, not open to impressions: they could only sense their own fear. They had no idea about the workshop's history. To them it was simply the hallway to their suffering. And even if they had known that on that very spot their illustrious role model had once sat, albeit under different conditions and with different expectations, it would not have brought them any strength. They would have seen it as a cruel twist, a sign of life's vanity. Even Tilling, who was craving some sort of sense of meaning, would not have granted it any significance.

3.

Toward eleven o'clock at night, two guards took Tilling up to the second floor. Tired, hungry, and disoriented by the abrupt change of surroundings, he stumbled several times, and was jabbed in the ribs by one of the guards. When he got up there he heard screams, audible in spite of the heavy felt hanging on the doors. He shuddered. When he was asked to remain standing, he felt a glimmer of hope for some reason. Tilling stood in the middle of the interrogation room. The light from the desk lamp was directed at him, blinding him, but he suppressed the wish to cover his eyes protectively.

Out of the blue, someone offered him a cigarette and he was asked to relate all he had done since the disbanding of the YSW. After lighting the cigarette, Tilling recounted what he assumed was already common knowledge. He had been a member of the Young Socialist Workers from 1931, and had taken part in several campaigns. Not knowing what lay in store, he refused to give the names of his friends who had not been officially registered members of the organization. Tracking them down had proved more difficult than anticipated. Six men entered the room and positioned themselves behind him with truncheons and whips. Even then, Tilling stuck to his given statement. It was viewed as unsatisfactory by all concerned.

In the course of the night, Tilling was beaten up several times. He tried to protect himself and covered his face with his hands and arms, but lost four teeth nonetheless and collapsed, exhausted by pain and hunger, three hours after the interrogation began. Violent, shaking movements took hold of him and Tilling found himself unable to sit down, even after a five-minute pain recess with some water to wash out his mouth. He was allowed to lie down. He experienced the next beating through a haze.

Shortly before dawn, Tilling was put in his cell. His body was a single mass of swollen flesh. The hearing was postponed until the next day on the advice of a doctor concerned by the faint pulse. The men who held the schoolboy's fate in their hands agreed to this as he was only reacting with the faintest of nods, and they could no longer make out what he said even when he really strained to be coherent.

Toward noon, Tilling was shaken awake. Along with the

stirrings of life came pain, which made him aware of his own body in a completely unprecedented manner. Tilling's referral papers had not yet been drawn up. The Gestapo officials had not anticipated that a first-time offender's interrogation could drag on so long. They were usually so easily manipulated. So his food was sent from the remand prison in Moabit, where he was still officially registered. It was an easy-to-digest gruel, specially prepared by the prison cook for those who had been given a "rougher interview" on the upper story of the Gestapo head-quarters. Sometimes he added a sticky sweet milk-rice, which also slipped down without chewing. The whole ration was poured into him, and when he had regained some strength, Tilling was dragged up to the second floor again at roughly three in the afternoon.

He seemed apathetic. He squinted at his torturers through swollen eyes. When answering his onlookers, he tried to fix his gaze on the face of a young-looking man, pale, with flaxen blond hair. He was the one who had given him the glass of water, and he had kicked him only tentatively, almost lovingly. As 6:00 P.M. drew near, and he had been tortured anew, he seemed to see reason. The information he gave was checked, and when it was proven true, he was sent off into a longed-for sleep with a morphine injection.

4.

All in all, Tilling spent three days under arrest. He did not face any criminal proceedings. With the exception of a leather briefcase — a present from his father with his initials stamped on the inside — all his belongings were handed back to him. He got back all the change he had on him when he was arrested. The briefcase, they said, smiling at him, could be picked up in a week's time. They knew that no prisoner willingly entered the building a second time.

To clarify the reason for his sudden, utterly unexpected change of heart — even after a further beating, Tilling had withheld the desired names — one event cannot go unmentioned. On the second day of interrogation, one official had held up the photo of Tilling's late father (the one he carried in his wallet), and torn it up in front of his eyes. In a fit of rage, Tilling jumped on the man. Surprised by the attack, the man was knocked over. The prisoner was then beaten and battered with truncheons until he sank moaning to the ground. Whether it was the tearing in two of the photo that broke the young man's resistance, or whether he could not bear the physical torture any longer, Tilling seemed changed afterward, and answered all their questions without further ado.

There Will Soon Come a Time

I WALKED ALONG THE CORRIDOR, trying to read my fate on the faces of the women who brushed past me, but my look rebounded off those pods of flesh, lifeless in spite of the red-painted lips. They were all feigning jollity. Embarrassed, they even averted their eyes as I came limping toward them. I could sense the curiosity I aroused, a repressed lack of respect to which I had grown accustomed. Only a child stared at my stick, shamelessly. He was whisked away quickly by his mother, her eyes begging forgiveness. Oh, that child did me such good! If only he had stayed a little longer I would have gathered courage again. I wanted to put an end to my journey, but did not know where. Was there somewhere a place I would be accepted, or was I damned to wander?

My despondency did not stem from disappointment, but rather from my physical condition. I had spent too much time by myself, alone, and would have liked to converse with someone. The merest amicable exchange, even on the weather, would have sufficed.

However, I knew all too well, though my brother may laugh at me: caution was imperative. In moments of exuberance, I had the tendency to tell all sorts of things. My ingenuousness in the art of dissimulation meant I often contradicted myself. Furthermore, I did not know what the prevailing opinion was, and could tie myself in knots making excuses as soon as I read disapproval on the face of my companion, and this was tiring in the long run.

I pushed at the doors, which yielded with a whine, swung my head first to the right, then to the left, as though relaxing the muscles in my neck, and gingerly stepped into the restaurant car. I had trained my eyes to comb every place I entered, and had developed quite a talent for observation, so much so that a nod or rapid turn of the head sufficed to take in everything going on around me, without anyone noticing.

The cutlery on the still immaculate tables sparkled up at me. There was only one elderly couple seated in the center of the area. The woman had discarded items of clothing that hung like dead leaves on the back of her chair. She was dressed too warmly for a winter's day, but there was nothing unusual in that. It was a month in which the weather changed constantly and played tricks on you, getting the better of you if you had taken along a warmish jacket just in case. Even in colder seasons, the sun could beat down, forcing drops of sweat from your pores, which backed up my long-held theory: the low flight of birds does not always portend a storm, preplanning generally does not pay, and prophecies are to be taken with a grain of salt.

The waiter motioned to me like a sleepwalker. Although the restaurant car was as good as empty, he had selected a corner table at the other end for me, next to the kitchen. I told myself he had probably chosen the table sensing I was a good-natured sort of fellow. I let him hang on to his belief and followed him along the narrow thoroughfare. Or was it his way of showing that my limp did not bother him? Was he teaching me some kind of lesson? Was he challenging me? I went through the carriage, head held high, listening to the tapping rhythm of my stick.

I passed by the couple and wanted to smile at the lady, but instead nodded a greeting at the lump of meat swimming in brown gravy on the gentleman's plate, which, I later discovered upon reading the menu, went by the name of "seasoned hunter sauce."

How apt, I thought, for the man bent over the plate re-sembled a hare, and it tickled me that the game occasionally ate up the hunter, although I knew in reality this was never the case.

The waiter pointed to the table. He had reddened hands, which he rubbed on his trousers before giving the table a wipe with a cloth. Embarrassed, I looked away and when he had whisked out his pad I ordered scrambled eggs with bread and butter. It had been years since I had experienced any pleasure in eating. The sweet taste of meat made me nauseous. I thought I could taste the animals' terror of death. And even without that, I had been a soldier for too long, had seen too many companions fall, not to be able to relate to how it feels to be sent to the slaughterhouse. Inevitably, my thoughts turned to one of them, a good fellow he was, who knew how to hold the position with a song on his lips.

The waiter made a face and slunk away to the kitchen with-out gracing me with another look. I was not a good customer. I had not even ordered a drink. How easy life is for him, I thought. I would happily change places with him. My criteria for judging people were vague, even to myself. Slowly I unfolded my napkin. I could go via the mountains — very beautiful at this time of year — or via the sea. There was much in favor of the mountains, but also something to be said for the sea.

Mountain dwellers are reserved. If a stranger comes by, they scarcely look up from their work, and let him go on without ask-ing where he has come from and where he is going. Mountain dwellers have a hard life: the soil is far from rich at that altitude, and it is a race to get the hay mown in time, to bring in the har-vest, and to drive the cattle back to the barn.

With my finger I traced the route on the map I had spread out on my lap. It snaked its way through the fawn-shaded areas. The waiter put my plate down on the table. I looked up and thanked him. The restaurant car had gradually filled up. Slowly I moved the fork to my mouth and observed the other guests. If it had not been for my mistrust, I would have noticed nothing out of the ordinary. I decided there was little point in conjecturing further — where was I meant to hide here anyway — and conscientiously went on eating my eggs. My talent for premonition, highly praised in the war by my superiors, had proven itself disturbing upon returning to the city. Why deny it? I could not bear the teasing and mocking anymore, I could not bear watching desires turn people blind.

My thoughts turned to the coast. I was very fond of it. How beautiful a coastal landscape can be, with its rolling hills and foaming surf. You lost yourself there in the face of that splendor. That was it, the decision was made. I would take the train that stopped at every village, and in between, too, should a goat or cow wander onto the track.

The sky was a fiery red in the first throes of sunset, casting a magical light on the fields. Soon it would be night. I became restless. I finished my sparse meal and wiped my mouth. There was the question of the suitcases. Yes, it was a little tricky with the suitcases. Three of them in all. I always got someone to carry them for a small tip. I had traveled through the whole country with them, but we had not yet crossed the border together.

The waiter brought the check. When he saw the tip I had left on the plate, he nodded several times approvingly. Would it not be clear to any official at the border control who saw me approaching with my suitcases that I was planning to leave the country with all my worldly goods? Was it not too much for a simple holiday-maker? Did not my suitcases announce my hopes of fleeing? The suitcases were dear to me, but they should not become an obstacle. I stood up. The waiter handed my stick to me as if it were a trophy. I thanked him, and he led the way. What a comical pair we made: the beggar king and his jester. Going through the door of the restaurant car, I looked back once more. The waiter waved at me. The tip had made him relentlessly attentive. I turned my back on him. Why should I concern myself with the benevolence of a waiter? I had serious problems at the time.

I do not want to hide my troubles anymore. My misfortune was not of my own making. I had conducted research. All to no avail. I was not to blame. I had no influence on my fate.

To steel my resolve, I turned my attention to a concrete problem. I would just take a small suitcase with a few things to wear. One bag I could kick along in front of me. Or would I draw attention to myself with just one bag? It could be assumed that the border control knew all the inhabitants of the area, could it not? Would he not find it odd that a stranger from far afield was traveling so very lightly? You cannot win, I thought, opening the compartment door. Whatever you do, you will look suspicious.

I looked at myself in the mirror and sat down at my place by the window, reserved by my open newspaper.

My hair was thinning, and the skin under my chin hung loose. As for my teeth . . . I should have had them seen to a long time back. To turn my thoughts in another direction, for seeing myself had had a sobering effect, I got out the map again.

Had I been traveling in the company of my brother and his wife, who still imagined themselves to be living in safety, I would not have hesitated in choosing the coastal route. Not everyone takes to the mountain air. People of a delicate constitution can suffer in the high mountains. Oxygen is thin, the paths are uneven, and the rain transforms it all to a muddy swamp. I lifted down my suitcase from the overhead net and got out the apple I had saved for dinner. Taking my penknife I made a long red spiral of the skin, then cut out the core. The apple was sweet and ripe. As usual, I would wait and see. Life had turned me into a fatalist. No, actually, not life but rather people had made me doubt my own will.

The train drew slowly into the town. I looked out. The sky was growing darker. An ugly grayness hung over the houses. I leaned my stick against the compartment door, put my coat on, and my scarf, too. First of all, I would look for a porter, then for a cheap hotel room. I sat down again — why tire the leg unnecessarily — and waited until all the others had got off. There was rubbish lying under the seats.

I gingerly stepped down onto the platform and nodded over to the porter. He had already been eyeing me expectantly, ever since seeing me limp on my cane to the door. As he was hoisting my suitcases onto his cart, I looked at the man who had been sitting next to me. He whirled his child around in the air, then put him down and kissed his wife. The child started to cry.

I silently pointed to the exit and bravely strode ahead. My leg hurt, and I had to stop several times to catch my breath. The porter overtook me, irritated. I was sorry for him. My ailments were depriving him of his second customer. I decided I would give him a generous tip. It was not his fault that my leg had been riddled by enemy bullets. Tiredness engulfed me. I slowly limped past the traffic controller. He let his signaling disc hang limply and looked like a redundant magician. The disc had brought the train to a halt, but now pointed downward. I stopped again. In front of me people rushed through the dark shaft that led to the outside world. Their shadows trembled in the yellow lamplight. It must have been after eight.

As I entered the tunnel, my eyes focused on the brightness at the other end. I saw that a crowd of people had bunched up near the exit. Perhaps a woman had fainted and her stretched-out body was blocking the way. Or the curious onlookers, the sort who garner pleasure from observing the misfortunes of others, were blocking the thoroughfare. Whatever it was, it had nothing to do with me. I continued for a few steps. Then I saw them. Two officials in uniform. They were standing at the exit checking tickets. I touched at my chest. Yes, the ticket was still there. I took the ticket out, stretched out my arm, then pulled it down again. Did it look suspicious to approach the man in uniform with arm outstretched? Could it appear as though I wanted to have nothing to do with the ticket? But this way, I thought, he cannot see my ticket at all and he will believe that I have smuggled my way into the station. I was uncertain and faltered.

Why were there two men at the exit? Was this not a perfectly ordinary station? Was one official not enough? I was pushed to the side. Why was my breathing getting quicker? Why were they looking at me? In a second I would hand over my ticket to the officials, cross the road, and go into the first hotel I came to. As every evening, I would try to fall asleep. I would press my head into the pillow and wait in vain for my fear to leave me.

I was now in the line that had formed in front of the exit. All around me legs crept forward imperceptibly. The beast is predatory, I thought, and even eats its own kind. The door swung open. I stretched my head up high and saw the porter waving over impatiently. A cold breeze caressed my exhausted body. It already carried the scent of coming spring with its linden blossom and anemones. Outside it was still. The official reached out his hand to me. All right, I thought, all right, and I looked at his hand. He had long, bony fingers.

Yes, there was a time when I could fall asleep whenever I so desired. How pleasant those restful hours were. The limbs grew heavy, the mouth opened, and you were carried into sleep as though in an unmanned boat. I leaned on my stick, which had left a dark trail on the stone tiles, and dug around in my pocket. I was not embarrassed by the dark trail. I had been on the run too long for there to be much left of me. Should they seize me now, at least I would leave behind a dark trail as a memorial.

My friends were right. All effort was vain. Despair had sunk roots deep in my heart. I had become a heretic because I did not believe in progress, because I did not want to bow down, and now I trembled in every gust of wind and found nothing to hold on to. What else is there to write, how should my story end? Are the last pages of my biography to be dictated to me? Do I not have any right to decide myself? Is such a rich, such an exemplary, life to end this way? And all that I had achieved, at the cost of great effort, all this was to be simply labeled absurd? Was my downfall to be a source of laughter, had I become amusing for the enemy?

The official tapped me on the shoulder impatiently and pointed to the line that had formed behind me. Caught, I thought, and handed my ticket to the official with a flourish.

Caught like a stag in the rutting season that raises its antlers up high and emits a powerful cry to entice its mate, but instead draws the hunter. Stretched out on the ground, the animal looks into the blue eye of the gun and hopes. Yet, even as the animal trembles, the hunter is pressing the trigger for the last time.

"Would you not agree," I asked, "that it is a crying shame to have to end in such a manner?"

The official took the ticket. He did not answer. But why should he. I knew the answer only too well.

The Leather Briefcase

Karl Kowalsky was arrested on a Thursday. He was sitting in a restaurant, bent over a bowl of pasta, when four SA men rushed at him. The attack caught him unawares, and he did not have time to reach for the pistol he had for a year kept next to him. After a brief struggle he was led away. Kowalsky, living in exile in Berlin since 1929, was betrayed by his girlfriend. She was up in the restroom on the second floor when the deed was being done, and on returning to the table she seemed composed. She was the one who had suggested this restaurant, a perfect venue for such an affair, peaceful and no escape routes. She was bumped off, by the way, a few months after Kowalsky's arrest by someone hired by the Komintern.

The first time I saw Kowalsky was on a Sunday. Ella Feigenbaum had invited me to tea. That was shortly before her brutal murder. I came somewhat later than planned and was led straight through to the kitchen. Kowalsky was leaning against a chair, speaking with a man whom I knew by sight. He was a translator with the Hungarian section of the Komintern. A small circle had formed around the two men. Although Kowalsky was debating heatedly with the man, he turned to Ella after every sentence and smiled at her. He was evidently beguiled by her, and she in turn hung on his every word.

Naturally, I was shocked. How could a man such as Kowalsky — I'd read all his writings, devoured every word — how could he act so silly because of a woman?

When Ella, knowing my admiration for Kowalsky, wanted to introduce me later on, I claimed a headache and left. I remember wandering aimlessly through the streets afterward. It was as though that small innocent display of mutual affection had cast me headlong into a chasm. Back then I did not understand my inner turmoil; today I realize that I was attracted to Ella and jealous of Kowalsky.

After that I heard nothing about him for a long time. He was said to have undertaken many journeys during those years, my student years, primarily to Moscow where he led an exciting life codenamed Cyrill. Several years later — I had become engaged in the meantime — I met him again in Café Comet. He had aged tremendously. His eyes alone still had that familiar youthful glow. Although not even half as prominent as Kowalsky — I was a modest union leader — I had the honor of being on one of the black lists, too.

I was captured in front of my home. I had just opened the door when a man asked me the time or something similar, and with a perfectly aimed punch to the stomach put me out of action.

As Kowalsky was led in I was standing next to three other comrades against the wall, legs spread, hands above the head. The Comet was one of many restaurants whose back rooms served as collecting stations for the SA. A polka was playing in the restaurant, I remember.

They took Kowalsky up front first of all. He was beaten and kicked consecutively. After roughly quarter of an hour they let him be. Strangely, they had not asked him a single question. I concluded from this that we were warmed up, that the real interrogation would take place later on.

Groaning, Kowalsky staggered over to us. We lay him down on the ground, his knees raised upward. They let us do this. I took off my jacket and made a pillow of it under his head. Kowalsky reached for my arm and pulled me down to him. His mouth looked like an open wound, and I could not make out what he wanted to say to me. Laughter floated through from the restaurant. Then I heard my name called. I loosened his grip and stood up. My heart was hammering wildly. They came to get me.

The second time I met Kowalsky was in the basement of the Gestapo headquarters. The Celebrity Jailhouse, as we inmates ironically called it, hoping, perhaps, to boost our spirits through this seemingly casual turn of phrase. I also saw Ernst Thälmann there, although I did not recognize him to begin with, as he had lost at least ten kilos. His face looked different, too.

Kowalsky was sitting on a bench outside the interrogation room, and nodded at me almost imperceptibly. It was indicated I should sit next to him. We had been expressly forbidden to talk to one another, so I couldn't ask him all that had happened to him since our last meeting. I knew that unlike myself — I had been taken to a precinct prison — he had been taken here that same night, and I could only imagine what effect those two days must have had on him both physically and mentally. Willi Gleit, a friend of mine who had already had the honor of being interrogated in the Prinz A. for having attempted to continue the activities of the SPD underground, had told me that the torture methods in the Gestapo prison far outdid those of the Columbia House.

We waited and waited. At some point it started getting dark outside. I wanted to smoke, to move, and above all else, to speak, but I stayed there motionless. I knew how you were rewarded for disobeying a rule. I had experienced that right at the beginning of my stay.

A man came up the stairs breathing heavily and there was a whispered exchange with the guard. Kowalsky and I looked at each other. A piece of paper was handed over, then Kowalsky was led away. Another two hours must have trickled by before the door opened and I was called in.

The first thing that struck me upon entering the interrogation room was the secretary. I had expected to be greeted behind the hateful door by uniformed Gestapo men, and instead saw a woman of my age, looking at me in a bored fashion over the top of her typewriter. I sat down on the chair and waited. The secretary inserted a sheet of paper and looked out the window. I was surprised how at ease she seemed with her job.

After a while the interrogator entered the room. He was accompanied by three other men, who had been in the political police force in Severing. I had already made their acquaintance. As they had been informed about my heart problem, the interrogation began with a good dose of coaxing. Then the questions rained down on me. Sometimes I was hit, not hard, only as a warning. The interrogator asked me to show some sense. He said that he only ate up communists, not social democrats. His exact words were: "You are neither fish nor meat: I do not go near such things."

When I was led back to the cell in the evening, I heard that Kowalsky had suffered a concussion. A fellow inmate, whose name escapes me, also told me that countless members of Neumann's resistance group had been arrested. He offered me a plate of cold soup that he had saved for me. I sat down on the wooden bed and began to eat.

Toward midnight I heard a rattling in the lock. I jumped up immediately. When the SS guard stepped in, I stared at him mutely. I was summoned again. With a pounding heart I followed him. Once upstairs I had to stand stock-still for almost two hours in front of the door. I tried to concentrate. I wanted to be ready for all their questions, but my thoughts kept drifting. I could not understand why everyone apart from Neumann had been transferred. Was he an informer or had he been done in? The door opened. I felt dirty and weak.

My interrogator offered me a cigarette. I declined and sat down. He came straight to the point and told me Kowalsky had committed suicide. This had the desired effect. I slumped down and shook my head, disbelievingly. It was only later that I learned it was all a well-thought-out lie.

Kowalsky is said to have been set free three months later thanks to international pressure. With the help of some friends, he made it over to France, then to Spain from where he fled when the fascists conquered Barcelona, and on to Moscow. He died of heart failure there, fallen from grace suddenly, shortly before he was supposed to be deported to one of Stalin's camps.

Before I could regain my composure, I was pushed down on the table by an SS man.

"Do you recognize this?" asked my interrogator.

I looked at him, confused. What did a briefcase have to do with Kowalsky's suicide?

I did not recognize the briefcase right away. I was too worn out, and could not see properly. It was only when the SS man opened the briefcase and pointed out the initials that I knew how they intended to break my will. I cursed softly. I was asked again if I recognized the briefcase. I was not capable of speaking and only nodded. The interrogator shook his head sympathetically. He was sorry for my mother, he said.

"Now both of her boys are in jail."

I asked him what he wanted to know. He promised to let my brother go immediately.

I stayed there for about two hours. Then I was given beer and sandwiches. I ate apathetically, as they patted me cheerfully on the shoulder. After a cigarette break, I told them more.

Yes, you've got to give it to them, it was a truly perfect method. First they destroyed what lent my life meaning, then my self-respect, and soon, I thought, looking at the man who had replaced the secretary, they would also destroy my body in the cheapest way possible.

Toward morning I was given coffee. Then I was taken to a cell, which had been emptied of my companions. A week later I was transferred to KZ Esterwegen. Although my trial was scheduled for the beginning of June, I stayed there for another two years.

I would like to mention another salient little fact: my brother had been set free the day I was taken there. He was, therefore, in no direct danger when I gave up the names they wanted. I discovered this truth several months later, but it did not play any role for me anymore.

Sacrificing Pieces

IT IS IMPOSSIBLE TO LIST ALL THE DIFFERENT FORMS mistakes may take. There are too many. According to probability theory, errors most often occur in unfavorable situations, when, for example, one believes that all is lost anyway. The following scenario illustrates the point:

A mouse sees a black shadow in the distance, and believes it is the cat lying in wait for it. Losing its head, it runs in the opposite direction, where the steel fangs of the trap are open wide in anticipation. Had the mouse, rather than scurrying away, reflected, it would have said to itself: "The shadow that I see could also be that of a fence or of a hedge. I will creep up to it softly, for I can't stay here motionless awaiting my fate. I will find out the origin of the shadow."

The mouse, however, lets its fear dictate its movements because from the very outset it is handicapped. It is a mouse and not a cat. It is the one that gets eaten and not the one that eats.

Often mistakes originate from a lack of thinking, which occurs when one uproots the subject from its familiar surroundings. If an opponent is not already weakened by its disadvantageous position, one should lure it into unfamiliar territory so that, with every step that it takes, it is faced with new decisions to make on its own.

1.

The first time that Harald Hartmund — a circumspect man who had started at the bank when he had just turned twenty and had recently been made head cashier of his branch — set eyes on Gerta Berg was a Wednesday. The meeting was not pleasant for either party.

Berg came as a customer to the bank. Hartmund was about to water his potted plant, a begonia, a superfluous and decorative thing on the birchwood table next to the cash register and several stamps. It had been a gift from his colleagues upon his promotion. Due to the economical lighting, it was dying. Hartmund was sadly contemplating the withering leaves, when Gerta Berg emptied a little bag of coins on the revolving disc, and asked him, in a penetrating voice, to change the pile into several notes.

Hartmund was annoyed and pointed to the sign that he had hung in front of his counter: it proclaimed in black and white that the position was closed now and, it being shortly before half past twelve, he was taking lunch, as stated in the union's regulations. He had set it aside for going over the words of a chorale, so as to be word perfect after work at the choir rehearsal he attended twice a week.

Seeing the precious minutes tick by, Harald Hartmund grabbed angrily at the dish as Miss Berg was stubbornly starting to arrange the coins into small stacks — she had not counted it up before, to add to the misfortune — and his hand brushed against his customer's in doing so.

"What do you mean by that?"

Hartmund apologized profusely — it was not one of the bank's policies to insult customers — and handed the woman three banknotes. One week later, Miss Berg entered the bank lobby again. This time, too, she shook the contents of her little linen bag on to the revolving dish. Whether it was the early morning lull that led him to do something he had never done in his whole career, or twinges of conscience, for he had not been able to put the unpleasant scene out of his mind, Hartmund asked his customer how it happened that she was carrying so much small change, thereby breaking the rule of discretion. The woman smiled and handed him an invitation to the fair in response.

Although he had intended to go to choir rehearsal, Hartmund found himself on the tram going out to the wooded outskirts of the city the following Sunday.

He looked around, bewildered. He could not recall ever being in such a place, and the garish colors on the posters hurt his eyes. After a while he came across his customer's tent. Here she was called The Great Samantra. Although he had been looking for her high and low a few minutes earlier, now that he had found her, he hung back. The poster depicting her scantily clad injured his feelings of modesty. He was just about to leave when Gerta Berg noticed him and called him over. Caught in the act, he sat down on a wooden bench.

The Great Samantra walked onto the stage right away. She had changed costume and was now dressed in a cloak with red sequins. After taking a bow, she unbuttoned it and threw it on a chair. Then, ignoring the catcalls of a man in the audience, she perched on the end of a long rectangular platform, center stage, draped with a black cloth, pulled herself up into a handstand, and went into a swift routine of somersaults and cartwheels and finished with a split. After she had performed some other figures, to a ripple of shy applause, Great Samantra's assistant, a ten-year-old boy, came out of the wings.

Now Hartmund realized which pockets those coins came from that he changed each week. He also put something in the hat that was held up by the assistant next to the exit to encourage reluctant customers to cough up.

Hartmund wanted to leave, but for some inexplicable reason stayed seated on the bench. He watched the gymnast Berg still onstage. She somersaulted and, as a kind of encore, turned a cartwheel, jumped in a single move back up onto the platform, and finished in an elegant second execution of the splits, arms stretched out to the sides. He was shaken. Never before had he seen such a mysterious dance. It seemed to him that the woman was floating. (He did not know, and could not know, that it was a simple case of a side split.) And she had done this dance, he was moved by the thought, when no one else was there to see it, when the tent was empty. At once he understood with all his heart what he had recently read in the introduction to a music book: that true art satisfies itself. He was tempted to burst into song. Instead he got up quietly and left the tent so as not to disturb the lady.

After that he did not see her for a long time. The fair had moved on. One lunchtime, when Hartmund had long since forgotten the scene in the tent, he was sitting as usual at one of the round tables in his local bar. He recognized Gerta Berg as one of the clientele. More out of politeness than interest, he bowed his head and asked her if she would care to sit with him.

"That would be nice," the gymnast replied, and stood up lithely.

Soon they were meeting regularly. On Hartmund's advice, Gerta Berg left the fair and started work at Kraus the optician's, who had taken her on in spite of her lack of experience. He was a lover of the Swabian bridal dance and whenever there were no customers in the shop, he let her perform dances.

Hartmund continued to go to the bank every day. But he no longer lost himself in work, and when he heard the hum of the clock above his head toward the end of the day, he trembled with impatience. He was distracted. One day, his mind on a movie he had been to see, he gave a customer who was withdrawing money from his savings account one note too few. It was only when the man had already left the bank that Hartmund realized his mistake. He meant to report it immediately, but after some hesitation, he popped the note into his pants pocket instead. With the money he bought two orchestra seats for the ballet to bring some joy to Gerta, who was missing the stage. From now on they were to attend a dance performance every Friday.

Although Hartmund was on his guard, only holding on to money of customers who seemed absentminded, and only ever taking small sums, as time went on there were some unpleasant scenes. He apologized each time and handed over the rest of the sum, but he had aroused the suspicion of a married colleague, who watched him like a hawk. Hartmund decided to give up his new hobby, but started again a few weeks later in spite of himself.

On the day of his twentieth anniversary with the firm, Hartmund tried to take a larger sum than usual. The day's climax was a celebration at lunchtime (the director who believed in rewarding loyalty in his employees had ordered a fruit flan from the bakery). The party atmosphere along with the glass of champagne at the beginning of the day made him reckless. The customer was an elderly lady with thick glasses, and she noticed the mistake in the calculation. In spite of Hartmund's repeated conciliatory gestures, she complained to his boss. The cashier was called to his office and asked to account for himself. After he had put the unforgivable mistake down to his insomnia, he was merely given a gentle warning.

A month later, Hartmund was sitting with his girlfriend in a vegetarian restaurant eating cabbage soup. Gerta told him that she was planning to give up her job.

"But why?" asked Hartmund. He heard very frankly that while Gerta Berg may have put her Great Samantra costume away in the cupboard, her restless feet had not been stored with mothballs. Should no replacement have been found for the Great Samantra, she would rejoin the fair, which would be making its stop in the city in a few days' time.

So now Hartmund became the recipient of regularly sent postcards whose glossy fronts depicted the sights of various cities. Although alone again, he did not change any of his habits. As he found pleasure in dance, he still went to a dance performance every Friday. And because dance was not only connected to Berg, the gymnast, but also to his discrepancies at work, he soon resumed holding back small sums of money. He did this out of nostalgia, not because he needed the money.

Now the director was also beginning to have his doubts. He decided to set a trap for his employee with the help of a trustworthy customer. Hartmund, blissfully unaware, held back his personal fee this time too, and as he was about to put the note into his pants pocket he was caught in the act. Hartmund could not explain why he had stolen the money. As he was one of the longest-serving co-workers at the bank and because they wanted to avoid a public scandal that could hurt the branch's reputation, he was dismissed in all discretion without the police being called in. After a long and heated letter exchange, he moved into the caravan of Gerta Berg, gymnast.

2.

If the enemy cannot be enticed down that dark path by means of an enthusiasm for art discovered at an advanced age, as in Harald Hartmund's case, you should try to awaken in him a passion for, say, alcohol or love or gambling that will stop him thinking in a reasonable fashion.

Moreover, should an exaggerated ambition be latent in the enemy, this is to be encouraged by offering up an unusual victim, thereby arousing the urge to attack.

The enemy leaves his cover and, surprised and flattered, takes a step forward. As there do not seem to be any obstacles in his path, he falls headlong into disaster. Overestimating one's own strength is one of the traps that defeats, above all others, strategists well practiced in conflict, because they are used to victory. But equally, underestimating one's own power can be dangerous, as this example illustrates:

On May 10, the opera singer Werner Kurzig was taken away by five young men in SA uniforms. Kurzig was sitting over breakfast with his friend, discussing a concert that was to take place the following day, when the men entered. They pretended they had been sent by the electricity board to check the meter. The maid, who had been in Kurzig's service for over ten years, and whose integrity was beyond any doubt, opened the door in good faith. Before she could call to her master for help, she was struck on the head and fell unconscious to the floor.

As though well acquainted with the opera singer's living space and habits, the men entered the dining room without any detours. They grabbed Kurzig. After damaging the grand piano in his study, they dragged him to the waiting vehicle. They drove to a fallow field south of the city. There they formed a circle around Kurzig, contemptuously called him "little lady," and ordered him to undress. Kurzig did what they commanded.

They rained blows down on the naked singer, using rubber truncheons and dog whips. They particularly aimed at his sexual organ. Then they pulled a potato sack over Kurzig's head and took his clothes, a silver ring, and a gold wristwatch.

About an hour later, the proprietress, Hilde Andacht, came across him lying there. Mrs. Andacht notified the police and called for an ambulance. Kurzig was taken to the university hospital. They found several bones were broken.

Kurzig's friend, the pianist Otto Wagner, escaped with a light concussion. The men had hit his head several times with a canelike object. It kept him in bed for a week. When he was up and about again, he went to visit Kurzig in the hospital. He spent several hours every day there in the company of his friend, who was convalescing slowly. He brought books to read from to distract him and cheer him up.

Wagner learned from Kurzig's agent that the doors of the opera houses would be closed to Kurzig from now on. Wagner, indignant about this turn of affairs, tried to set up a singing evening with the help of some influential friends from the music world. But he could not find a suitable hall. The owners of those that were possibilities (three of them) feared rioting.

Although the incident caused quite a stir among the public and was unanimously condemned by the press — not only was Kurzig an exceptionally fine singer, he also enjoyed a certain popularity due to his friendly nature — several important concerts were canceled. By the end of the year, Kurzig felt compelled to emigrate to a neighboring country. There he remained, after a failed attempt to revive his career, in a modest guest house until his death.

Although Kurzig tried to persuade his longtime friend to go abroad with him, Wagner stayed behind in Germany. They did, however, keep in touch with each other.

When Kurzig was declared an enemy of the state some months later, Wagner publicly distanced himself from him. One year later, he was appointed director of a large opera house. That same year he got married to a young actress, whose career was just beginning.

Wagner never saw Kurzig again. He learned about his death from a common friend. That was on a Wednesday. Afterward Wagner went to the opera house, where a rehearsal of *The Magic Flute* was taking place. Fifteen years earlier, Kurzig had had his big break with this opera. Wagner could still remember how he had stayed seated, stunned at his place up in the gallery as the last note of Sarastro's aria faded away: he had never heard a sound of such purity. He had looked down in amazement at the small man who seemed to him at that moment like a god even as he fumbled awkwardly at the heavy folds of the burgundy velvet curtains and popped out under the spotlight, like a tongue out of a woman's red mouth.

3.

Victory used to be easy. In silent agreement, enemies would throw themselves into the heart of the fray. To take victims, even if it involved some risk, was a matter of honor. And to offer up some tasty bait, soon to prove inedible, brought many to their knees. Yes, in those days defense tactics took a backseat to methods of attack. The strategist did not consider what he could lose; he thought of victory, and this was often the upbeat of a domino-like succession of sacrifices.

Nowadays, if you want to come into contact with your enemy, you first of all have to cunningly coax him out of his shell. Many ways have been tried, many ways remain to be discovered: each new case demands the creative ingenuity of the strategist. However, there is only one method of attack that stimulates even the most indifferent of people. In technical terms, it is known as strategic placing of casualties or, even more categorically, sacrificing of pieces. It has everything to do with the clever exploitation of circumstances planned in advance, and the main shape this exploitation takes is that of a perfect circle. The opponent is coerced by the carefully plotted ambush to give up his best men, and then to sacrifice himself. Yes, he who has never looked upon the whites of the enemy's eyes as he dies shamefully has never known victory.

Three years later, Otto Wagner, in the meantime having become the director of the most important theater in the city, was invited one afternoon to come to the Ministry for Theater and Film. When he arrived, he was asked to give an actress by the name of Kernig the main role in a play that was currently being rehearsed and was to open the season.

Wagner did not initially understand the secretary's request. There was no doubt that Kernig was not up to the part. She had neither the talent nor the looks — she was a powerfully built, bulging blond — to successfully portray the tragic female lead. And, he took the liberty of responding, the role had already been given to an excellent actress, who would certainly do a fine job. He was referring to, as you will doubtless have gathered, his wife.

"Yes," replied the secretary, growing impatient, "I agree with what you say, but there are other factors at work here."

He told him something that Wagner should have been well

aware of as director of the most important theater in the city: Kernig, the actress, was with the rich and influential Paul Raeder, one of Göring's close advisers. Therefore, it was a *fait accompli*. Wagner promised to set the wheels in motion and went back to the theater with an uneasy feeling as he imagined his wife's anger.

Indeed, Mrs. Wagner, usually rather careless, was taking this performance very seriously. She had already gathered historical background material, with the help of the dramaturge. It was piled high on the drawing room table, waiting for the actress's fine, carefully manicured hands to start leafing through.

The following morning she learned via her husband's secretary that she would be taking a vacation from work. Without even putting on her coat, she ran back to the apartment, went past the maid without a word, and smashed Wagner's records against the bedroom wall.

Meanwhile Wagner was spreading his bread with fresh butter in the rustically decorated dining room of a small inn. He was aware of his cowardice, and felt wretched. But what else could he have done? The season started just five weeks from now, and he had to conserve his strength if he wanted to have a successful fall. As the mere thought of a fight with his wife was enough to exhaust him, and to a certain degree also bore him, he was hiding out for a few days. He pushed his plate to the side, lit up a cigarette, and compassionately thought of Heller, his secretary. He would bear the brunt of his wife's fury, and would have to be promised a raise for his troubles. Wagner planned to give his wife a present: the lead role in a play to be performed at Christmastime. She would sheath herself in a white toga, and bemoan the fate of women.

But things turned out differently. During rehearsals, Mrs. Wagner's glance had chanced upon the young dramaturge Johannes Schellenberg. Until then he had struck her as insignificant, but now his general knowledge changed that indifference to enthusiasm.

Young Schellenberg had taken advantage of the beautiful

actress's interest. As they looked through the old books and catalogs that he had lugged over to the Wagners' apartment, he
inched closer and closer to her. After a few timid days, a passionate relationship flamed up between the two of them. They kept it
secret for obvious reasons.

For quite some time, Mrs. Wagner had felt a weariness with
her husband and her marriage. It had now reached a point of
aversion; without being aware of it she was looking for a reason
to leave her husband, to whom she felt duty bound.

When she saw herself crossed in such a cheap manner — his
passing the buck of bearing the news was like a slap in the face to
her — she felt such anger that she told the dramaturge what had
long bothered her about her husband. She did not spare a
thought about the destructive results of her confession.

The next day the whole theater already knew what had been
disclosed during a minute of weakness on the velour sofa. Wagner knew nothing of it.

While the newly engaged actress Kernig was at the minister's weekend house, the dramaturge at the Wagners' apartment,
and his secretary, Heller, was spending Sunday with his mother,
Wagner was marching through the woods, humming a Mozart
melody. After an expansive dinner, he went to bed early. The
next morning he planned to take the first train back to see how
things were simmering at the theater.

He got to the theater around ten. He did not notice the
stolen glances in his direction. He opened the door to his office
and was relieved to find it empty. He ordered a pot of tea with
milk, and took out the message book. Bored, he read his secretary's delicate tidy handwriting and reached into the cookie tin
that he always kept on his desk for energy. When he read that he
was to contact the ministry immediately, he dialed the familiar
number.

When he discovered that for moral reasons he had to resign
from his post, he went to the toilet and threw up.

He was made to wait half an hour, then was led into his boss's room. Three men whom he did not know and who were not introduced to him demanded he give them the names of his friends. Wagner did not understand. Was he being threatened? Was this a joke? He was married, after all. He had married the most beautiful woman in the Reich. Agitated, he got up, and walked back and forth in the room. Did they not believe, then, that that chapter of his life was definitely over? Was he to fall from grace for the sake of an old long-forgotten story? Wagner started to explain. The men brushed his words aside, they wanted names, only names. The calm, even polite way they reprimanded him showed they were serious.

A week later Wagner traveled to his sister in Bavaria. It had been recommended that he stay in the country. There, as in days gone by, he gave piano lessons. He could live fairly well from the interest on his savings and the income from his lessons. His wife, who in the meantime had divorced him, came to visit once. As she was in the midst of rehearsals, she did not stay long. She told him that the play in which Kernig played the lead folded after just two weeks, and had some other juicy anecdotes from the theater world. She also brought him records she had purchased for him. He felt like a convalescent, but did not know which illness he had been diagnosed as having.

Later that month, just as he was helping his sister get the comforters from the linen chest, two men entered the house. They ordered him to go with them. Wagner pulled on a jacket and off he went.

There was another interrogation. They questioned him about famous actors and musicians. Four hours later, he was dismissed and went for a walk in the park. The leaves had turned red and yellow.

The priest persuaded Wagner to give concerts in the church during the week. During one of these concerts he noticed a man among the sparse audience whom he had never seen before, dressed in the clothes of a city man. Although there was no proof, and although he believed the ministry had no further interest in him, Wagner felt eyes on him from that day forth. Now, even during the music lessons, which he otherwise gave with his heart and soul for he loved children, his thoughts were occupied by the interrogation with the men.

One Tuesday he was picked up and taken to the local police headquarters. He had been on his way to the church, as he had a concert that evening. The head of the police who had received his file, told him that his piano lessons were suspended as of that moment.

Wagner understood that this was meant as a further insult, and decided to accept it without a word. When he was dismissed, he went to the church and till evening practiced the piece he was going to perform.

Dusk fell. Slowly the room filled up. Wagner recognized the local community leader and nodded to him. His sister and some neighbors sat on a wooden pew. After the brief time he always took to pull himself together, Wagner mounted the three steps, twisted down the stool, and took his place at the organ. A short smothered cough pierced the stillness. Wagner raised his arms and touched the white keys with his fingertips.

After the concert he stayed at the organ for a long time, fulfilled and pleasantly drowsy. His reverie was broken by one of the neighbors, who had taken her daughter to church, asking a question. He looked around. His sister, his coat over her arm, gave a sign of impatience. The neighbor's daughter tapped him on the shoulder. She was a stolid ten-year-old girl, with breasts beginning to jut out already, and her open moist mouth betrayed a sensuality that would be the cause of many a headache for the parents before too long. The neighbor drew nearer.

"But you are . . ." she said, and pulled at the collar of her daughter, who wanted to be free of her mother's grasp. She had seen his wedding with the actress in the magazines and asked him whether he still saw the actress in spite of the divorce.

"It's really for Anna, my daughter, she admires her so much."

Wagner shook his head. He had not seen his wife for months, nor spoken with her. She was in the movies now, and accompanied in public by the minister.

He got up and went over to his sister. She held out his coat. The neighbor followed. She asked him whether what he had just played was Schumann. She remembered from the magazines that he was a Schumann expert.

"Schubert," said Wagner, "Schu-bert." He had once been seen as a expert interpreter of his songs.

"Ach, Schubert," said the neighbor.

"No, no," answered Wagner, holding the door open for the lady, "this composition is by a contemporary musician."

He switched off the light, and was the last one into the yard. They went along the little path together.

"Did you like it?"

"Yes," replied the lady, "It's rather strange, but beautiful all the same."

"Schoenberg," said Wagner. "Master of twelve-tone music, Arnold is his first name."

"Like my brother-in-law," said the lady, and told him how her Arnold had just suffered a hernia while carrying a crate of beer. "That will teach him a lesson."

"You are right." Wagner nodded. "Pain is a good teacher."

When they got to the front door, he patted the child on the head. Then he took his leave and hurried into the kitchen. As always, his sister followed, out of breath. Wagner unbuttoned his coat, took off his gloves, washed his hands, and sat down at the set table.

Smiling, he unfolded his napkin. He had told the lady the name of the composer, but had failed to mention that he had tumbled from grace and ought not to be played anymore. He had tried to explain this work to her, its greatness, and the freedom that swelled with every note. He was sure that it was this that really led to the ban on the Jew Schoenberg.

"What do you think?" asked Wagner, smiling over at his sister as she placed two steaming plates on the checked tablecloth. "Freedom is something truly beautiful, wouldn't you agree?"

With a relieved sigh she sat down next to him and reached for her fork. Wagner shook out his napkin. Yes, he thought to himself, beautiful and vast are the paths of freedom.

Lea, or How One Learns to Doubt

When a child learns language, at the same time it
learns what is to be investigated and what is not.
When it learns that there is a cupboard in the room, it
is not taught to doubt whether what it sees later on is
still a cupboard or only a kind of stage set.

— Ludwig Wittgenstein, *On Certainty*

Something was different today. Lea opened her eyes and looked
at the chair next to her bed where yesterday's clothes lay folded.
Daylight penetrated the room through the slits of the blinds,
making a geometrical pattern on the wall. She rubbed her eyes
with her fists, then scratched her back.

Why was it so quiet? She sat up and listened for footsteps.
She knew her mother's hesitant tread: it sounded as if she had
forgotten where she wanted to go after the first step. Lea turned
to the wall and felt for the corner of her blanket, sucking her
thumb. Any moment now her mother would come through the
door and sing, "Wake Up, Sleepyhead." Then she would tickle
her toes.

Lea liked her mother's smell, and breathed it in deeply with
delight when she was allowed in her parents' bed. Of course!
Mother had told her yesterday before bedtime. Today Granny,
Grandpa, Aunt Dora, and Uncle Reinhard were coming for
dinner.

She got out of bed and stretched. Granny would have a
present for her, perhaps the little wooden horse she had asked
for, and Uncle Reinhard would forget his Haggadah as he did

every year. They would get one from the library. Father would give her the key, and she would get a penny from Uncle Reinhard for helping him out of a tight spot.

She went into her brother's room, which was also now the new girl's bedroom. She had only been with them for a week, and her name was Claudine. The room was empty. Lea opened the door that led into the corridor.

It was always the same. No one helped with the housework. Not even Erika was a help, and now, to top it all off, they had delivered gladiolas. Yellow gladiolas. Cemetery flowers. She had ordered a longish low bouquet for the center of the table and two small round ones for the ends, but certainly no gladiolas, and definitely not yellow ones. She could have put up with white, red, even shades of pink, she was not petty, but not *yellow*, for God's sake. Now Erika would have to put out the yellow napkins. Did she have enough? Mrs. Lewinter made her way impatiently through the newly decorated kitchen, letting her gaze rest briefly on the wall cupboard, the spice rack, the sink, and the tap.

A prime example of carelessness. She would have to change shops. It certainly wasn't the first time that they had tried to sell her the dregs. With a green dishtowel, Mrs. Lewinter opened the oven door and jabbed at the cake. She was too good-natured. Or was she simply not cautious enough? The assistant had taken her order. A strange young man; he had a bitter smell about him. Not unpleasant, just unfamiliar.

Another half hour or so, thought Mrs. Lewinter, then I can take the cake out of the oven. She sank down onto the kitchen chair and drank her second cup of tea.

Why didn't Mother come? Erika should have called for her, too. Breakfast was probably over long ago. Lea was not in a bad mood. No, she was not. She gave the door a slight push and went into the corridor, which she hated because it was dark, had various turnoffs and blind stretches; she especially hated it when she wanted to get into her parents' bed at night. She halted in front of the electric meter and turned back. She had forgotten to put on her slippers. Mother had forbidden her to go barefoot through the apartment, lest she catch cold.

She liked being sick. Mother brought her pieces of cut-up apple and made her favorite food: tomato soup with boiled white rice that floated on the surface of the soup bowl, like a fleet of white sailboats in a red sea. With her tongue she pressed each grain against the roof of her mouth.

Lea pushed open the kitchen door. Maybe Mother would let her have a bit of chocolate cake. Erika had baked it the night before. If I could have a glass of milk with it, thought Lea . . . but she knew she would not even be allowed to lick the extra chocolate icing off the side of the plate. The cake was to remain intact throughout the day, then in the evening Mother would cut it, with all eyes trained on it. Lea stretched, went up to Mother, and was taken in her arms.

Since the birth of her son, Mrs. Lewinter had worried about Lea's behavior. When she came home with the newborn child in her arms, her daughter had greeted her by biting her hand. Hours later she could still feel the pain. Astonished, she looked at those little red indentations again and again. Her daughter's violent reaction had taken her aback. The first weeks had been difficult. Too much to take in, she thought, drinking down the last of the bitter coffee. She would have liked to sweeten it, but restrained herself in the face of the sumptuous dinner that evening.

Worst of all was the thumb-sucking. How many tears, how many promises and presents had it cost to wean her off that habit.

She did not delude herself. She saw the chubby legs and the frizzy hair, but that could still change, and of course the nose Lea inherited from her father: it sat enthroned, big and awkward, on the little one's face.

Mrs. Lewinter pushed the salt shaker to the middle of the table and looked at her daughter. She pushed back her chair.

"Sit up straight, and stop swinging your legs."

She went to the cupboard next to the oven, opened the baking drawer, cut a large triangular slice of cake, and took it to her daughter at the table.

Thank you, dear God, thank you for making Erica burn the cake. Lea pulled the plate to the edge of the table. She wanted to eat the slice very slowly. First the icing, then the top layer of sponge, then the cream, and then the base. She liked the spicy taste. It made her think of the time she and Father went on a picnic together in the vacation. They had baked potatoes in the campfire. She would go into his study soon, for he usually took a break around now. With the help of her fingers, she counted the time on the kitchen clock. Ten minutes, she thought, and probed her front tooth with her tongue. It was loose and soon would fall out.

"Can I go and see Father now?" Lea put her plate in the sink.

She looked questioningly at her mother, who was making little balls out of yellow mush. In the evening they would float next to the flecks of fat she hadn't been able to spoon out of the chicken soup.

"First of all this little chocolaty monkey is going to get washed."

Her mother held her hands under the cold stream of water and sprayed Lea. She loved the expression on her daughter's face when she was disappointed.

"My little messy monkey. My sweet little monkey. Mama's little angel is going to get washed now."

Lea buried her face in her mother's dark-blue dressing gown and fiddled with its belt.

Somehow everything had sorted itself out. Lea had calmed down after a few weeks. Her birthday party had certainly helped. She could still picture the magician's furious face, coming into the living room where she and the other mothers were sipping coffee. In whining tones he had complained that her daughter had encouraged the other children into taking apart his case and props to see whether or not he was a real magician.

Mrs. Lewinter smiled. She gave him twice the normal rate so as to avoid haggling with him in front of the other ladies. Although she didn't feel he deserved it.

It had been a stressful day. With a corner of her dressing gown she wiped the steam from the mirror above the sink. She tried to remember what little Beatrice's mother had told her about that man. A careless, slovenly woman. Gossip, gossip, gossip, thought Mrs. Lewinter, and all that from the mouth of such a tart. She soaped her daughter's back.

"Behind the ears too, my angel. Mother sees everything, hears everything, and smells everything, just like the three monkeys."

"No, not smell, the third monkey holds his mouth shut, not his nose, so that he doesn't have to speak."

Lea got out of the bathtub, leaving a puddle on the white tiled floor. Her mother wrapped her in a towel and rubbed her body dry.

"Quickly into your room and put on your undershirt for me so you don't catch cold again."

Lea hated undershirts. Nor did she like tights, hats with ribbons that tickled her neck, or shoes with buckles. But there was no getting around her mother today. She could tell by the way her lips were pressed together. She would really have to watch out. She put on her bathrobe, took a deep breath, and ran into her room.

That child hadn't an ounce of grace. Other girls of Lea's age were already young ladies. She herself had been coquettish, too. As long as she could remember, she had always wanted to please boys, and later men.

A woman has to take care of how she looks. Her appearance

is her weapon. Cunning was part of it, too, of course. Plenty of cunning, diplomacy, and a willingness to compromise.

Mrs. Lewinter put her hands in the pockets of her dressing gown and left the bathroom. Yes, you had to compromise. What dreams she had had. But that's natural when you're young. Then her husband had come along. No handsome prince on a white steed, but with a car at least. What was Erika up to now? Mrs. Lewinter opened the door to the new nanny with her son. He waved his arms in the air when his mother looked at him. How helpless these little creatures are, how affectionate. She would feed him lunch today herself.

At least three hours had gone by, and her father had still not come out of his study. And the new nanny was busy with her brother, Erika was not there, and her mother was in the kitchen. Lea was hungry. If Erika at least would come to play with her . . .

Lea plumped up her pillow, shook out the heavy down quilt, smoothed the sheet, and placed her folded nightgown under her pillow, as her mother had taught her a week ago.

With a sweeping movement she threw the stripy daytime cover over the bed, took two steps back, and contemplated her handiwork.

Something was off-kilter. She tugged at the right hand corner of the quilt: she wanted the blue and yellow stripes to run parallel to the line of the bed frame. Now there was too much material on one side, and not enough on the other. The cover was difficult.

Laboriously, Lea heaved the bed from the wall to get in at the left side, and her eyes fell on a blue book cover. Using two fingers she fished out the volume, which she had been looking for all week, from the narrow gap between the bed and the wall, and threw herself on the bed.

Now Erika could take command. Mrs. Lewinter gave up the helm. She left the ship. Not a sinking ship: up to this point everything had worked out better than expected. No dirty underwear on the bathroom floor, no leftover food on forgotten plates that she would discover at the very moment the guests were arriving. And with a bit of luck, nothing would be eaten ahead of time.

There had been that incident with the cucumber. . . . She had planned to decorate the fish with it and Erika had painstakingly cut it into wafer-thin slices, then twirled them into little spirals. And her husband had simply picked at them on the tray while reading the newspaper.

He could not understand her fury at all. He found the whole thing ridiculous. Of course, he never understood why she got worked up. A couple of friends are dropping in. We don't need a cold buffet. It's just the family. Just the family! It was laughable. Particularly the family! But if everything weren't so clean and tidy, if there wasn't always something to eat . . . where did he suppose all the meals came from, and the freshly ironed and starched shirts?

She kneaded her neck with her left hand. She had that headache again. It always came on when she was anxious. I could do with a hot bath, she thought, and decided to take a nap.

Mrs. Lewinter massaged cream into her neck with large circling motions, and energetically stretched her chin upward. Five minutes of facial gymnastics a day were enough, the beautician had said. A, O, I, E, Mrs. Lewinter articulated the vowels loudly and clearly. This was meant to keep wrinkles at bay.

She stood on the scales and noticed with satisfaction that she had lost a pound. Men could fool themselves easily. But for a woman the signs of aging could not be ignored. She screwed the cap off a little bottle, dipped a cotton bud in the oil, and dabbed the skin under the eyes.

She remembered her first period and how she had run to her mother, scared by the bleeding. Her mother had told her that from now on she would have to be careful, but she did not know what of.

She had been disappointed. She had imagined it would be much more romantic. She had kept her bra on out of modesty. Not that there was anything to see back then. Mrs. Lewinter pulled back the covers and slipped into bed. Poor Emma, she thought, and fell asleep.

Father had left without even saying hello to her. And her mother had not let her into the library to see him. Now she was in the library, and Father was no longer there. Lea could not understand it.

Mean. It was simply mean of her mother, she must have known that her father was going out. She had done it on purpose. Lea tore up the picture she had painted for him in india ink. He wouldn't get that picture, nor any other ever again, her mother either. She ran into the kitchen, through to the drawing room, and, when she did not find her mother there, up to her parents' bedroom. The closed door told her Mother was sleeping. She did not intend to spare her. She threw open the door and kicked it shut behind her.

"You are horrible. Horrible."

Lea stood in front of the bed and started to sob.

"What happened?"

Had she slept too long? Mrs. Lewinter was seized by panic and scrambled for the alarm clock that was on the bedside table next to a novel by a contemporary author, recently deceased. She was jinxed, she could not rest for even half an hour.

"You knew it. When you told me to get washed, you knew it."

Mrs. Lewinter looked at her daughter and decided there was no point in trying to get back to sleep.

"What did I know, my little angel?"

Lea kicked at the dressing gown that had slipped from the chair with her new patent leather shoes that already looked like hand-me-downs from an older sister. She raced out of the room. Mrs. Lewinter sighed and pushed back the covers.

Her mother knocked at the door. Lea did not open it. She did not even consider opening the door. She would stay in the bathroom for a long time. Lea turned the tap on and splashed her face. Then she watched herself crying in the mirror. Her eyes were red and swollen, her chin was quivering. She sat down on the toilet lid, stood up again, got the towel from its holder, sat down again and pushed the towel between her back and the wall. She would stay in the bathroom for an hour at least.

Lea crept to the door and put her ear to it. Nothing . . . nothing stirred. Neither Erika nor her mother. But perhaps there was something after all? She slowly turned the key. The corridor was empty. She stepped out, went to the kitchen, passed through the living room. There were voices coming from the dining room. Lea stood in the doorway and looked at her mother. She was discussing the seating plan with Erika. Oh, how she hated her mother.

Mrs. Lewinter combed through her wardrobe. She could wear the bolero dress of printed piqué or the beige blouse with the puffy sleeves, but the suit she wanted to wear with it was at the cleaners. That left the wraparound skirt that disguised her hips to advantage, or the severe gray woolen dress, which looked delightful on her as her delicate feminine features meant she suited a boyish cut.

Well, I'll be wicked, thought Mrs. Lewinter. Not that she would have been wicked. Anyone who was closely acquainted with Mrs. Lewinter knew that it was all a carefully constructed game, that she, like the barking dog in that proverb, had never yet bitten. Although there had been plenty of opportunities. She herself did not know why not. Out of love, or feelings of duty?

Mrs. Lewinter decided on the woolen dress. She would

wear the pearl earrings with it and the lascivious little sandals that fastened round the ankle. She observed herself in the mirror, lifted the skirt, and turned sideways. Not a bad figure, she thought. Since I started massage, my legs have firmed up. Mrs. Lewinter smiled to herself.

Once she had been in love with another man. The excitement had not been good for her. For months on end she had not been able to sleep. Especially not when her husband said offhandedly, over lunch for example, that the other man would come around the next day. She was in a daze every day. She could not concentrate on anything else knowing that he was in the library with her husband, that there they were under the same roof, only a door separating them, a mere centimeter of wood. She felt his presence in every part of her body.

Her husband, of course, registered none of it. And nothing happened. Eventually she arranged never to be home when he came by. Mrs. Lewinter folded up the silk blouse that she had gotten out of the wardrobe and laid it back on the pile.

She could not understand what people found so nice about it. One could not think straight anymore and behaved awkwardly. She had hated herself back then. But now that was all in the past. She was glad that tranquil nights had returned.

"Not here," said Mrs. Lewinter, shooing Lea off the bed. She laid out the sandals for Erika to polish. "Go and play."

Lea didn't want to go to her room. Nor did she want to play. She sat on the floor and clung to her mother's legs. Her mother shook her off and gave her a little slap.

"Go on, my little one, go through to Erika in the kitchen."

Lea got up and nipped her mother's arm.

"You little witch. Go away."

Lea shook her head and started to cry. Everything had changed since her brother came along. She sank down on her knees and clasped her mother's legs with both arms. Her mother shuffled to the door and called for Erika. She banged against the edge of the bed, but the pain did not bother her. She would not let go. No way would she let go.

This could not go on. She was exhausted. She had sent Erika out with the little one, although there was so much to be done. She'd had to promise that Erika would buy that dreadful stuff that sticks to your teeth and makes them rot.

She licked the spoon and added a pinch of pepper and nutmeg. Then she stuffed the mashed potato into the piping bag and pushed out fat rosettes onto the baking tray. Pommes duchesse: elegant and inexpensive.

She went into the dining room and cast a critical eye over the table. She adjusted a fork, lined up a knife, stepped back, and viewed the set table appreciatively. She had gotten out the silver cutlery. Her pride and joy, inherited from her grandmother. Very lovely, she thought, in spite of the yellow gladioli. She jumped. The doorbell always gave her a fright. She hurried through the corridor and opened the door furiously.

"Can't you remember your . . ."

Bewildered, she looked at the two men standing in the doorway. She smiled, and hastily ran her fingers through her hair.

First they went to the playground. Then Erika bought her some cotton candy. She pulled it off the stick using two fingers and let it melt on her tongue. She still wanted to have a ride on the pony, but Erika said there was no time for that. The guests would be there soon.

Lea fiddled with a piece of chalk, now completely moist.

"Will you give me a piggyback?"

"No."

"Just to the front door."

"No."

"Pretty please."

"Shh, be quiet." Erika took a firm hold of Lea's shoulder.

"You're hurting me." Lea rubbed her arm.

What was up with Erika now? What had she done wrong? She had not done anything. Erika yanked the child, about to cross the street, in the opposite direction.

"Let's have some ice cream."

"But we have to go back home." Lea looked at her plump nanny. She didn't understand. And then she caught sight of them, by the front door. Lea wanted to break free and run to her father — he was sitting in a big black car — but Erika held her tight.

"Let me go."

That was why they had sent her out. That was why she was allowed to eat cotton candy. That was why Erika wanted to buy her ice cream even before dinner. Everything was clear now.

"Let me go."

She watched her mother go into the car, she watched the French au pair, whom she could not stand, had never liked, hand over the bundle that was her brother. Lea tried to break free from Erika's arms. Everyone knew about it. Everyone apart from herself. Her father, her mother, even her little brother, would drive away in the big black car.

"Shh, shh, my darling. Mommy and Daddy will be back very soon."

Lea sank her teeth into the woman's hands. Even Erika had known about it.

"Hush, hush. Mommy and Daddy are just taking Leo to the doctor because he is sick."

The stranger stepped into the car and shut the door. Erika stroked Lea's head. The car drove slowly past them.

Lea looked at her father. He was in his shirtsleeves, and stared downward.

They were all lying. Her parents were not going to the doctor's. Her brother was not sick. They were going away on a journey. They were all going on a journey in the big black car. And her father didn't look at her, and her mother didn't even think to wave. But she had seen her. She had even turned around.

Why hadn't they taken her with them? Was there not enough room? She could have sat on her mother's knee. She could have made herself really small. Why hadn't they taken her with them? Lea looked at Erika, who was rocking her in her arms.

"Shh, shh, my sweetheart, shh, shh. Mommy and Daddy will be back soon."

"You liar."

Lea kicked Erika, who let her. Once, twice, three times. Everyone was going on a journey with the two men. And she was left behind, all alone.

La Ronde

1.

The Scouring Cloth

The life span of a scouring cloth
Can be noticeably extended
If its center
Is darned with a patch
Made from the leftovers of the old
Cloth, ruined
In the center.
In addition, one should
Always wring out scouring cloths
Following the line of the thread.

La ronde was begun by Miss Barbara Dahl, the accountant, unemployed for over a year. For reasons not completely understood by Miss Dahl, her long-term employer, naturalized since 1918, Richard Kahn, a full Jew, had his citizenship revoked. When he was expelled in the middle of 1934, Miss Dahl found herself abruptly deprived of her salary. Whether because she had "served" a Jew, or because there was a shortage of jobs, Miss Dahl could find only temporary positions. She worked at an optician's, for a fur dealer, in a bar, finally spent several months sitting at the information desk booth in the Dresdner Bank, was dismissed for not recommending the fixed-rate bonds warmly enough, and, having tried her hand at cleaning cameras, was now devoting herself to sewing clothes.

She found this activity very enjoyable. She loved the diversity of the materials, caressing them lingeringly with her fingertips, and the whir of the sewing machine she had bought for Christmas.

Since she had not learned the seamstress trade and was not confident enough to try out her own designs, she had subscribed to a woman's magazine that had patterns in it. She thought it would help her progress. It was produced by the Party and opened Miss Dahl's eyes to the true nature of Kahn, her erstwhile employer, and offered plenty of other worthwhile information to work with.

It so happened that this very magazine was having a competition. The third and final part of it consisted in creating a new look from old scraps of material, a task to which Miss Dahl had dedicated herself with particular fervor for quite some time.

If she could not win one of the top six money prizes, Miss Dahl would have been happy with at least the mounted flower prints (she had just recently bought the framed, color picture of the Führer), and so decided to take part. Not long before she had made a dress for her neighbor out of an out-of-date checked jacket and a light-colored linen skirt that was too tight. As the dress had turned out very nicely, and everyone had admired it, Miss Dahl got out the pattern, wrote down the material requirements on the back along with the instructions, and sent it off to the fashion and housekeeping editor.

To Miss Dahl's great surprise, she received a letter three weeks later, briefly but warmly informing her that she, Miss Barbara Dahl of B., had been chosen as first-prize winner. Not only was the fashion expert extremely enthusiastic about her design, so too were the deputy editor and the editor herself. The money arrived the next day. Moved, she read the congratulations card adorned with a lovely saying. Then she went through to her neighbor, informed her about their victory, and gave her a present of a copy of the magazine: she had laid aside four at the paper shop.

Luck, against her for so long, was smiling on her again at last. After a nearly two-year sentence of unemployment for her lack of racial awareness, she was given a job in a large bakery, just a month after being crowned the Queen of Recycling. The famous salt pretzels, known to one and all as "crick-cracks," were made there.

2.

Second prize went to Mrs. Helga Pfeifer. If the first prize was intended to commend the imagination shown by one reader, the magazine wanted the second prize to draw the attention of readers in all the provinces to the practical sense of a housewife, mother of four boys, who had immeasurable experience in recycling old clothes.

Mrs. Pfeifer resisted any unnecessary frills and instead sent in her suggestion on how worn-out elbows on sweaters could be prevented for a considerable length of time — not forever, unfortunately. The only indulgence she allowed herself was a title as a heading to the ten sentences or so of explanation, written on a page out of one of her son's exercise books.

"Elbows on Sweaters are the Bane of Our Lives" was not only practical, it was also easy to carry out. Mrs. Pfeifer suggested removing the worn-out elbow and changing it with the other one, by swapping over the two sleeves: the right sleeve sewn into the left shoulder seam, and the left one into the right seam. Mrs. Pfeifer was unanimously declared second-prize winner and four weeks later the prize was sent to her along with a letter of congratulations. Mrs. Pfeifer deposited the check at her bank. Since the letter had encouraged her to treat herself to something, she ignored the pleas of her three youngest sons, did not buy a single penknife, went to have her hair done, and bought a telescope marked down thirty percent.

Now it turned out that those same three sons had taken up a new hobby a few weeks earlier. Their equally enthusiastic classmates wholeheartedly urged them to pursue it. It involved closely observing the carpenter's wife, living directly across from them. She got dressed and undressed with the window open and no curtains. Her anatomy was discussed in detail in the schoolyard.

To quench their thirst for detail, the sons borrowed the telescope, although it was strictly forbidden. No sooner had their mother left the room than the eldest son pulled the telescope out from under the bed, rolled up the blind, and, wrapped up in his blanket, waited for the light to go on in the room with the window. But nothing happened. Slowly, he went from floor to floor, ignoring his brothers impatiently tugging at his arm.

Mrs. Pfeifer was sitting beside the radio, drained, when a quiet but determined quarrel broke out in the children's room because of the telescope: the younger brothers also wanted a look at what had drawn a soft whistle from the eldest.

"What is going on here?"

In one fell swoop, Mrs. Pfeifer opened the door, went into the dark interior of the room, and saw the telescope being passed from hand to hand. Whether he wanted to draw attention away from an imminent scolding, or because the sight had really shocked him, words came bubbling out of the eldest son about what he had seen. Mrs. Pfeifer snatched at the telescope. Sure enough. Two men were sitting closely entwined on the sofa, stroking each other's hair.

That very evening, the indignant woman told her husband what was going on in the other building. Mr. Pfeifer congratulated himself for having such an alert son, went up to the fourth floor, found out from the neighbor the name of the elderly man living over the way, conscientiously noted down the name and address of the relevant person, added to it a brief written explanation, and handed over everything in a white envelope to his boss, who was a member of the Party. One week later the elderly man was led away. Mr. Pfeifer, on the other hand, was given a raise in salary.

Mr. Bernhard was arrested for his asocial behavior, noticed by a source that would remain anonymous, and taken to a bright green building. After a ten-hour interrogation, in which he saw reason, he was allowed to go home. There, he drank a cup of strong freshly made tea, packed a few items of clothing, and left the country that same night.

Five weeks later Operation II S was successfully completed. Twenty-five men in total were arrested for breaking § 175 of the Civil Code, as they were strongly suspected of having sexual relations with members of their own sex.

3.

Because of the strict legislation, ten of the twenty-five men had gotten married. Another four lived with their parents. Only three of the men had frequently been seen in the company of someone of their own sex.

All the men were freed after the first intense interrogation. Four of them tried to escape, thereby proving their guilt. Three of them were rearrested after their attempt to escape failed. Only one of them managed to leave the country, but he was tracked down two years later in a small harbor town and turned in.

Two of the homosexual men, one of them a sports journalist whose captivating coverage of the Olympic Games was still fresh in people's minds and the other a young workman, hanged themselves.

Eight men active in the public sphere, among them the respected theater director, were fired on the spot. Private businesses that employed a further nine of the men were casually advised by courier in an informative manner to do the same, which they promptly did.

Six men, a bookseller, a real-estate broker, a liquor-store owner, the owner of a menswear store, a printer, and a glazier, had to sell their businesses to trusted members of the Party within the month, to avoid enforced expropriation. Two businesses, those of a publisher of Bibles and of a carpenter, were liquidated due to incompetent management.

All the men had a second interrogation, sometimes even a third or fourth. Preventive detention was imposed for anything from seven to ten days.

With the exception of an industrialist and the son of a high-up Party member, in twenty-three cases a file was opened that would be available at all times to any Party official conducting research. On the cover of the file was the name, age, and address of the person concerned, along with a certain abbreviation for internal use.

In the hope of recognizing typical patterns of behavior, which could prove useful in identifying more men, the files also contained incidental details of the private life of the accused. All the witnesses — domestic help, work colleagues, friends, family, and neighbors — told all they knew about the subjects free of charge.

Twenty-three of the twenty-five men lived in the city, two in a smaller suburb, ten in rented apartments, nine in apartments they owned, and six in houses.

After their interrogation, fifteen men were sent to a labor camp. When the wife of one of the prisoners asked about him, she was told laconically that things were better for her this way.

Three of the fifteen men died in the labor camp, three were freed after ten months, and nine were put in a train along with Jewish and political prisoners bound for Oranienburg concentration camp.

Within the first four months there, three of the men died, one of typhus, one of starvation, one was hanged.

Another four men were shot a few months later because of their pink triangles. Two men survived.

All the men had to sign a declaration in which they confessed that even in their early youth they had been guilty of perversions. Some of the men claimed during the public "morality trials" that they posed a particular threat to National Socialist society and asked that they be sterilized.

In the case of five of the twenty-five men, the mothers were still alive at the time of arrest. Six men still had both parents, four had only a father. Ten men had already lost their parents before their arrest. The parents were sent a letter the week after their son's death. In it, the camp commander informed the parents of their loss and named weak cardiac muscle as the cause of death.

Four of the ten women whose husbands had been arrested for asocial behavior filed for divorce. The others maintained contact during the early stages of imprisonment.

Five of the ten women with homosexual or bisexual husbands had children. Three children were given up for adoption. The children, aged between one and five years, took on the adopting family's name. For the sake of better integration, the children's mothers were forbidden to visit the new families.

Only two children turned against their fathers and refused to talk to them. One was the sixteen-year-old son of a doctor, who had been demoted from group leader to simple member of the Hitler Youth. The other was the twelve-year-old daughter of a civil servant.

In the case of nearly all the men, work colleagues, acquaintances, and neighbors knew the reason they had been arrested. Only five people — the childhood sweetheart of the publisher, a widower without dependents and neighbor to a male nurse, the acquaintance of a shopkeeper, a church minister, and a colleague of the accountant — tried to help and stand by the men or their families.

4.

One of these people was Miss Barbara Dahl. Just before lunch one day eight months after winning first prize in the sewing contest, she was summoned to the private residence next to the factory. She was extremely surprised, since she had set foot in the director's and his wife's house only twice. She quickly tidied her desk, nervously ran her fingers through her hair, tucked her blouse into her skirt, and set off, her heart thumping with anxiety.

The director had looked her up and down and observed to himself what he had already noticed as a student: education is unbecoming in a woman. Then he told the intimidated young lady that he had heard so much about her competence that, in spite of her youth, she was to be appointed head accountant.

"Ah," said Miss Dahl, happiness robbing her of speech, and clung on to the chair for a moment. She knew nothing about her colleague's dismissal. She was too excited to think clearly and to reach the logical conclusion about her promotion. She was only to hear about it from the security man who had accompanied her to the director's house and was now waiting for her outside in the garden under a pear tree. The conscientious and courteous Mr. Mehler, who had been her superior until a few days before, had been sent packing without notice.

Three weeks later Miss Dahl visited the Mehler family because she felt sorry for the wife and the two children and was curious about their situation. Her trained eye took in the neglected state of the clothes of the children and Mrs. Mehler, now separated from her husband. Passion stirred anew in Miss Dahl.

Not wanting to irritate the woman, who was obviously too proud to accept financial help, she offered instead to recycle any old children's clothes. After asking several times, she was given two faded outgrown playsuits belonging to the youngest son, which the woman had laid aside in the kitchen cupboard to use as cleaning rags. Mrs. Mehler did not subscribe to the magazine that had awarded Miss Dahl first prize, and knowing nothing of her husband's colleague's sewing, did not want to take any risks: therefore she cautiously left the better-quality outgrown items safely in the wardrobe.

How surprised she was when Miss Dahl came back a few days later with a playsuit that looked brand new. She enthusiastically quizzed the young woman.

Soon they were meeting regularly at Mrs. Mehler's house or in a pastry shop famous for its cream cake. They talked while the children were looked after by a distant cousin.

Although Miss Dahl was seven years younger, she felt responsible for her new friend's fate. Mr. Mehler's savings — for over eight years he had deposited a fifth of his salary in a savings account, which he had assigned to his wife's name before his arrest — were considerably reduced now, and Miss Dahl's modest support could not cover the costs, so Miss Dahl got her friend, who had been a secretary in a small firm before getting married, a part-time position at the baking factory.

Now the friends saw each other every day at work, and left together at the end of the day. Following the advice of Mrs. Mehler, who did not think it wise to push one's luck in these uncertain times and worried every evening when her young friend set off for home, Miss Dahl moved into an attic apartment, ten square meters bigger than her old one, two floors above Mrs. Mehler. It had become vacant when the tenant, a single widower without dependents, died. Much to Mrs. Mehler's irritation, he had bequeathed his two canaries to her.

This was the happiest time in in the life of Miss Dahl, who had long resigned herself to being without company. It was also the most productive, since after all those restless years she was finally content and could give her imagination and talent free rein, with Mrs. Mehler seeing to the economic and household chores. During this time she created what must be considered the high point of her sewing career: a black dress with a fitted bodice praised by all. She made it for Mrs. Mehler from a dinner jacket and a white shirt of her former husband. From that day forth, Mrs. Mehler would wear it every Sunday to coffee parties, while her husband was some hundred kilometers away, digging holes in a field with a shovel.

Two Wedding Rings (Gold)

THE RECKTENWALDS HAD BEEN MARRIED FOR THIRTY-FIVE YEARS when Detective Reinhold Mehring, conducting the body search that all prisoners had to undergo prior to entering preventive detention, relieved them of their golden wedding rings.

Although this body search and the resulting inventory of the prisoner's personal belongings had been part of Mehring's duties for more than five years and he had established a routine designed to make the rather unpleasant process as quick and painless as possible for him and for the prisoners, he was irritated this time around.

He did not understand the serenity and faith radiating from the couple standing in front of him, despite the surely disagreeable circumstances in which they found themselves, and did not know how to act in front of them.

During all his long experience — Mehring belonged to the crafty old foxes in the police station and was highly respected by everyone on account of his dependability — he had learned that there were two types: the stubborn and (borrowed from his favorite author) the "pallid murderer."

To deal with the prisoners in his custody as quickly and as painlessly as possible, he had developed different methods for the two types. In the case of the stubborn sort, who let everything wash over them apathetically as though someone else's fate was taking its painful course in the room, his colleagues let their authority be felt. He, on the other hand, addressed the prisoner in a pitiful tone, sighed again and again, and did everything he could to convey sympathy, following his impulses completely. Mehring acted this way since he had noticed that even the most hardheaded case was not impervious to slow, cunning, creeping self-pity, that even the stubborn sort would break down when confronted with a sympathizing soul, whereas raw shows of power only strengthened their determined denial of facts.

Should the prisoner, however, already show outward signs of feeling intimidated — eye contact and the position of the hands were good indicators — Mehring would look at him with severity and swallow the surge of emotion in his throat.

Nothing was more embarrassing to him than a wailing person, oblivious to the world in his grief. He could not bear the sight of a sobbing female, and found the sight of a man who had lost control repugnant.

Mehring looked down at the fine gray lead of his propelling pencil, then back at the couple standing in front of him, waiting. He had to admit to himself, reluctantly, that although their file stated they were enemies of the people, he could not help liking the lady and her elderly husband. And had they met in other circumstances, at a family party or at the local pub, he would have been able to put his finger on what it was he found so irritating in the married couple's attitude.

But Detective Mehring could not allow himself to reflect upon human dignity, not in his office, and certainly not the dignity of two prisoners. For he understood, as every child in the Reich did, that the enemy of the people was double-dealing, impudent, cowardly, and dishonest, that the concepts *enemy of the people* and *dignity* must not be uttered in the same breath, particularly not by a detective assigned the task of conducting body searches on the prisoners.

What's all this? Mehring thought, shaking his head vigorously, and he asked Mr. Recktenwald to take a seat on the chair opposite. The way the old man pushed the chair back, jolting it rather so that the chair legs left the ground, took him back to his youth. He remembered his father pushing his chair back with that same impatience to let him, Mehring, pass by him after the meal.

Mehring felt the same irritation, the same helpless fury rise up in him that he had felt years ago whenever he saw his father's white folded hands resting on the kitchen table, the harbinger of approaching humiliation. Although they were resting peacefully on the clean tablecloth, they could spring into action at any moment, like a predator catching the scent of its prey, to land on his face with a cracking slap. He hated them all the more as it was inconceivable that he defend himself against his father. Mehring got up and walked to the window.

"Read this through, please," he said pointing to the inventory, lying on top of the heap of the Recktenwald's possessions.

"If everything is correct, sign it."

He looked at the facades of the houses across the way. A woman was stretching her full-figured torso far out of the window and cleaning the glass with wide circular motions. Like a greeting, thought Mehring. Scrutinizing the building's gleaming dark green front door, he saw his father again in the woolen jacket that he wore over his shirt in the evenings, more comfortable than his daytime waistcoat, but more fashionable than the dressing gown he put on just before going to bed. He saw the white cuffs of the shirt protruding from the jacket that had gone fluffy from all the washings, and his father's thickly veined hands. And it suddenly struck him as odd that he could remember all these insignificant details, and yet could not recall how he himself looked as a boy: whenever he encountered his father in his thoughts, he was always the man he had become over the years.

"I beg your pardon?" Mehring turned round and walked up to Mrs. Recktenwald.

"Couldn't I?" she asked. "It means so much to me. I've never taken it off, ever."

Mehring looked into her timidly smiling face, then down at her hands. She was twisting the ring with her left-hand thumb and index finger. A nervous tic, thought Mehring, that she doesn't notice anymore. He sat down.

"No," he said. "I'm afraid that won't be possible." When he saw her disappointed face he added that he was sorry.

He understood the woman's reasons. Nevertheless it would be impossible for him to make such a decision.

"Leave it be." The man slipped the ring from his wife's finger and threw it on the table.

"You have to understand that . . ." Mehring began, then stopped when he saw the man's hunched posture, a curved vault of anger.

There was no point. He would not be able to make them understand him. They wouldn't understand his methods. They didn't know the department. Didn't know the rules of the department. They didn't know what it meant to carry out this work, that no exceptions could be made, or else everything that was meant to last for a thousand years, that was being built to last for eternity with his participation, would completely collapse like a house of cards. He pressed the button that made the bell ring outside.

"If you please," he said as the policeman came in, and indicated they were to go now.

That was enough for the morning. Impatiently he ran his fingers through his hair and stared at the door closing behind the couple; it clicked shut with an easy motion that angered him, for it did not seem to fit with the surroundings of an office. Such is my reward, thought Mehring with a sigh, and walked over to the sink.

He did not often become flushed, hardly at all these days, and only if something pleasant happened. Now, however, touching his face, he felt the heat coming off it. He went back to his desk and straightened out his writing tools: the inkwell, the blotting paper, and the fountain pen holder he had been given for Christmas, complete with its fountain pen made of solid silver that produced graceful loops when put to paper. Then he picked up the Recktenwalds' declaration. He would deal with the remaining formalities after lunch. He still had to note down the reason for arrest, place of arrest, the code at the top of the form, and any distinguishing features. None, thought Mehring, not even a mole, and added the form to the stack of papers to be dealt with over on the right-hand side of his desk. He put on his jacket, straightened the sleeves, and walked over to the door. He already had his hand on the door handle when he turned around and returned to his desk.

One could never be too careful. He knew everyone in the office, of course, but the sergeant's wife was critically ill. A lengthy affair. Poor man, thought Mehring, I don't want to lead him into temptation. He took a box, wrote the couple's name on a piece of paper that he had cut in half, and pasted it competently on the lid of the box. Then he took the inventory, read out the first object on the list, fished it out of the pile, and put it in the box, and scored through the word with his pencil. He worked quickly, with concentration.

When he got to the ladies' watch with the leather strap turned black from wear, he paused and, after holding it up to the window to check, added that it was a gold-plated watch.

Finally, he reached for the rings. Although they lay uppermost on the pile he had kept pushing them aside. Two wedding rings (gold). He slowly drew his pencil through the four words. He was about to put the rings in the box when he noticed that they were engraved on the inside.

Mehring peered at the curved writing and read the words. They made him pensive. Hesitantly, he placed the rings in the box, sealed it, and fished out a rubber band from his desk. He pulled it round the box and slipped the declaration together with the list beneath it.

He would countersign the list afterward and also fill his fountain pen, which was barely writing now. He opened the desk drawer and pulled out the newspaper he had not managed to finish that morning because of all the subpoenas. He was especially interested in the tragic tale of the actress and had deliberately saved it up for last. Mehring rolled the paper into a tube, bounced it off the table a couple of times to cheer himself up, and went off to the local pub. He was slowly working up an appetite.

After greeting two of the regulars, and exchanging a few words with the waitress, he ordered the day's special and a small beer. While he was waiting for his food, he turned to the culture section.

"Oh, yes," Mehring said, smiling at the waitress as she put his glass on top of a round beer mat, "There is something very nice about a beer like this."

And then he could not help thinking of it again: of the rings, two wedding rings made of gold, now in the safekeeping of the Reich, and also of the Recktenwalds, whom he had duly passed on to the responsible authorities for custody, according to the regulations, and of the man, and of his parents who had the same words engraved in their rings back then, the same or something similar, for his parents' generation had still believed in those alien-sounding words, devoid of purpose.

Oh, yes, he thought, and then his food arrived.

A Fundamentally Flawed Attitude

(The Powder Compact)

THE FEBRUARY 27 ISSUE of the *Berlin Law and Court Journal* reported that a ruling had been passed by the District Court of Berlin on January 19, 1937, citing the purchase of a silver-plated powder compact from a Jewish store as a marital offense.

The marriage of the parties concerned, Dieter and Vicki Walter, who were both very young, had lived together for a mere five months, and hadn't known each other much longer than that, was to be considered failed due to reciprocal fault. The court noted that the defendant's fundamentally flawed attitude had revealed itself to the plaintiff through the act of purchasing a compact from a Jewish store.

Vicki Walter must have been aware that her husband could not approve of the purchase as it would create difficulties for him as a Party member and in his capacity as local group leader: the purchase was at odds with both his lifestyle and his philosophy.

Quite spontaneously, claimed Mrs. Walter, she decided to go into the store. (It was the O.B. Department Store, which had been in the Jewish hands of the Oppenheimer and Baum families ever since its founding, a fact with which the defendant must have been familiar through her husband's information project; Mr. Walter, along with two other Party members, had drawn up a list of all the Jewish stores and pinned it in strategic locations all over the city. One of the lists was outside this very department store.)

She had not recklessly planned the purchase. She had come, she declared, from the market and was carrying her shopping bag full of ingredients for lunch, which she still had to cook. She planned to make potato salad, and added to the normal groceries were two kilos of potatoes and six bottles of beer, which meant the bag was very heavy. She had to stop several times to catch her breath. The handles of the bag were cutting into her hands, too.

"I did not deliberately stop outside the department store," she said. "I went as far as I could, but my hands were hurting."

She noticed the compact, she said, when she was having a quick look around.

"I can hardly stare at the ground all day, just because the whole place is full of Jewish products," she retorted, when her husband asked why she had looked particularly at this shop's wares.

The compact was in the shop window. Mrs. Walter spotted the compact in question immediately. She had always wanted a compact like it, as her husband knew. She had spoken of her wish to possess such a compact on various occasions. The last time was around her birthday, but her husband hadn't listened. He hadn't given her anything, neither a compact nor anything else.

She therefore saw it as perfectly within her rights to buy the compact, to which she had taken an instant liking, and without a moment's hesitation she went into the store.

In response to the question with what means she had planned to purchase it, she replied that she had used the sum leftover from the housekeeping money, which she had saved up over the last two weeks, as a reward for her economizing.

"The housekeeping money is mine," she said. "I am the housewife," thereby irritating her husband, who was of the opinion that any leftover money should be returned to him.

"We could have decided together what to do with the money," he said.

The plaintiff admitted that the comment "It's my money, not yours" had left a particularly bitter aftertaste.

"She has no right to keep anything of mine since she shows no interest in my political activities, nor in the repercussions of her actions. I had had it up to here," he said.

When asked why she left the store in such a rush, the defendant replied that it certainly did not stem from any feeling of guilt, contrary to her husband's belief. She had got a shock from seeing the time on the clock above the exit. Half an hour had passed, and she noted to herself she would have to dash to get lunch ready in time.

"He," she exclaimed, pointing at Mr. Walter, "would have a fit if his food wasn't ready and waiting for him on the table." This made the courtroom chuckle.

"It certainly could not have been as straightforward as that," contested the plaintiff. If she had not been feeling guilty, why had she not shown him the compact, or at least mentioned it?

Mrs. Walter replied that she had refrained from mentioning it because she knew he would ask to have the housekeeping money back to finance his political activities, although it was money that she had saved. The thought had not entered her head, even back home, that the store was a Jewish one, and that she was now the proud owner of a Jewish compact.

Mr. Walter interjected that therein, to his mind, lay her offense.

"She is the wife of a local group leader," he said furiously. "I spent four whole evenings at least with two of my men in the kitchen, drawing up the list of Jewish stores."

"I, however, was not allowed to enter the kitchen." She could have listened from the sitting room, countered her husband. She could have made herself familiar with the required information anytime thereafter. The list was laid out along with other material on the sitting room table. Thus it was well within reach.

"I don't have any time to read, I have to make potato salad," retorted the woman, making the courtroom laugh again.

It was high time he explained how he seemed to know every

detail, demanded the defendant, expressing her suspicion that she had been spied upon.

He had found out about the purchase of the compact by chance.

"She," said Mr. Walter, pointing at his wife, "was observed by a guard strategically placed in front of the store to ward off would-be Aryan shoppers."

The guard was leaving for lunch when he turned round, with no particular aim, and caught sight of the defendant entering the shop. The accused, the plaintiff went on, had chosen her moment well. She had not, however, reckoned with the guard's vigilance. Thus, in spite of taking precautions, she was caught in the act.

The guard, devoted to Mr. Walter, regarded it as a matter of honor to sacrifice his lunch hour, to remain standing in front of store, and carefully follow the course of events. The accused left the store twenty minutes later, smiling contentedly and sporting an O.B. shopping bag. Mrs. Walter then went directly home to their common apartment, but held the bag for all to see, the entire way back.

"That shocked me particularly deeply," said Mr. Walter. "It didn't even cross her mind to hide the bag discreetly in among the groceries. Any old neighbor could have seen where the local group leader's wife spends her mornings."

Everyone, he added, knows the logo printed in red on those bags.

"She had been making fun of my political activities for quite some time," said the plaintiff. He lent no credibility to her theory that her open behavior emphasized her innocence.

"A friend of hers stirred her up against me." The plaintiff named a neighbor who lived on the floor below them. She was also the one who contacted the police on hearing the woman's cries for help. They arrived three quarters of an hour later.

Mr. Walter said he had found out about the purchase after a meeting. The guard, respecting the situation, approached him afterward, when the other members had already left, thus show-ing more compassion and sensitivity than his own wife.

He had questioned her about it immediately. To begin with, she had denied it. When he told her she had been seen, she called him a dirty rat.

Even after several warnings she was not prepared to hand over the object she had purchased from the O.B. department store.

"I had to search the apartment."

After a cursory look in the kitchen and the sitting room, he ransacked her wardrobe. In no time he found a compact in among her underwear. He had never laid eyes on it before and she could not explain where it came from. As its place of safe-keeping struck him as more than a little suspicious, he held on to it.

It was only after the subsequent argument regarding the compact that he struck her. He hit her once, possibly twice but certainly no more, hard in the face. He did not do this in a fit of rage, but rather to teach her a lesson. She grabbed hold of his arm and demanded he hand over the compact.

"She wanted the compact, spoke of nothing else, and didn't listen to what I had to say," retorted Mr. Walter, as his wife pointed out to the room the areas of the face where bruising had occurred. He added, "She started screaming, 'Give me back my compact, give me back my compact.' I had to hit her."

According to Mr. Walter, in this instance she also showed a lack of sensitivity. The neighbors were forced to take notice of her because of her shrieks.

He then filed for divorce immediately. When the police had gone, she refused, the plaintiff went on, to spend even ten min-utes more under the same roof with him. She left for her mother's. She sent her mother to him the next day, and she had asked that he make up with her daughter. He told her he would give her another chance. He had made her return as easy as pos-sible, and was even willing to forget the incident.

She came back the following day, but still refused to speak to him. A whole week went by this way and he spent as much time as possible at the Party, to escape the unbearably oppressive atmosphere at home.

"A week later, she finally opened her mouth. I was extremely excited that evening because it brought the end of a project we'd been busy with for two weeks."

Together with a companion from the Party, a teacher, he had drafted one hundred manifestos, which were to be read throughout the Reich.

"We sat down together in the sitting room after dinner. I lit a candle and began reading the text to her. She listened passively, playing with the tassels of the tablecloth. I tried to ignore it. As I read the last section, she smirked. I asked her what was so funny and forbade her to smile. She held her mouth tight shut, like a stubborn child, and listened like that without moving."

He had tried not to feel provoked, and read on to the end. He had not shown his annoyance. Then he had asked her whether she had anything to say about it.

"And what do you think she said when I asked her for her opinion?"

She asked, said the plaintiff, where her compact was.

"That was her only utterance. It was obvious to me then that it was all over between us."

Mr. Walter stated that he did not harbor any feelings of anger toward his wife. He put her behavior down to youth.

"Vicki, when all is said and done, is not a bad person," he said, and when the grounds for the sentence — his wife's fundamentally flawed attitude — had been read out, he wished her the necessary maturity to change her colors soon.

50 Kilos of Gold Fillings

1.

My name is Ernst Fuchs. In 1908 I first saw the light of day in a sleepy little town on the Polish border. It had a beautiful gothic church tower and a marketplace where the local farmers sold their wares twice a week. There was also an inn where high society liked to gather on a Sunday to talk about everything under the sun over a midday drink.

My father had a general store. He stocked just about anything that could be of use in our town, from raisins, schnapps, and smoked fish to cotton thread.

There were two fat catalogs on the counter. They were sent to us twice a year and were full of illustrations of what you could order, prices including postage. Should you be looking for something special — a baptism gift or a wedding present — you would come to my father, leaf through the brochures, and get his advice.

My father was the contact to the outside world. He loved keeping up to date with it all and so he traveled to Danzig or Berlin more than was strictly necessary. We were all ears when he returned from one of his trips, and he told us his stories at bedtime. They seemed more incredible to us than Grimms' fairytales, inhabited as they were by electric kettles, trams, and every imaginable machine. We always awaited his return impatiently, in anticipation of a present.

My mother hardly ever helped out in the store. She didn't have a particularly strong constitution. The four pregnancies had certainly taken their toll on her physically. A year after I entered the scene, a child was stillborn, and I don't believe she ever got over that emotionally.

Although my father worshiped my mother, or so it seemed to us through our children's eyes, he didn't like to have her around him in the store. He also tucked himself away from us whenever he could.

I'm sure this was the only reason he went fishing on weekends. He certainly wasn't fond of the taste of fish. When I was still in shorts, I was allowed to go with him sometimes. This soon petered out though because I couldn't keep quiet — show me the child who can.

I can barely remember the births of my two sisters: Katharina was two years younger, and Charlotte, known as Otta, came a year later. For some inexplicable reason, however, Käthe's arrival is associated with an image of a shiny red toy train rumbling round in a circle, and a small iron barrier that I excitedly raised when the train drew near. Perhaps I'd received this as compensation for the small catlike crumpled sister that suddenly appeared in a cradle in my room. Or maybe I'd seen a picture of it in one of my father's catalogs and wanted it, knowing of course that my parents might be a little more open to persuasion right then. I'm really not sure now. Anyway, it doesn't play such an important role.

When I was about four years old my parents employed a nanny. She had thick brown hair that she wore pleated and rolled up around the ears. I adored her. She cooked, cleaned up, and if my mother was resting, or having a friend for tea, she would sometimes look after us children. She is the one who armed me with the fairies, giants, and witches that I re-create at my godchild's bedside.

Our nanny, whom I called by her last name, came from a very simple background: both her mother and grandmother had been maids. She would have become one too, if she hadn't been lucky, becoming an employee of my father and enchanting our childhood.

She baked an orange cake for us every Friday. And thus, quite unintentionally, she instilled in us a sense of time. The cake did not only signify the start of the weekend. Without this dark brown object, we would have known nothing of the importance or, dare I suggest it, the existence of a religious day.

I was to have many opportunities later on to sample orange cake — it is regarded as one of the few culinary specialties of the town I live in now — but never, not even abroad, did they excite such pleasure as those early ones: that sunny smell, spongy, so light that it crumbled at the slightest touch, the base just a little moist from the runny warm butter and the juice of the oranges, sprinkled with a mixture of almond chips and powdered sugar like the snow of the first day of winter. It would give us children short delicious hiccups, which became in their turn a weekly family tradition, as we each shoveled in our allotted slice hurriedly to ensure a second helping.

Twice a year we were spruced up and sent to a photographer. These sittings seemed to last an eternity. All movement was prohibited and you were supposed to laugh at all sorts of childish and unfitting remarks: we did so out of feelings of pity and impatience rather than any genuine desire. What torture!

The day before I always went to the barber. Or rather I was dragged to the barber by my father, because I hated and feared him. He joked about cutting off my ears as well as my hair if I didn't keep still.

The nanny cut my sisters' hair. She casually pleated it into two pigtails, then with one snip cut off several centimeters of hair. With long hair, the precision of the cut isn't considered all that important.

I think that at moments like that — most of the time I was quite content as I was — I envied my sisters for being girls. Although I understood fairly quickly that the barber was just kidding, it was only when I was older that I could shake off the unsettled feeling that possessed me when I saw a pair of scissors.

Those numerous photos taken in front of ever-changing backgrounds could tell a historian far more about the tastes, fears, and dreams of our time than the silly statistics so fashionable today, as though figures could describe our reality. Those photos have of course disappeared without a trace. I have no idea who took them when my family was driven out of their house one night. I keep the hope alive that one day while out taking a Sunday stroll I will come across my father, my mother, and my rather awkwardly smiling sisters at some flea market, among orphaned cups without handles, headless dolls, and other old worthless objects. They could only mean something to me, surely not to anyone else.

There's one photo I remember particularly vividly. It was one of the few I enjoyed having had taken. I am in a summer sailor's suit with shorts, standing in front of a tropical background. There's a palm tree, some bushes, and a brilliant blue sky. I have just turned six, and this is my official birthday picture. In my left hand, slightly twisted, I'm clutching a hat, in my right a walking stick or a riding crop. This time I am not supposed to laugh. Instead I am meant to look serious and important. I look into the black hole of the lens and imagine I am a plantation owner in America. We had just received a letter from my father's brother. He had emigrated to America at the turn of the century. My uncle had come into quite a sum of money and his fortunes were often the topic of my parents' conversation at the table.

My uncle hadn't made his money, as my vivid boy's imagination liked to think, by growing sugar cane. He had set up a flourishing chain of express dry cleaners. He had invented a then complicated (later simplified) chemical process with which the most stubborn of stains could be removed from clothes without their having to be washed with soap and water.

Nowadays everyone has heard of dry cleaning. But when my uncle introduced it, one can imagine the reaction.

My uncle sent us a shiny postcard of a row of nicely dressed employees he used as an advertisement. Although the layout of the card wasn't the best, praise is certainly due for the way my uncle managed to exploit a prejudice as a selling ploy. The saying on the upper portion of the card in the shape of a garland read, *Was ist denn das? The death to dust!*, playing on the mistaken belief that we Germans are even more cleanliness-conscious than other nations.

There's not much to tell about my school days. I attended the local primary school, then spent some uneventful years at high school. It was a few miles away from home in a small provincial town. My father took me there every day.

These trips were very embarrassing for me. Throughout my youth they were the constant source of what seemed to me then unsolvable problems.

I did not want my classmates to see my father delivering me at the school gates. Most of the students were from the town and arrived on foot. There was nothing I longed for more than literally to walk with them, not to be the exception.

I've heard it said more than once that grown-ups envy children their imagination, courage, and independence. I view this contention as romantic nonsense.

How often has my godchild, a charming if ordinary example of her species, asked her mother for the exact same doll that her friend has? How often during a dispute between mother and child is the final secret weapon drawn and driven home with power, namely that X is allowed to, so there can be no possible reason on earth for her not to be allowed to as well: and who gives a fig in these cases about the rules of logic or observes the natural claims of knowledge and experience? However forcefully the mother insists that what her daughter wants is unhealthy, dangerous, foolish, or expensive, she has to concede that if the friend is allowed to, it can't harm her daughter either.

Yes, I strongly believe that it's only with the passing of years that one discovers that in the course of a life, one has to cast off not only one's own prejudices, but also those of one's parents, aunts, uncles, as well, of course, as those of one's time. It seems to me one of the greatest and perhaps most beautiful paradoxes that one only starts to grasp who one is and what life is about when death is nigh.

My father would not give up this daily routine. And since I would never have dared tell him the truth, because it would have hurt him, I fell back on lies. Back then I made up lots of lies: the weather, possible depressions or highs, was my favorite topic.

I was only an average student. My reports said the same thing every year, in a sort of leitmotif: is hardworking, but dreams too much.

I was bored in German class and hated Latin. I couldn't retain the names of the various spears, lances, and pikes that were forever being talked about. I didn't see the point.

Our teacher, a certain Mr. Schubert — names are often deceptive, he was no romantic — was one of those classicists who take their subject incredibly seriously. For seven years, the time required to drink in the great subject, he marched us briskly through the battlefields of Bellum Gallicum, rather than contenting himself with some risqué poems by Catullus or Tibullus.

I was reasonably well liked by my classmates, though exactly why, I'm sure they could not have said. I was an inconspicuous sort of a boy, on friendly footing with everyone, but I didn't form any particularly close friendships. When teams were picked for soccer I was always next to last to be chosen. It was my good fortune that there was another boy in the class who was not only short-sighted, but also pudgy. Throughout school he relieved me of the humiliation of being last.

It wasn't that I was unathletic: I always had a real aptitude for running. Nor did I fear physical pain in any way. I just couldn't muster up any enthusiasm for the game. Deep in thought, dreaming, I would stand slightly apart. From this distance the absurdity of it all struck me — twenty-two boys with almost religious humility, in short pants, racing after a little ball.

Yes, what I'm trying to say is that this place of knowledge didn't overly stimulate me. I viewed the time at school as a duty one had to fulfill in one's youth, from which one would be liberated on becoming an adult. And so it could have gone on right up to graduation had it not been for the arrival of a new biology teacher. He first ignited that passion that has remained with me throughout these years. This biology teacher was a religious man. He saw his belief in a higher realm confirmed in the conformity and diversity of creation. He was thrilled by the smallest, most banal elements of it. I've never known anybody who could recite the various methods of planting potatoes in such an excited and lively manner. His young listeners were swept along without his even trying. He led us on to previously unknown peaks of imagination. And so it actually seemed quite natural to me, when to my surprise I graduated with better results than expected, to devote myself to medicine.

In the meantime, Katharina had become engaged. During the summer vacation my mother and sisters had been working feverishly preparing for the wedding. A larger new table had to be bought, a menu concocted, wedding announcements printed and sent off.

I can still remember the quarrel that ensued because of the fabric and lace ordered for Katharina's dress from a well-known textile trader in Berlin. The manufacturer named the silk Florentine Pollen. I can remember the name so well because as far as I could see there was nothing Italian about it nor anything that resembled pollen. With my youthful know-it-all attitude, I informed my sisters that a plant's pollen is nothing other than small particles of masculine sex cells. My sisters looked at me with pity and compassion. How could I, a mere representative of the male sex, possible hope to understand that reality is of absolutely no interest where feelings and impressions are concerned?

At that moment, I really felt sorry for my sister's future husband, ten years her senior and an employee of an insurance company in Danzig.

2.

How can I describe the impression Berlin made on me? The buses, the painted red lips of the women, the lighted advertisements urgently flashing the names of products: everything was astonishing and exciting for me.

I had spent my childhood dreaming of the city, filling in any blanks left by my father's stories. Yet, as I paused during one of my lengthy walks and looked around at the blossoming trees, the cars driving by, I had to admit that the city wasn't at all as I had imagined it as a child: it was more scintillating, noisier, it took me by surprise. The Berlin I had conjured up irrefutably resembled the little town on the Polish border where I had grown up. A little bigger perhaps, more beautiful, but a small town all the same. I had done nothing more than diversify, with a few strokes of variation, what I already knew. Yes, I had violently come up against the barriers of my world, for the unknown is always outside the realm of the imaginable.

I put it down to my youth that places of entertainment and diversion made the greatest impression on me. The cafés. Still today I think of them with such wistfulness. They have gone.

Of course there were cafés in our little town too. But what a difference between the snug rooms smelling of fresh baking that you go to in the afternoon to eat cake, and those huge noisy buildings.

Whereas there you admire the wide choice of cakes with their delicate icing — the central focus of such a cozy café is always the glass display cases through which the carefully arranged goodies can be viewed — in the coffeehouses of the city it is not the cakes but the guests who are on display. If any remnant of the afternoon cake culture clings on there, it is only in the guise of an already slightly misshapen slice of apple strudel past its prime. But that didn't bother anyone.

Armed with my friendly disposition and my monthly allowance from my father, I had soon settled into a routine at the café five minutes from the building where I had a room. As soon as I arrived a tray appeared in front of me with a cup of tea, a small milk jug, a glass of water, and two buttered halved rolls topped with ham. I always ordered another two of those later on. I wholeheartedly enjoyed this.

I would sit there for about an hour, reading the paper, chatting with some of the other locals, or with the waiter: toward eleven, when the breakfast guests had gone and before the lunch customers started to arrive, he took a short break and often stood next to my table. Afterward I either went home, or made a short detour to the university. If nothing else seduced me, there were always the morning screenings at the movie theater.

At first glance, these theaters were just like those in any small town in which the same films were shown two weeks later. They had display cases with photographs, a box office, someone who checked the tickets at the entrance, and an usher: usually a middle-aged woman, who, just before the lights went down, sold raisins, nuts, and chocolate.

No, what made these theaters so different from the others, whether provincial theaters or the luxuriously decorated theaters on the avenues, were not any architectural details but rather the expressions on the faces of the moviegoers. I saw more careworn and disillusioned faces in those matinees than in any railway station or hospital. The people who went to the movies in the mornings did not go for pleasure, nor because the film interested them — any other film would have done just as well. It was seldom that one would see, as one did on the weekend, a boy bursting with anticipation clutching his week's pocket money in his sweaty palm to hand over in exchange for a ticket to see his favorite hero riding through the black and white prairie.

The morning showing was the domain of the unemployed. They bought the reduced price tickets because they had nothing better to do. They didn't enjoy this pastime. They were aware of their lack of usefulness. I think that very little has changed on this front, in spite of the great progress that's been made in most areas today. It's not going too far out on a limb to suppose that in order to enjoy doing nothing, you've got to have money.

Starting out wasn't as easy as I'd imagined. First, I had to transport my few belongings, then a furnished room had to be found. Back then people were streaming into Berlin. The city attracted not only youngsters from the provinces like myself, but also Poles, Russians, and Eastern Jews hoping to find happiness there. The property owners made the most of this state of affairs. Their hands weren't tied by any law and they often asked for unashamedly high prices.

I searched for three whole weeks. As my hopes sank, so too did my criteria. I viewed so-called artist's studios the size of dog kennels, rooms that were so damp that the wallpaper was sprouting greenish flora and fauna, and, curiously, plenty of basement rooms. Where were the airy and bright brothers of these gloomy stepchildren? I never set eyes on them. Instead, I became acquainted with the innards of the city, traversed Berlin's colon and intestines, into which I'd been sucked along with the masses of other newcomers.

Finally I found it. My first room. It was rented out by a respectable lady, who looked like a red-cheeked Mother Goose. I passed the cross-examination, and moved in that very day. I was to live there until shortly after graduation, which was all to my good.

The landlady, complete in starched white collar, was an old-fashioned but generous person. No expense was spared to make the small family as comfortable as possible. She had made us her responsibility. We were never cold in winter, could wash whenever we wished. There was warm water all day long, and electricity was not rationed. Our bedclothes and towels were changed once a week. We could, should we be in the mood, join our head of the house and her two cats in the sitting room. Yes, this place could have seemed a bourgeois Arcadia, if one thing, as is the case in any paradise, had not been prohibited. We weren't allowed to invite any member of the opposite sex into our rooms. Our landlady did not take any risks. The apartment was locked up at night. If two charming young women hadn't lived there too, I'd have been hard pressed to have all the precious experiences you shouldn't miss out on in your youth, since they are of overriding importance for the healthy development of all the senses. One was a student, the other a salesgirl. We quickly became friendly, and they often visited me at night.

I soon felt at home, got into the habit of smoking along with some other vices, and started university in the fall as the first signs of excess were making themselves visible.

3.

Although I wasn't too turned on by the subject matter to begin with, still, looking back wistfully at those long lazy days, I was a conscientious student. I received good grades and was given an assistant's position. First of all I sterilized the bone chisels, the extraction pliers, the mouth mirror, and all the other instruments, the very sight of which make some patients think unjustly of torture instruments — dentists who get any joy out of hurting helpless patients are few and far between. Soon, though, my professor trusted me enough to let me perform the straightforward checkups.

I loved fashioning bridges for my professor, who then placed them against the patient's dark red gum. What I enjoyed most was the minutely detailed work, matching the color and shape of the porcelain teeth.

Never were patients so joyful and full of anticipation as just before being fitted with dentures. They had survived the agony, the tooth chiseled down to a stump and other teeth taken. The opening of the mouth heralded the moment in which the dentist would liberate the patient from his humiliating situation: he would no longer look like an old man. He would be able to smile the smile he used to: broad, flashing, displaying all the new teeth. At such moments, I stood behind my professor to catch a glimpse of the dark throat. Some of the gratitude that filled the room also settled rightfully on my shoulders.

If only the daily routine of the dentist consisted solely of such experiences, I would have been absolutely satisfied with my chosen profession. But one also had to drill, to pull, to fill. All of these little maneuvers, truly child's play from the medical perspective, left me a wreck for several hours afterward.

The patients' inhibition knocked me off balance. I couldn't find the right words to comfort them, I didn't know what to do or say to win their full confidence. I was sure that the pain I would cause them was bearable. And yet, I could not approach that unscalable wall of fear that formed between the patient and me as soon as I leaned over him. It was noticeable through the hunched shoulders, the hands clamped tightly either on to the chair arms or over the chest, and, most unpleasantly, through the excessive saliva.

I was and remain a theorist. I much prefer writing articles about transplants to carrying them out, and thus am in no way suited to the dental profession. But I had started studying, and couldn't just give it up halfway through, so I kept going. I spent some pleasant, interesting years and graduated in 1932. I wasn't going to put my diploma to great use, incidentally, opening as I did an antiquarian bookshop a few months later.

4.

In order to graduate I not only had to pass successfully the written exams, I had to perform successfully three forms of dental treatment. I had the two dreaded ones, filling and root work, behind me. But with, of all things, my hobby — dentures — I made no progress. I couldn't find any suitable patient. The people who came to the university to be handled seemed to prefer their old, rotten teeth to a set of new replacements, practically impossible to damage. They clung to their teeth as a child to its misshapen one-eyed teddy bear. The child wouldn't trade it in for the world, certainly not for a new doll. The mother can only surreptitiously wash it quickly at night when the child has fallen asleep, since he won't stand for the briefest separation from his beloved companion.

But that wasn't the worst of it. I was not, of course, the only student. Along with me, a hundred other students were on the hunt for the patient, who, once caught, would be led under the envious eyes of the classmates through the large treatment room to the chair. He wouldn't be allowed up before he'd been fitted with dentures or at least a bridge, which the professor would then examine.

Rumor had spread that extraction was the name of the game at the university: beware fresh-faced dentists clad in white coats with an eager expression, coming your way.

What was I to do? I didn't have an aunt whose premolar should be ground down to a stump, no sister-in-law or cousin to sacrifice themselves for the sake of the family. I was an independent bachelor whose family lived in a little town on the Polish border. In spite of being sociable, my circle of acquaintances was mostly made up of classmates and fleeting female acquaintances. I had to think of something. And because I had to, I found a solution.

Following my intuition, I went to the Herbert Gertler Foundation. It was a Sunday afternoon. I was not let in right away: the seminar nurse had forgotten to mention my visit and so I had to wait in the reception area while the concierge looked for her in vain.

Impatiently, I went for a walk along the corridor. When I was almost at the end, I heard music coming from behind wooden double doors. Hesitantly, I opened the door and saw a hall painted green. At the end of the hall twenty inmates of the foundation were sitting at a long table. They were looking at a trolley piled high with plates of cake. A nurse was pouring drinks into the cups. She had a tired, bored face.

A woman of around fifty with a muscular body and red-dyed hair was dancing through the rows of empty tables, singing folk tunes. She had a beautiful voice. Although she tapped affably on the shoulders of some of the old folks, no one took any notice of her.

The nurse handed the cake out. Now the remaining two members of the singer's audience turned away to follow the emptying process of the cake trolley. The singer stopped singing and, shrugging her shoulders, came over to me. I offered her a cigarette, and smoking we contemplated the patients. I remember this informative scene in precise detail. The greedy, joyless way the old folks shoveled in their cake conveyed a sense of hopelessness that I could not relate to.

After an eternity I was led to the staff nurse. She promised to relay my unusual request and we went up to the second floor. It turned out that there was indeed a sprightly old lady, eighty-four years of age, who needed new dentures urgently.

Berta Kurzig was an exceptionally stubborn woman, not unfriendly, but exhausting. She was of the opinion that nothing in life is free and greeted me with suspicion. She kept looking for the catch, the small print that she had overlooked. She kept waiting for me to give something away, to see a dishonest gleam in my eye. When a week had passed and nothing of that sort had occurred, I remaining polite and determined, she sent her granddaughter to me. This young lady was no less contrary. She stared at me with green cat's eyes, and the large tortoiseshell glasses couldn't disguise their distrustful glint.

Had I found another patient, I would most certainly have left Mrs. Kurzig to the hands of fate; my patience was wearing thin. But I didn't find any other patient. So I turned on my charm with the granddaughter. After one arduous week, I gained her acceptance regarding the fate of her grandmother's teeth, and three years later regarding her hand in marriage.

126

5.

But beforehand, although this was very unusual at the time, Klara and I moved in together. Klara had to give up her apartment since the owner, a greedy and in every other respect truly unpleasant person, had raised the rent. And I did not want to stay a subtenant any longer either. We decided to give it a shot.

Klara's uncle, the opera singer Werner Kurzig, found us a three-room apartment in a house built at the turn of the century. A fur dealer lived on the ground floor. The entire first floor was taken up by a dyeworks specializing in feather dusters. Then came the Brackmanns, a friendly family; the father was a teacher and I often played chess with him. After that came a gentleman who collected coins, and his sick mother, two other tenants whom I didn't know, and finally, under the eaves, Klara and I.

We were good, quiet tenants. We said hello to the neighbors when we met them on the staircase, carried back the shopping of various exhausted housewives, and did not complain when the Brackmanns' daughter trotted up and down the major and minor scales for a whole hour, martyring the piano because she had to familiarize herself with the celebrities of German music.

Nothing bothered us, made us restless, irritated us. We were the golden generation, the children of good fortune. We had experienced the war only through the veil of childhood that makes everything hazy: for us, it was limited to the waving of flags as the soldiers departed for battle, and later, when all was lost, to the telling of bad jokes, in which a completely stupid Jean or Jacques came out on top. Even the cripples, who populated the streets with their vendor's trays, didn't frighten us since we were used to the sight of them. We knew that these men had been mutilated in the war, but they did not act as a warning to us.

We were presumptuous enough to believe that the horror cabinet of war, the invalids, the hunger, the widows with their swollen eyes, had brought everyone to their senses once and for all. We believed in progress as in a new god; we believed that one can learn from one's mistakes and that glorious days were coming our way.

We enthusiastically discussed the education of workers and the salvific function of art. We handed out pamphlets, wrote manifestos, and saw neither the coarseness nor the bitterness that was slowly crawling into people's hearts.

Yes, we were presumptuous, because we considered ourselves untouchable, because we thought that luck was on our side. And had anyone said to me then that my life would be destroyed in less than three years, and that I would lose everything that was dear to me, I would have laughed in his face.

6.

We had been together scarcely four months when Otta called one morning. Something in the way she asked me if I was fine made me realize that something dreadful must have happened.

My father, who was brimming with good health, collapsed suddenly after dinner while he was in the sitting room reading one of the novels he selected from a Berlin publishing house every month. On coming back with the cup of tea that she always brewed for him after lunch, my mother found him sunk down in his chair and thought that he had dozed off. When she went up to him, however, to take the book out of his hand and to cover him up because he always felt the cold, she saw that his eyes were open.

My father died two days later of the aftereffects of a heart attack. He had not regained consciousness.

Charlotte took care of everything. She sent for Katherina and me, ordered the coffin, placed the death announcement — I had not managed to put together a decent text — and looked after my mother, who clung to Otta like a small child and allowed herself to be washed, dressed, and fed without resistance.

We set off immediately after the phone call. The train was packed and we had to sit next to a group of young men who were recounting their adventures with a certain Elizabeth. Klara watched me anxiously throughout the trip. She must have noticed in my face and bearing that I was close to losing control. She didn't know — and I would never have told her, for I seemed a monster to myself — that it wasn't the men's laughter that disturbed me, nor their overexuberant *joie de vivre*, which was painted on their smooth faces and threatened to flood the compartment. What was tormenting me was that I couldn't stop listening to their stories. In fact, I could not identify a trace, a shred, of mourning within myself. And I was consumed by an unspeakable fear. What would happen, what would my mother, Klara, Otta, think of me if I did not partake, if I remained unmoved, if I was incapable of any feeling? For everything drew me away from mourning: the men in the compartment, the brown and white cows we passed, the river, the poplar trees. I tried to imagine my father in the act of dying, but was always jolted back to life, which was taking its normal course all around me, and finally gave up.

When we arrived, I went to Father's room immediately. The curtains were drawn as if he were still sleeping. The familiar smell of my parents, the light that shone through the heavy curtains and made the objects in the room seem red, and the bedside table with Father's notebooks and half-empty glass of water still on it — no one had thought about getting rid of the beaker of fluid — all of it reminded me of my childhood Sunday ritual when I was three or four and my mother came to fetch me to creep up to the bed on tiptoes, and to wait there in the bed next to my father, who would pretend to be asleep until my mother came back with the breakfast tray, which she put down carefully on the little table. And as my mother was throwing open the curtains and then the window, my father would sit up and twirl me around in the air laughing, and I would cry out in joy and fear. I settled in between my parents in the bed. Cold morning air

129

poured into the bedroom, and we ate freshly toasted bread, drip-ping with butter.

And all of a sudden I grasped the whole unjustness, the absolute indecency, of the situation I could not come to terms with and which was all the more awful because no matter how hard I tried I could not change it. I was going to lose my father. In several hours, strangers would enter our apartment, mutter tried-and-true words of condolence. Then they would wash him, dress him, and take him with them. And there was nothing I could do. I did not have anyone to lay the blame on for this mon-strosity, no one against whom I could vent all my anger, to forget during a few moments of rage what could not be forgotten. I was losing my father and then I would lose my mother, and that is just the way it is, the most normal thing in the world. And although there is nothing more apparent than those words I had recited a hundred times, "dust to dust," their whole meaning struck me then for the first time, and this comprehension finally tore me from my childhood years, from this well-fed and chubby-cheeked world that, like a chess board with black and white squares, was divided into good and evil and where good prevails, always prevails, and death is accepted merely as the final and toughest punishment for scoundrels rather than as the nat-ural end of life.

And I understood that soon I would not see my father at all, that these were the last hours I could contemplate this familiar face, the small wrinkles etched under his eyes, the stern mouth. I took his hand. It struck me as so white and fragile and I kissed it and told him what he could not hear now and never would — I had, like all men, forgotten how to show my father tenderness — I told him I loved him.

And although the pain and the feeling of weakness re-mained, those hours spent with my father reconciled me to his death, for through the love that I felt for him and dared to expe-rience at his deathbed, I absorbed him into me.

7.

How did I learn about Hitler's election victory, through a radio report, in the paper, or was it the concierge who knocked at my door excitedly to tell me the glad tidings? I don't know anymore. At that time, unbelievable though it may sound from today's perspective, I lent it little importance. The Day of Potsdam, Mother's Day, Father's Day, the Day of Labor, the Day of German Gymnastics, what did these celebrations festooned with cheap firecrackers and gunfire, instigated by the brown rabble to intoxicate the people, have to do with me? They couldn't impress me in the slightest with all that. I found all the fuss quite ridiculous. And now all of a sudden an entire people was throwing the right arm in the air whenever someone entered or exited a room — the *homo germanicus* would soon not only differ from other types of people in their discipline, but also in their overdeveloped right bicep — well, that did not astonish me either. And although I actually considered myself a perspicacious person and some acquaintances suddenly disappeared to who knows where, at first everything carried on as before.

I opened a bookstore in two small rooms covered in cobwebs in Große Hamburger Straße. That was in February, a few days after Parliament was dissolved. I was sure the location would bring me luck, because it was next to the building where my favorite author had spent his school years, and also near the old Jewish graveyard. Three months later I returned the shop, without kicking up a fuss, to the safekeeping of the spiders. In the name of stamping out lies, branding treachery, and keeping the German language pure, my entire stock had been burnt — with the exception of a rare volume of Japanese woodcuts and a book illustrated with watercolors of butterflies. And who on earth can run a bookshop with the brimstone butterfly or the Great Fox in its autumnal guise?

I found a position with the Kulturbund Deutscher Juden,* founded in June '33. It was a place where dismissed actors, directors, and musicians could find work. I worked for Alfred Spira, who was employed until '33 by the Stuttgart Regional Theater, and a little later by Dr. Walter Levie, a cultivated and very reserved man. Levie often spoke of a manuscript he had edited shortly before the Aryanization of his publishing house. Before it could go to press it was literally torn from his hands, for the employees of the so-called Jewish publishing houses, i.e., Ullstein, S. Fischer, Reiss, and Cassirer, were harassed by house searches, murder threats, and the regular confiscation of books and manuscripts.

Naturally this "spontaneous indignation about Jewish inflammatory writings" was nothing more than a well-thought-out ploy to push the owners into selling their publishing house.

Levie claimed that the novel was one of the most beautiful and important works of contemporary literature. The manuscript in question was the last of a then unknown writer, who had died several years earlier of consumption. Levie had received the manuscript from a Czech journalist, who was to become famous many years later for some letters written to her.

With the help of an influential friend, Levie tried to rescue the manuscript. Yet, although he received a stamp of permission from the responsible office, the novel was never returned. Via the publisher, Dr. Lehmann, he discovered several weeks later that the "nonsense of the eastern Jewish cultural Bolshevist" had been burned the day it was seized.

Levie often spoke about the novel — it became a kind of obsession — yet apart from a garbled rendition of the content he could not say much more than that it had 254 pages and twelve chapters and the hero died after just seventy pages.

I comforted myself — if it is at all possible to comfort one-

---

*Cultural League of German Jews.

self about such a loss, but we lost more than just our master-pieces at that time — I comforted myself with the thought that the author would certainly have liked that technical description of his final work. I thought of him then as I do now, in opposition to the current popular opinion among academic circles, as an author with unmatchable black humor.

8.

While Albert Spira and Walter Levie saw to the administration of the theater, I was entrusted with the publicity work. I helped out with editing the *Monthly Rag*, but my main job consisted in procuring permission for performances from Hinkel's office, or, more precisely, from Cultural Minister for Special Papers Hinkel. Hinkel, after 1945 classified as "not significantly guilty," had several editors working for him who, red pen in hand, read through any plays to be performed by Jews. As grotesque as it must seem to present-day eyes, not only were the dramas of Schiller and other plays of pure German spirit off-limits to Jew-ish directors, but Jewish actors were not allowed to pronounce certain words, like *German*, *blond*, or *pure*. I remember an exchange of letters I had that went on for ten days with one of Hinkel's officials about a Molnár comedy and in particular the mediocre line "Farewell, blond and unfaithful briefcase," the official eventually coming up with the inspired idea of replacing *blond* with *fair*.

We were just rehearsing *The Merchant of Venice* when I heard, I couldn't say where, the news that Klara's uncle, the opera singer Werner Kurzig, had been beaten up by a mob of SA men. He had become the object of their hatred for not hiding his homosexuality. Werner left the country that year. He offered to help us leave, too. He had friends in Paris and Amsterdam, who would have found work for me. We spent many sleepless nights in the kitchen, not knowing whether we should emigrate or not.

We decided not to run away like thieves. This was our country after all.

Klara started to complain of stomach cramps. She would also suddenly feel sick, especially in the evenings. I was worried, and although she had strictly forbidden me to do so, I called my university friend Johann Marburg, who told me to bring her around without delay.

9.

Johann was a gastroenterologist and his practice was above an electrical goods store that gave the impression its back room might contain radios from homes that had parted involuntarily with them.

My God, that was a grotesque situation. I was standing next to the receptionist of my friend, holding forth on chronic and acute gastritis with my freshly gathered knowledge garnered from an antiquarian medical dictionary. Next door Johann was examining my wife. I tried to pick up something of the proceedings inside, but could see only his white back through the half-open door. I sat down and smoked a cigarette. I must have been on my third already when I heard Johann tell my wife she could get dressed again. I got up. Johann opened the door and came over to me. He indicated I should follow him into the surgery. We sat down in silence. I wanted to hear the diagnosis, but didn't dare ask. Johann looked at me for a long time, shook his head, and sighed. Then he took his prescription block out of the drawer, wrote something on it with a flourish, and, as I slumped down like a cold soufflé, handed it to me. I must have looked absolutely dismayed as I read my friend's verdict: "Congratulations, you old ass."

Johann burst into peals of laughter. Then he shook my hand, kissed my Klara, who was visibly moved, and invited us out for lunch.

10.

We celebrated our wedding with immediate family, and limited the celebrations after the ceremony in the town hall to a meal in a small restaurant.

To our mutual amazement — we'd been living together for almost three years before getting married — it was only in those months following the wedding that we really got to know each other. Without being able to pinpoint exactly when the change took place, I found myself adding warm milk and two sugars to my coffee in the mornings, and, as though the fact that I was now a married man had changed my taste buds, instead of the hot golden-brown fried potatoes that left a delicious fatty pool on the plate, which I dipped a slice of white bread into, I ate steamed chopped carrots and other vegetables whose existence I had deliberately overlooked in my youth.

And I wasn't alone. Klara also put old habits to one side, adjusted to me, became my wife, so that every day that "thing," for which there's no suitable word in the language, grew between us: something that comes into being when you realize that the gestures of the other, how she pushes her hair out of her eyes or how he dabs his mouth with the napkin, have become familiar, when you notice from afar the other's gait. Something that overcomes you, too, when torn from sleep, you feel the warm regular breathing body next to one, the sight of which calms the anxious heart so that its beat slows down until it's at one with the other's heart and melts into its pulsation.

11.

Seven months after our wedding, David was born.

I remember his first smile. It took us by surprise one morning, when I was awkwardly changing his diaper. No one had told me how charming this first timid toothless smile would be.

I remember our first walk in the park — we were so proud — and all the little shirts, caps, and socks that suddenly appeared in our linen cupboard.

I've already mentioned the spectacular dismissal of Jewish journalists, musicians, and actors. Then came the "Jews Not Welcome" signs, on the benches in the park, in front of shops and restaurants, the distinguishing *J* in the passports, the smear propaganda in *Der Stürmer*, the death threats, the exclusion of Jewish lawyers, and many other forms of harassment.

Yet nothing could compare to the Nuremberg Racial Laws in all their monstrosity and well-organized madness. On November 15, 1936, I was sentenced in the name of the German people to two years' imprisonment at my own expense for breaking paragraphs one and five of the Law for the Protection of German Blood and Honor: note the "at my own expense."

For those who may have forgotten what this was all about: race defilement, of course. As a so-called full Jew, I had come up against the law protecting German blood and German honor by marrying on December 15, 1935, the German-blooded Klara Kurzig.

One rainy day I was arrested. Klara was just feeding David when the knock at the door came. He was emitting little noises of satisfaction, and fell asleep red-faced from the effort at her breast. One of the officials was wearing a light-colored trench coat, the other, who put the handcuffs on me as though I were some kind of dangerous criminal, had a curly mustache, outdated then. It lent him a certain respectability.

Two years to the very day, I was released. My time there had passed reasonably uneventfully, apart from the snide remarks of a fellow inmate, a petty thief with ambition, who hoped to slime his way into the favor of the prison staff.

Klara was waiting for me at the exit. I didn't recognize David at all — how could I? He had become a serious little boy, had lost his mop of blond curls and his baby chubby cheeks. Klara had changed, too.

I had learned from a friend that immediately after my arrest she had been forced to walk the streets with a sign around her neck, denouncing herself as a Jewish whore. Klara was a very proud woman. I felt this humiliation must have broken her, for there was something in the way she looked at me I did not comprehend. Now I know she was despairing even then. With her innate practical sense she had long since realized the hopelessness of our situation, whereas I was still dreaming of a better life in another land.

Our financial situation had severely deteriorated. The money that my mother and Klara's grandmother sent us was not sufficient. Through a friend of her mother's, Klara had found a part-time job in an office. We were extremely surprised, for she was, being married to a Jew, race despoiled, after all. We made a definite decision to emigrate. I asked for emigration papers and worked at the Siegfried Scholem publishing house in Berlin-Schöneberg while we waited and waited.

We moved into a furnished one-room apartment on the first floor of an art deco house, whose over-the-top flourishes and stucco facade threatened to crush the stunted birch in front of it. Klara had clumsily hung striped blinds in front of the windows. Whether she wanted to protect David and me from the world looking in at us, or to spare us from looking out, I do not know. Whatever the reason, reality caught up with us nonetheless.

A few months later I was arrested again. This time they came toward seven, just as we had sat down for dinner. I have heard that this (along with nighttime, of course) was a favorite hour for the Gestapo to make their arrests, for they could be sure not to find an empty nest. There was always a logical reason for the way the Gestapo proceeded: I cannot vouch for the others. First of all, I was taken to an assembly camp, and then, because I had a previous record, to a concentration camp, KZ for short in German. To begin with, I worked in the kitchen there, where I was a dishwasher. I couldn't complain, for at least I had something to eat, unlike the other prisoners.

Whenever I could — the guard was strict — I stole a raw potato or a slice of bread, which I swallowed on the way to our barracks. At some point, I had long stopped counting the days, I was transported east.

Nothing there resembled what I had experienced before. I worked in an ammunition factory, then in the orderly's office, then in the hospital building. Several months later, I was called to the commander of the camp. I was afraid: he was known for his dangerous humor. I looked at the skull and crossbones on the badge on his collar. I don't believe I looked him or any of the numerous guards in the eye throughout my detention. I only dared to many years later when I was giving evidence at a trial and was forced to identify Adolf Vogt, a member of the Einsatz-gruppe, and I found that incredibly difficult to do.

The commander was eating. I stood in the corner of the room and waited. When he had emptied his glass, he fetched my file and read it out loud to me. He asked me why I had not mentioned that I was a dentist. I didn't understand his question. I was incapable of establishing any link between the camp and my life.

12.

Fate can play some capricious tricks. When I was still wet behind the ears, my father told me again and again that I had to study to make something of myself. I did not always share his opinion, but studied nonetheless for his sake. And now the fact that I had studied something that I was not interested in was to save my skin; my cowardice with my father — for I had never dared to contradict him — was going to help me. I was given a new area of work and, because my value had gone up as a doctor, more bread.

Along with two dozen other dentists, all with their yellow stars like me or red and pink triangles, I dug for gold. After the men from the work unit had opened the doors and thrown out the corpses that stood upright, pressed against each other in the chambers, I opened the mouths with a hook.

Even in death, one could recognize the families. They held hands tightly as they died. Using pliers and chisels, we broke the gold teeth and crowns out of the jaws and put them into cans. We filled a can a day, sometimes two. We worked quickly, concentrated hard, for as we were extracting, the Ukrainians were refilling the chambers.

I can still see the corpses today. Not people, not women, children, and men, but jaws that had to be pried open. And the sickly sweet smell grows no less, the smell that came from the uninterrupted cremation of bodies. It penetrated the whole area and informed all those living in the surrounding communities that annihilation was at work.

That is my life, then. It does not stop there, but the rest of it is not worth the telling. I was liberated in 1945. When the Russian soldiers came to us in the camp and saw what had happened, they wept. We could not cry anymore.

I was taken to a sanitarium, I had tuberculosis. They thought I would die, that my body was too weak. I wanted to die, but I survived. Then my search began. I learned from the Red Cross that my mother, Käthe, and Otta had been killed in another camp. God rest their souls. I could not find out anything about Klara and little David. They had been taken away by the Gestapo one winter afternoon, but what happened then no one knows.

I hope that they did not suffer too much, that little David was not afraid when he saw the black coats, that it happened quickly. I hope that they were placed in a row in a forest full of firs and pines, and that the soldier was good at his job. I hope that they fell onto a soft carpet of moss and leaves, next to one another, and that the snow, the all-encompassing, soothing snow, was their shroud.

13.

I am coming to the end of my story. In '56 I opened another bookstore. People do not read as much as they used to, and nothing decent is written anymore, but books are and will remain my passion. I did not marry again, although once — that must be some twenty years ago now, too — I was almost talked into it by a blond widow with a poodle. In retrospect, I can only thank my lucky stars that I have an inexplicable (but who can explain everything anyway) aversion to overbred dogs.

I busy myself with my godchild, who is starting school next year. With her two front teeth missing, she looks like a little vampire, but a very sweet one. Once a week, I go swimming and otherwise I lead a peaceful and unremarkable life.

I did not go back to Berlin until last year, when the mayor organized a gathering for former Jewish citizens. We were taken from the airport to a festively decorated room where a dry turkey and all the trimmings awaited us. The city had vastly changed. Not for the better. I have never been back to my birthplace, that sleepy little town. What would I do there? Nothing remains of what I knew.

I recently read in a report that Special Operation Reinhard collected 11,730 kilos of dental gold during the war. I calculated my contribution and think that this figure best sums up my life. But what am I saying? I have seen so much, terrible things, but also beautiful things, and when I sit in my shop and a customer holds forth on his views on art and literature, with the contented air of a connoisseur, as though pulling a particularly white pearl of unique purity from a resisting oyster (everyone has an opinion these days), then the few exquisite moments of my life come to me again. And it is with one of these that I wish to take my leave of you: when I asked Klara to be my wife, at the same time going into why she should not accept my proposal, she looked at me with her sparkling green cat's eyes and I saw myself reflected in her pupils, her big, round pupils, and I heard my breath catch in my throat, and she laughed in a deep voice, raw with tenderness.

One Hundred Furs

H<small>E CALLED HER TOWARD MORNING AND ASKED FOR HELP.</small> The ringing telephone had jolted her out of a dream. She did not immediately recognize his voice. She connected it to her dream: she was with Vicki, an old school friend, and they were trying to scale a wall. Only when he used his own affectionate name for her did she register what was going on. He told her she should hurry.

She hastily pulled on her clothes, which lay in a heap by the chair, and crossed the hallway. So as not to waken Bettina, who had forbidden her to leave the house, she carried her shoes.

She stopped in front of the door on which the name of her little niece was stuck in bright paper letters. While her sister and brother-in-law were quarreling in the living room, she had played hide-and-seek with the child. The little girl asked what was wrong, over and over again. She could feel the tension, but could not understand it. She had carried her into her room and laid down on the bed next to her. Then she had sat down in the kitchen and downed three glasses of cognac, one after the other. Wolfgang and Bettina had joined her. Together they emptied the bottle. After a while, her brother-in-law had gone through to the bedroom. Although he shut the door they could hear his sobs. His soft weeping frightened her. He had not cried since the murder of his sister, Ella. Everything else he had taken in silence: losing the right to vote, the J in their passports, his admission to the bar being revoked. She did not comprehend why the attempted assassination in Paris had unbalanced him so.

She listened to the steady breathing of the sleeping child, saw the untidy shock of brown hair sticking out from under the covers, and could not help thinking of Ella. She had seen her only fleetingly, once or twice. Ella had given the speech at Wolfgang and Bettina's wedding. She was very witty and had made everybody laugh, and she, Eva, had been full of admiration. A few months later she had been stabbed to death. She kicked the stuffed toy dog that guarded her niece's door — it looked like it was laughing at her maliciously, its felt tongue hanging out — went to the door of the apartment, and turned the key twice.

Everything was still asleep. Only the occasional single light was going on in the uniformly gray facades.

In the twilight, she thought, the houses and everything around them are curiously beautiful. She pulled her coat more closely around her and tightened the belt. She had actually wanted to wear her fur coat, her engagement present, but had decided not to, not wanting to draw attention to herself. Her quick little steps echoed on the cobblestones. She crossed the street, went along the right-hand side, and hurried past the empty site where a detached family house was to be built.

She had once read — where exactly she wasn't sure, or perhaps they were Alfred's words — that a city changes far more quickly than a person's life does. That was true. She had the feeling that everything was rotating in this city. Yes, even lifeless objects were getting restless.

The streetcar was almost empty. Only a few workers were sitting on the wooden seats, their faces creased with fatigue. She sat down in the last row, next to the window, which steamed up immediately from her hot breath. Bettina would be awake now and would have read the note she had left in front of their bedroom door. She would crumple it up into a ball, furious, and flatten it out with her hand to read it again.

The streetcar stopped. Two men jumped down and wandered over to a group smoking in front of a gate. As the streetcar jolted into motion, she turned around and looked at the men. They were going through the factory gate, laughing. She got out at the next stop. She only knew this neighborhood when it was bustling with people; the peacefulness disoriented her.

As she passed the café where Alfred and she took lunch, the waiter, in the process of taking the chairs off the tables, gave her a long and penetrating look. Frightened, she clutched her chest and went on. She went as far as Kantstraße, turned right, and stood stock-still. Disbelieving, she stared at the pavement. It was covered with splinters of glass, shreds of paper, pieces of wood and metal. She had not wanted to believe her brother-in-law, who had spent the whole evening claiming things would go from bad to worse now, that the Reich citizenship laws were just a little taste of what was to come. Now she could see it for herself. She wanted to run but forced herself to walk slowly, and read the words that someone had painted in white on the walls and shop fronts:

JEWISH PIG

GO AWAY JEWS

THE JEW IS OUR MISFORTUNE

DIE JUDAS

DO NOT BUY FROM JEWS

When she reached Alfred's door, she realized her dress was drenched in sweat. She entered the shop. The table, the chairs, the glass case he had constructed just three weeks earlier, were smashed to smithereens. Softly she called his name, but there was no answer. She went to the display room and found him in the changing cubicle.

"Alfred, Alfred."

He groaned. She sat down on the floor next to him and started to cry.

2.

There had been ten of them. He had seen them in the street and thought nothing of it. He had bolted the door and felt safe although he had not yet let the grating down. He had gone into the back room to cut the fur that Schröder was to work on in the morning. Schröder had offered to stay. He had heard about the operation because his brother-in-law was in the SS. He had thanked Schröder, but would not hear of it. Schröder was not a well man and there was his wife to consider.

He had believed that they would not be able to get at him, and looked up in bewilderment when he saw a man standing in front of him. How had he gotten in? he asked. That the door must have been broken down did not even occur to him to begin with. The man answered by beating him with a truncheon. Then the others arrived.

They kicked him and dragged him out into the street. He could still remember that the streetlights seemed very bright to him. He could also remember the amused faces in detail, leaning over him, saying all sorts of things he could not follow.

They wanted to force him to set his shop on fire. He refused and was beaten up again. He shut his eyes and submitted to it quietly. They threatened him. An SS man cut his shirt open with a knife. He would do the same to his dirty Jewish skin, if he continued to disobey orders. He acquiesced. A woman passed him a flaming torch. He hurled it through the door. It went out right away. They left him an hour later and loaded the furs into a truck. Painfully, he crawled back to the building, and leaned against the wall. As he watched them piling the furs one on top of the other his thoughts turned to his father, from whom he had inherited the store. He also thought of his first trip to Russia, taken with his grandfather when he was four or five, and of the impish old woman who had given him a present of a foxtail.

"Let's go," said Eva. "We can live with Bettina for a while." She helped him to his feet.

"Come on, let's go."

3.

The street had come to life. About ten people were standing in front of the store, looking at them with curiosity. No one said a word. He was leaning heavily on her. They made their way laboriously along the street.

Two doors down, the windows of a tobacconist's had been smashed in, and across the way those of a stationer's: it was managed by a widow and he ordered his visiting cards from her. They stopped so he could catch his breath.

"Look at them."

He pointed to a group of people, scouring the ground in front of the stationery store for anything of value.

When they were passing the café, the waiter helped them inside and told them to stay seated until he had ordered a car. The room smelled of fresh morning bread rolls. The regulars, mostly shop proprietors with a good hour before opening time, had not yet arrived. She went to the phone next to the cash register and called her sister. After she had explained briefly what had happened, she asked her to call the doctor.

"Tell him it's urgent and he should come before his morning rounds," she added, and hung up before Bettina could start with her reproaches.

When she went, she saw the second waiter. She had not recognized him right away for he was still in casual wear. He was sitting there spooning bright red jam out of a big container with a

146

wooden spoon into glass dishes decorated with fruit. There's strawberry jam today again at long last, she thought, and immediately reproached herself for being able to think such thoughts at a moment like this. She sat down again and tried to compose herself by looking at her hands. She felt the tears coming.

"I shouted, but . . ."

"Ssh," she said. "We'll be home soon and then I'll tuck you into bed."

"I asked them to leave me the sign. You know the one, the family sign. I said my great-grandfather . . . you can have all the furs . . . but the sign . . . they just laughed."

"You shouldn't talk now," she said, and gently laid a finger on his mouth. "You mustn't get worked up."

With the help of the waiter she heaved him up and brought him to the door. The taxi was waiting outside. She carefully settled him into the backseat, pounded her coat into a ball, leaned him forward, and put it behind his head.

"They whipped me like an animal. Like a dog. Then they loaded my furs into a truck. And laughed . . . they were grinning as they did it . . . like a dog . . ."

"Shh," she said, shutting the door, and told the driver the address.

They drove off slowly. As they passed the shop, she looked out of the window. The shards of glass had already been swept away. She looked at the sign that his great-grandfather had mounted on the wall outside, a century ago. Alfred Blumenfeld and sons. Four generations of furriers. She stroked his hair gently. Someone had nailed a plank across the door frame.

A warning, she thought, a warning nailed to the door. She took his hand.

In These Sacred Halls
One Knows Not of Revenge

(Watches)

WHEN HE WAS AWAY, they had called his home and summoned him to the police station. He was to give testimony as a witness. He did not go, he knew it could only be a trap. His wife advised him to hide at a friend's in Stuttgart for a few days.

"And then?" he asked, and stayed at home as though nothing had happened.

They came on the third day, on a Sunday. They did not say where they were taking him.

"You will see for yourself soon enough," they said, and asked him, not impolitely, to hurry.

He gave his daughter a good-bye tweak on the arm and promised to bring something back.

"A doll," she said, "with a baby carriage," and as she watched him go, she clung to the faded hare her mother had sewn together from scraps of material.

He had seen the synagogues burning. Even in his sleep, he had heard the blazing cupola of the synagogue in Fasanenstraße collapse. In the middle of an ever-increasing crowd that had gathered around the building to stare in silence at the flames, he had thought of a sentence he had used to introduce the first publication of a contemporary dramatist, who had since become well-known. This is only a timid prologue, he had written; what follows will become history. A clumsy sentence, he thought, but very fitting.

He was taken to the police station and asked to take a seat. A drunken man was led in. Everybody knew him, and greeted him by name. He was singing a song about a merry baker.

"He used to be a baker," the policeman explained, leading Bernstein to a cell. He lay down on the wooden bench and shut his eyes.

Half an hour later, two men came up to the iron bars and unlocked his cell door. They told him they were taking charge. He should get a move on, they were waiting for him in the car, he had once been a famous man. He smoothed down his jacket and followed. It was only in the car that he realized they were talking about him in the past tense.

The shards of glass that had still littered the pavements a few days before had been swept up. Only the boarded-up windows revealed something had happened here.

When they drew up in front of the community center they asked him if he were a good gymnast. He did not understand the question and looked at them.

"You'll do a few gymnastic exercises now," said one of the men, and opened the door, smiling. "It's good for the health."

He walked as though in a dream, stumbled down a low step he had not noticed, passed rosebushes, and entered the brightly lit hall. It all seemed unreal.

He was told to place both hands on a wooden table. He spread his legs and an SS man searched him for weapons.

"Nothing," said the SS man, and went up to an elderly gentleman. He knew him by sight. He was called Recktenwald and worked for the same newspaper as he. Beneath his coat, he was wearing only pajamas and was freezing.

"A lovely bright blue," said the SS man, and smiled at Recktenwald.

He was pushed forward. At another table a man took his watch, watch chain, and the change that he always carried in his pants pocket. When the SS man had counted the money and thrown it into a cash box, he looked at the watch.

"Gold?" asked the SS man.

He nodded. It had been a present from his father for his doctorate.

The SS man turned around and placed the watch in one of the four boxes on the table behind him. While the SS man was filling out a form, he looked at the labels on the boxes. He read: pocket watches — gold and gilded. Pocket watches — silver. Wristwatches — gold and gilded. Wristwatches — silver.

"Sign."

The man who had confiscated his belongings held out a sheet of paper and a pen. He winced. Then he signed.

A line had formed in front of the third table. The foreman was asking a young man his name. The man said his name and was slapped.

"Name," repeated the foreman.

The man protested this was the only name he had. The foreman gave a sign, and the young man was led away, sobbing softly.

When his turn came he had understood what was expected.

"Jew," he answered to the foreman's question, who nodded, satisfied, and to the question, "What sort?" "Jew Justus Bernstein."

Then he gave his address.

He was taken to a smaller room, acting as conference room. The chairs had been placed against the wall, so that an empty space had been created in the middle. He joined the other ten men who had been arrested that night. The journalist Alfred Neumann, the publisher Siegfried Scholem, and a sociologist were among them.

"Get down," came the command.

He got down on his knees.

"Crawl."

He crept on all fours through the room, crawled the length of the room, went round in circles, and lay down as ordered, face down, arms stretched out. He was sweating.

A man approached him. He saw the points of his shoes. The brown leather was worn away and scratched in places. He wanted to protect his head with his hands, but lay motionless, shut his eyes, and waited for the kick. After a while, they were ordered back to the big room.

An officer came in and went from group to group. The way in which the others greeted him showed his superior rank. The officer walked up to him and looked at him for a long time. Then his face lit up.

"But I know you," he said. "You are the . . ."

He said he was.

"How old are you?" the officer asked and nodded acknowledgment when he got the answer.

"You are in good shape."

He turned to the next man and prodded his belly with his thumb.

"Your belly has grown fat from the spoils of our Reich. We will be able to rid you of that lard. What is your profession?"

"Cantor," the other man replied.

The officer laughed and turned to Bernstein.

"You are a music lover, I read that somewhere."

"Yes," he said. "I am a member of the Friends of Chorale Groups Society."

The officer shook his head.

"Were. You were a member. Now you are nothing."

He turned back to the cantor.

"Then sing the aria from *The Magic Flute* for your brothers in faith, and sing yourself free."

The cantor took a deep breath, and started to sing.

2.

Toward dawn, they were taken into the courtyard. They immediately clustered into small groups. They discussed what might happen. No one knew.

Someone reached a couple of bottles of milk and bread over the wall. He saw cracked hands, used to hard work.

He greedily gulped some down, and passed the bottle on. An elderly man whispered his name and address to the man over the wall.

"Tell Inge," repeated the man, over and over, "she should take down the pictures. She should take down the picture in the bedroom. She should also take down the one in the living room. . . ."

He went over to the elderly man and tapped him lightly on the shoulder.

"It's all right," he said. "Everything's fine."

They were led back into the room and ordered to lie down. He unbuttoned his jacket and crouched down. The elderly man crawled over, stopped in front of him, introduced himself, and asked what they could do.

"I don't know any more than you," he said. "They want to intimidate us, and then they'll let us go."

Maybe, he thought, maybe it's even true, but he did not really believe it. He took off his jacket and balled it into a pillow. There was no point in speculating.

Just under an hour later they found themselves being led through a street full of gawking faces. A woman, who was dragging a short-haired sausage dog behind her, spat on the ground as he went by.

"Ugh," she said. "Pack of Jews."

At the side of the road were two trucks. While he was waiting to climb in, he glanced over at the houses opposite and saw a woman hanging covers over the balustrade. He thought of his wife and daughter, who had certainly not slept.

A few weeks earlier, they had talked about what they would do in an emergency. He had reckoned with his arrest, but had not imagined it would come so quickly. He had applied to emigrate, and thought he still had a few weeks at his disposal.

She is still at home, waiting for a sign. She is not with them. She has certainly not stuck to our agreement. Oh, he thought, please let her already have gone, she'll be in Holland tomorrow, and then they will be safe.

The driver looked sleepily down at the street. Gradually the sidewalk was emptying.

He sat next to the young man, who immediately grabbed hold of his jacket. He gently pried himself free, took his hand, and spoke softly to him. He had no idea what he was saying, but the words had a calming effect on him too.

They were taken to the Silesian railway station. He had hardly ever been in this area. He was seeing some of the streets for the first time. They stopped in a tunnel. They had to climb down.

"Hurry up, hurry up," the SS men shouted at them.

They stood in a line and were counted.

"Eighty-three," said an SS man, and tapped him on the chest: "Remember that."

Several special carriages had been set aside for them, joined to the end of the train. It was a normal passenger train, the travelers were already seated and waiting. The train's departure had been delayed because of them. On the platform a group of workers hurried past them. One of them had a large leather pouch clipped on to his belt. His breakfast is in there, he thought, and realized he was hungry.

He was placed next to two SS men, who were guarding the compartment. He listened to them. They were quietly talking about what would happen to the prisoners. One of them mentioned Dachau and Sachsenhausen. Yes, he thought, that will be it for sure, as he had already heard talk about them. The other one, who got out at the first station to fetch water, said something about the "expiatory sacrifice of Jewry."

When they came to a standstill for several minutes between stations and were overtaken by an express train, he considered for a moment what would happen if he were simply to stand up. He imagined walking past the two guards, turning the handle, opening the door, and walking out.

Shot in mid-flight, he thought, or they would take my wife and child. Oh dear, he thought. If only they've already left, if only they're already at the border. Let it be so, please. He dropped his hands into his lap and listened. Behind him a voice whispered:

"Guard, is the night almost over? Guard, is the night almost over? But even when morning comes, it will still be night."

The Gold Coin

As is the case with most collectors, Blumenfeld's passionate desire to accumulate things was awakened in early youth. He could not remember when and why he began. His mother, now deceased, liked recounting that she had first noticed his collecting mania one spring morning. During her quarterly cleaning spree, she and the cleaning lady pushed his bed to one side and came across about fifty chocolate wrappers.

Blumenfeld was six then, a melancholic child prone to puppy fat and kept to a strict diet by his mother. To this day he could remember the jumble of joy and fear that filled him as soon as he drew near the fine foods store on the way home. He bought a chocolate-covered cream wafer there every day. He did not eat it immediately. He hid it between the exercise books in his schoolbag, so that the heady feeling increased through the afternoon, reaching its climax in the evening when his mother left the room and he took the first bite.

Was it fear of his mother coming across the chocolate wrappers in the trash can and stumbling upon his secret? Or did the placid child need the excitement the knowledge of his guilt occasioned, prolonged by smoothing out the gleaming, silver paper, folding it with his sleepy hands, and placing it behind the bed? The pile grew bigger and bigger and with it heightened his state of physical and mental tension.

His mother suspected this childhood episode had given his dormant collector's zeal the kiss of life. Blumenfeld had never given much thought to whether he was interested in the chocolate-scented wrapper as an object in its own right, or only as evidence of his misdemeanor, but he did know that when he came home one afternoon to find his mother holding out the foil wrappers reproachfully, he had felt disappointment, mixed with relief. With that an abrupt stop was put to both the midnight snacks and the diet.

The subject of his rather famous collection came to Blumenfeld; he did not come to it. He was given it as a present on his twelfth birthday by his father's youngest brother. Saddened that he was the only son not to have gone to college, taking over his father's fur business instead, his uncle hoped with this Roman coin to awaken his little nephew's interest for history. It was a subject in which young Blumenfeld had yet to achieve any satisfactory result, and without mastering it, so thought his mother and uncle, he would amount to nothing in educated circles.

Blumenfeld thanked him politely, and the coin with its detailed noble head of a glorious general covered with the green patina particularly coveted by experts was mislaid that very afternoon.

It was not until four years later that he was to come into contact with the future subject of his collection again. He was in a public library, because a girl from his class spent her afternoons there, and was leafing through an illustrated volume of coins, next to the dictionaries and encyclopedias by the entrance.

Blumenfeld had selected the book randomly and, as he was looking over to the table where the girl was sitting, he indifferently turned to the middle pages. Suddenly, his glance fell on a blown-up photograph of a well-conserved coin. It was made of silver and on it was the head of a bull, whose dark, flaming nostrils were strangely exciting to him.

That same day, Blumenfeld went to a shop that — along with stamps, seals, and medals — had two shelves of coins. He had not noticed it before, and bought a silver taler, reasonably priced, since it was widely available.

Within just a few months, Blumenfeld, whose zeal for collecting had now settled upon a suitable subject — beforehand he had hoarded anything and everything in his room, sometimes truly bizarre objects that he exchanged for others when they bored him — had put together a fine collection. He was advised by the shop owner, an experienced numismatist who was kind to the young man and spent many an hour with him in the back room.

Soon Blumenfeld was not content with the usual coins, and to the numerous silver talers and birds' heads from Bavaria and Bohemia, rarities were added, with hippos, elephants, and lions that grinned at him with mouths of nickel, silver, or copper when he took them out in the evening to polish them or simply to hold them in his hands.

These coins were his pride and joy. Tracing an uneven surface with his finger, he thought he could feel the sweat of the artist hundreds of years ago, carrying out a prince's or emperor's order, and powerfully striking the hot metal with his hammer, to press the pattern in with the pressure of the blow.

Only the human hand could produce the irregularities that were the reason Blumenfeld collected the coins: the hand grew tired and struck with less strength at the end of the day. And he thought he could tell — he published his notion, hotly debated but never disproved, in a series of articles in the numismatics magazine — whether a coin had been crafted in the evening or in the early morning. The nighttime coins had technical deficiencies, deeply moving like the pallid, sickly skin of a young girl.

Only once did Blumenfeld almost allow himself to be led astray and to neglect his collection. He had by that time established himself as an expert on classical coins, although he also from time to time dipped into coins from other periods. He had met the lady in question — the confusion of feelings was occasioned by a woman — in a lawyer's office to which he went to straighten out a question about his mother's will. Blumenfeld had just turned thirty-four.

The lady was called Vicki Walter, recently divorced, had a shy smile and small tripping footsteps, and was employed as a secretary in the lawyer's office. His first and last words to her were an apology.

It was actually an insignificant story: Blumenfeld had brushed against an inkpot with his stiff loden coat in passing, pouring its contents over the secretary's desk. After some clumsy words of apology, which fortified the first impression he had made on the secretary — of being an untidy but likable person — he invited the young lady to dinner.

He was not attracted to her. Rather he felt duty bound, and did not cover up his mixed feelings when he met the secretary, who had immediately and wordlessly wiped away the signs of his absentmindedness with a sponge.

Although to start with he looked at his watch impatiently — Blumenfeld did not like to be robbed of time he could be spending with his coins — he had to admit, after meeting her three more times, that he liked the woman. As she seemed to like him too, the inevitable happened. And he could not help thinking at night, when she had left him and he lay a little longer in bed, that what the Greeks called fate was smiling on him, too.

In fact, the woman had entered his life like the churning waters of a flood after a storm, and had torn down all the protective walls Blumenfeld had carefully erected, believing he was content with his life.

Thereafter there was a feeling of emptiness. Blumenfeld did not pretend to love the woman. He had his carefully spent youth behind him, was standing at the threshold of a new chapter of his life, and contentedly looked forward to a peaceful future made complete through her presence.

The engagement date was set. Blumenfeld began unhurriedly looking around for a larger apartment. This was around the time he decided to catalog his collection, which had grown considerably from its modest beginnings.

Blumenfeld asked his prospective fiancée, experienced in such matters, to help him. They started one Sunday. Carefully he took the first little paper bag from the cupboard, opened it, and slid out a Roman coin of raw copper with the head of an emperor famous in the history books for his gluttony. He slowly raised it to the light, squinted at it, and stated in brief technical terms its period, country, denomination, and inscription. He took out the second coin when the data of the first were recorded and it was back in its little paper sack. And so they continued through the afternoon, taking just one short coffee break to relax.

Toward evening, an uneasy sensation started gnawing at Blumenfeld, almost imperceptible to begin with, invigorated as he was from seeing the coins, but gathering in strength the further they progressed. They had already filled about seventy cards, when he realized, while regarding a groschen, what had been irritating him: he had forgotten to mention the condition of the coins. Blumenfeld paused and explained to the woman that the work they had done thus far was incomplete.

"What?" she demanded. "All those things all over again?" She was referring to the coins she would have to unwrap for a second time.

Blumenfeld did not answer; he just nodded sadly. When she left him that night as usual, he said to himself that there was no such thing as perfect happiness, that the expression she had used to describe his coins had slipped out of her otherwise shy, smiling mouth by accident.

Nonetheless, although Blumenfeld had forgiven her immediately, some of the magic surrounding their shared happiness had evaporated.

After that he saw the lady less and less frequently, much to his mother's delight, and in the winter he broke the relationship off altogether. When the first birches were blossoming,

Blumenfeld bought a coin he had wanted for ages, so beautiful that the other coins paled in comparison. It was an example of the high point of Greek coin minting, a silver drachma. On its reverse side was the finely crafted, beautiful head of the nymph Arethusa, Daughter of the Night. Blumenfeld gazed at the coin before going to bed, and laid it on a velvet scarf by his bedside at night. He thus found his inner peace again. The secretary was already forgotten.

One year later, his mother died. With his cousin's help, Blumenfeld saw to the formalities and quietly buried his mother next to his father, deceased twenty years earlier from a heart attack. Using his inheritance — a respectable sum his mother had gathered carefully over the years — he bought thirty coins that had been missing and were necessary to confirm his reputation as an important collector and expert on numismatics. It must have been then that something struck him that can only be viewed as a kind of momentary madness: intoxicated with the diversity and appearance of his collection, he got it into his head to acquire one specimen of every classical coin, and thus to possess what every numismatist longingly dreams about: a complete collection.

Blumenfeld put an advertisement in the numismatist's magazine, expressing his wish to purchase well-known pieces from the classical period. Within a week, he had received two answers. Delighted, he wrote back immediately announcing his imminent visit.

It was in this way that he got to know Dr. Heillein, a quiet man of advanced years, who was indirectly to save his life.

Dr. Heillein was a bachelor too and lived in an apartment so small that it would have been as little worth mentioning as the terraced building it was part of, had his collection not drastically improved the first impression.

Overcoming his natural reserve, Blumenfeld, after introducing himself and taking off his coat, went up to the shelves and, extracting a velvet cloth and a magnifying glass from his pocket, looked at every piece laid out there. Step by step, he went round the whole room, then turned to the man standing patiently by his side, who waved him through to the bedroom.

Speechless, Blumenfeld sank down on the bed. Even in Berlin, he had never seen such treasures. There were silver pfennigs from Gratz next to kreutzers from Vienna, Roman coins of raw copper next to golden guilders and delightful Greek tortoises. The crude fare he had taken in a restaurant near the station weighed down like lead in his stomach; nor did the man's explanation, feeling obliged to account for the largesse of his collection, cheer him up. He slowly got up and on the host's invitation took a glass of wine, toasting good health and the prosperity of numismatics. He left shortly afterward and fell into a deep and dreamless sleep in his hotel room.

Like a cloud chased away by the wind, one that had prevented his seeing clearly, Blumenfeld's delusion waned after this meeting. He understood that it would take more than one generation to build up a superior collection, perhaps more than two.

To avoid ending up a pauper, as his mother had predicted, and to spend the years left to him calmly and peacefully, he decided to give up collecting. Since he had doubts about his willpower, he put his plan into action that very week.

Two weeks later, Blumenfeld had sold all of his coins, apart from the Daughter of the Night, which never left his side. With the proceeds he acquired a little house in a fishing village in the French Riviera, where he spent his days in a most pleasant fashion.

So it came to pass, then, at noon one late spring day, that Blumenfeld was drinking his first glass of red wine, brought to him out on the terrace on a wooden tray, along with some olives by his part-time housekeeper, a middle-aged widow who had only recently shed her black attire, at the very moment when five of his relatives were arrested, during an operation planned two weeks earlier, as a consequence of the religion to which they belonged. (Blumenfeld did not hear until two weeks later about the operation and never fully understood its implications.)

Nor could his subsequent handling of events — selling the Daughter of the Night to spend the proceeds trying to buy the freedom of his younger cousin Alfred, his fiancée, and her niece Andrea — be attributed to his perception and understanding of the political situation.

As surely and confidently as he could estimate the year a coin was minted, so was Blumenfeld's capability to comprehend political events limited, for he could draw no relation betweeen them and his own reclusive life.

Blumenfeld only felt, without being able to put it into words, that the Daughter of the Night with her domineering beauty was keeping him from the life offering itself to him in a new unfamiliar light in the figure of his shy, smiling house-keeper.

The Future

(A Department Store)

THE YOUNG LADY DID NOT MARRY, as expected and generally hoped, Reinhard Lipmann, but instead a certain Karl Schneider, whom she had gotten to know at the university: he played an excellent game of tennis and cut a fine figure in jodhpurs. She was a daughter of Oppenheimer of Oppenheimer and Baum. And the young man? He was nothing much, apart from being very fond of the young lady. The reason for this was, why hide it, the capital O that shone next to the illuminated capital B on the roof of the department store.

He had a doctorate in business and wanted to achieve the maximum profit possible with the means at his disposal. He therefore carried out random spot checks to test the father's readiness to pay up, garnered the affection of the mother through certain services and gifts — an open ear, bouquets of flowers, and lots of chocolate — and after a month in which he did not show his face, knowing that for something to be of value, it not only had to be useful but also scarce, he received, as a reward for his careful calculations, a golden watch. A beautiful apartment in 5 Hölderlinstraße followed. And three years later delightful twins, clad like he and his wife, exclusively in Oppenheimer and Baum (O.B. for short).

Fourteen years later, when the old man died, the two charming sons by this time towering above the desk in his office

and equipping themselves secretly with O.B. cigarettes, magazines, and other distractions, Schneider, husband of the young
lady, still a lady if no longer as young as all that, was the man
appointed director of the O.B. department store by the board of
directors and the major shareholders; that is to say, by himself
and his wife.

In a word, he inherited. He inherited the department store
and along with it the writing desk made of oak, which he had had
his eye on for a long time and behind which, albeit briefly, he felt
completely at home. And so he sat down behind the heavy
oak table, blackened by the passing years, and reflected and,
although advised against it for several reasons — the aryanization process was enough to make a man of German origin think
twice before opting for ruin — had his name changed from Mr.
Karl Schneider to Karl Israel Schneider, the Mr. being left off for
Jews.

He did this because he did not want to divorce his wife, the
Jewish Liselotte Sara Schneider (maiden name Oppenheimer).
He had grown to love her over the years. Nor did he want to be
separated from his sons, the two Schneider twins. Among the
store's employees, they were now privately known as the Jewish
bastards, because they were the sons of an Aryan and a Jew,
which made, if one were to calculate exactly, two half Jews, or if
you added, divided, multiplied — you could do whatever you
wanted with Jews — one full Jew or four quarter Jews or five
fifth Jews or eight eighth Jews.

Logic dictated otherwise, but he could not do it. The market value of Jews had sunk. But he could not do it. He knew the
time for betrayal was upon him; however one looked at it, there
was no concrete use to be found for Jews, yet they had become
vital to him, more important than the O.B. department store for
which he had married the young lady almost twenty years ago.

He converted. In 1939, he converted. Then he sold off the
store cheaply. He could not keep it of course, he was a Jew, not

from birth, granted, but nonetheless a Jew, and so the store had to be aryanized. It was purchased by the estate broker Paul Raeder with a flawless family tree and a blond spouse with an impressive bosom, for an eighth of its value.

And he, what did Schneider buy with the proceeds? For the price of 1,033 marks and 75 pfennigs he purchased three passages on a boat to Casablanca from Hapag. Three, not four, as he wanted to wait until he had tied up all the loose ends.

After all, theirs had once been one of the most important and most highly respected families in the country. Numerous ministers had dined with them. There was a lot to do. There was the department store, which had to be aryanized, as was the case for chain store Leonard Tietz Corp., later called Kaufhof, and for the chain store of the brothers Alsberg, bought up by the purely Aryan employee Horten and continued under his name, and for the chain store Rudolf Karstadt, which was taken over by the Didier Works in Wiesbaden, the Münchmeyer Insurance Group, and four banks.

Then there was the apartment to be aryanized, and the houses, and the summerhouse, aryanized, and the three cars, and the family bank account, and the business bank account, and the insurances and the shares, the bonds, the paintings, the carpets, the sculptures, and everything that a person collects in a lifetime: what he had hoarded, what his wife had held on to, and her father, who had been an art collector, and her grandfather, also an art collector, and her great-grandfather with his medals, and her grandmother and great-grandmother.

He took it stoically. He who opts out of the realm of justice will have his downfall one day, he thought. He asked for the necessary documents for emigration as three members of the Schneider family were fleeing to Casablanca, slipped a banknote into the official's hand, and when the emigration office could no longer see any reason, no legal impediment, to prevent the three members of the Schneider family from emigrating, Schneider submitted the inventory of their move in two copies. When two weeks later he had received no answer he made his way personally on foot to the foreign exchange office, slipped the official a banknote, and after a further two weeks received permission according to foreign exchange law for:

2 Bundles of Cleaning Cloths and Accessories
20 Mathematics Exercise Books
1 Flashlight
1 Little Box of Fake Jewelry
4 Handkerchiefs
1 Suitcase
6 Coat Hangers
3 Nightgowns
2 Knitted Waistcoats
1 Underskirt
4 Pairs of Underpants
1 Blanket
7 Pairs of Stockings
3 Brassieres
1 Pair of Slippers
3 Scarves
4 Belts
1 Pair of Ladies' Shoes
2 Bags
2 Pairs of Stockings
5 Dresses
1 Umbrella
3 Tablecloths
3 Ties
1 Shirt
2 Suits
1 Traveling Rug

Permission according to foreign exchange law was denied for the following items:

Winter coats
25 Sanitary Towels
1 Set of Stationery
1 Coral Necklace
1 Shoe Cream
1 Sewing Set
1 Package of Persil for Washing Clothes on the Voyage
1 Package of Sea Sand Almond Bran for Skin Care
1 Pair of Men's Shoes
14 Bars of Chocolate
1 Box of Pralines
1 Carton of Cigarettes
4 Novels, English Binding

And when all this was decided, he took his wife and sons to the ship.

His wife wept. He wept too. That was no problem, though, for they had received permission according to foreign exchange law to take four handkerchiefs they could dry their tears with.

He said good-bye to his family, hugged his sons, kissed his wife, telling her to be brave, and handed her an envelope of money that should keep them going until everything was over — a matter of a few months, they thought, or perhaps a year.

He stood for a long time, watching the gray point on the gray horizon of the Hanseatic city until it disappeared. Then he turned and left. He still had a bit of money in the account. He still had some friends. But he had no more hope.

He was a businessman and knew the facts: the Jew was good business. Stealing his fortune was a fruitful affair. The little bit of effort bore no relation to the profit, for many civilians helped with the plundering free of charge. Soon the simple operation would be restructured into a regular branch of business.

The future held no bright promises. He sighed and entered the department store. He exchanged greetings with the secretary and went into the office that had not belonged to him for several days now. He opened the drawer of the desk that also was not his anymore and took out a revolver. He had not declared it, therefore it had not been aryanized and still belonged to him. He held it to his temple.

He sat there, with everything going on as normal outside, and thought about Paul Raeder. He had given him a jovial thump on the back at the signing of the contract. He thought he had to make it clear to him too, that one could not so good-naturedly overlook the injustice that had taken place. He looked out the window and imagined the blood-flecked desk where his successor would take his place — surely after suicide at least the man would start having his suspicions. He imagined his secretary racing into the room as soon as she heard the shot, and the cleaning lady who would have to wipe away the blood with soapy water, and the numerous employees — they would whisper, their hands in front of their mouths. He sat like that until dusk, then laid the revolver back in the drawer, and left the store through the service entrance.

Out on the street he stopped beneath a lamppost. He took the golden watch out of his pocket, the one he had been given by his wife, and looked at the face.

"Good God above, good God above," he whispered and saw the first salesperson push open the door and go out into the evening.

He could tell by the way the man walked on the cobblestones that it was an apprentice, whose calves were not yet hurting from all the standing.

"In the shoe, toy, or tobacco department," he said, or maybe — there being no male staff in the ladies fashion, underwear, or household goods departments — in the tool department, ironically known in the store as Daddy's Hunting Ground.

Oh, how he would love to change places with the young man. How he would love to be going home to mother after a busy day at work. Or to be going back to the first room he could call his own. A room with a washbasin, and a girlfriend waiting for him. He was a strapping young lad, and was sure to have a girl already, preparing something for his dinner.

On the weekend, he thought, watching the young man light up a cigarette, they would go to the movies. Or they would simply stay at home, sitting next to each other on the bed, hatching plans, just as he had once done before he was married.

Back then everything had seemed possible. He wanted to embark on a career, or if necessary join the civil service treadmill like his father. And then, because he could not make up his mind, and had not yet had his fill of student life, he started a philosophy course. Outside the lecture theater he got to know a young lady. He liked her immediately, and liked her all the more when he found out that she was the daughter of the old O. They had married. He had believed that now nothing stood in the path of his dazzling rise. Back then he had many dreams.

He put up the collar of his coat and looked up at the familiar illuminated writing, not yet dismantled, on the roof of the building, and at the advertisement: "The Temple of Your Desires."

He had introduced the slogan four years ago, just before Christmas, against the will of his father-in-law. The old man thought the slogan blasphemous. A department store, he had shouted angrily in the office while selecting the spring fabrics with the representatives, is not a holy place. People's desires could not be satisfied by material goods. Schneider smiled. He had always wondered how this uncompromising man had made his fortune.

He got out his notebook and looked up the name of a university friend, whom he intended to stay with. Soon he would join with his family. They would be waiting for him. For how long, he could not tell.

"If only everyone was like the old man," he said, thinking of his father-in-law's face when he had argued with him that value was dependent on the market.

"There are values," the old man had thundered in response, "that are eternally valid."

Schneider had smiled cynically and answered that where there was no recognition of a deficiency, there was no need to remedy that deficiency. The old man had refused to speak with him for two weeks because of that. His wife had had to act as mediator between them.

He went into a café and asked whether he could make a quick call. The future would decide which of them was right.

You Have Cast Out Love

1.

I am a useless person. I do not like working, get up late whenever possible, and can never turn down a drink. I do not drink to drown my sorrows. My ambition is not sufficient to be wounded by failure. I am not striving for any success. I am neither content nor worried, and do not take it to heart when my mother scolds me for wetting the bed again.

My mother says she cannot keep up with all the washing. My urine will be the ruin of her health and her white hands, of which she is so proud. Although she turned seventy last year, they do not have any of the blotches typical for elderly hands. I am sincerely sorry for my mother. But my bladder pigheadedly insists on its autonomy. In spite of various attempts at dissuasion, I cannot prevent it from emptying every night.

After lengthy deliberations, my mother and I have reached a satisfactory compromise. For simplicity's sake we have accepted the disturbing occurrence. Grudgingly, for an organ should not push itself so much in the foreground. But after all, we couldn't spend every evening trying to tame my bladder. There are so many activities that are far more interesting. I could further educate myself, for example, read a book. If there is no hope of a physical recovery, the gray matter should be stimulated at least. Most edifying of all for me and my soul would be a glass of schnapps, of course. What a noble sight is a little glass of schnapps! But let's get back to the point.

My mother's vanity won over her social qualms. For a week now the lady concierge, an evil-smelling, gossipmongering woman, has come to collect the laundry. Soon all the tenants are bound to know that our sheets are soiled more often than convention allows. The lady concierge, of base character, gets such pleasure out of incriminating me.

Unfortunately, I am the one who has to pay. It is not a question of money with Mother, she is very generous: it's the educating principle. She is of the opinion that a reduction in my pocket money could affect the working order of my bladder. She is not far wrong with this strategy, a mild form of blackmail. While measures of punishment no longer have any effect on my conscience, grown degenerate over the years, I have nonetheless noticed that the flood of urine has lessened over the last few days, very probably because I can't drink so much in the evenings now because of financial reasons.

I don't drink to drown any sorrows. So why do I drink? A deep question, a fine question, one that deserves being toasted with the raising of a glass.

I drink at home in the afternoons, and in the bar in the evening. Both with company and alone. I drink out of greed, or if you like, out of enjoyment.

Sitting up at the bar, I do not raise my glass to anyone, do not look around, and do not seek contact of any sort. My shoulders slightly hunched, I concentrate my full attention on the sense cells in the mucous membrane of the nose and tongue that receive the pleasure of smell and taste of the schnapps.

The very sight of the clear liquid sets me aquiver. Before even touching the glass my skin begins to prickle. Patches of color appear on my face one by one. Should anyone distract me at this crucial moment, by asking nonstop questions, for example, about what I would like for my dinner tonight, I feel suffocated, as though an animal was pressing down on my chest.

Only after the first gulp does the pain subside. And then, in ever-increasing circles, penetrating my entire being, a feeling of happiness spreads, such happiness as is known by few people. It ebbs away immediately, so I have to refill my glass. I am back to the starting point: hands trembling with longing, breath catching, pulse racing with an irregular beat. After a deliberately drawn-out pause as I raise my glass to someone, for the torture of waiting contains overtones of the release, I moisten my lips with the acrid liquid. And so I continue until my senses are exhausted and my body pleasantly limp. Then all is well with the world.

Ah, schnapps, sweetest schnapps, my beloved firewater. How can I glorify you? How to describe you? You are my life. You are my mother. My homeland.

Sit and wait. Sit and wait until stomach, intestines, and liver, until each and every nerve is drenched by you. Until my blood is joined in union with you. I would love to have you in my blood, to have you in my blood permanently.

Ah, schnapps, sweetest schnapps, palatable treasure. Most beloved of the spirits, my brother, my colorless romance.

I've grown to love you. Have given you my repentant heart and hereby solemnly declare: at any time schnapps can raise me from the state of dullness my mother delivered me into. It gives me a sense of purpose and lends meaning to my life. With its guidance I am privy to knowledge preferable to the sobering examination of my own time. By playing games I conquer my quota of life I never asked for. Is that then not evidence enough of the profit a clever man can reap from alcohol? What is a cirrhosis of the liver in the face of all the possibilities opened up by schnapps?

My entire body trembles, sweating hot and cold, at the thought of the money running out. Fold my hands in prayer, and silently beg that schnapps hears me: do not desert me. Do not grow weary of me. And when morning comes, and I wake with a splitting headache, I find another little bottle in the wardrobe. One last mouthful under the bedside table, missed by my mother.

173

That is what I drink to: to the development of my creative initiative under the influence of alcohol. To creative plans and shapes after the sixth glass of schnapps. To my razor-sharp mind and wealth of imagination as far as finding new hiding places goes.

The old hag doesn't like you. Why, you have already taken her husband, you should let her son be. She declared war on you then. Wants to save her son. The son must not acquire a drinker's liver, and his room is checked. After all these years.

Nonetheless, I chalk up lots of points. I am, after all, a learned swindler, a master of creeping, pretending, and covering things up. And if she does find it, and pours it out, then I repay her brutal behavior by shitting in my bed. Make a steaming pile, then the old witch shouts, and peace resumes.

Ah, schnapps, dear schnapps, palatable treasure trove. My fruit schnapps, my cherry schnapps, my most beloved damson schnapps. You bring me fulfillment, you give me meaning. You mold me and my body. Over the years I have bloated, grown broader. My translucent pallor is thanks to you. This is my lordly title. This is my mark of Cain, my pride and joy. When I look at my naked shapeless body in the morning, I see your work everywhere.

With my lips I kiss you. With my tongue I lick you. I breathe your fruity aroma. Carefully I try you, so that you unfold in me, that you open up in me, that you give yourself. No one else, no one, do you hear me, can caress me as you do. And I am a *primus inter pares*, have gathered certain experience, but no one comes close to you.

2.

You call it a degeneration of the human race. You talk of a brain riddled with alcohol. Liver, stomach, intestines, kidneys, all done in. What remains then? A human wreck.

His odious offspring must be wiped out in advance, you say. At this point, we must be brutally frank. He is a good-for-nothing. He just costs money. There is no reversing events for him now, and even if there were . . . who would want him anyway?

I ask to be queried on the matter. Am glad to comment on my life, past or future. I have talents you know nothing about — let me explain. Then you will see that your suppositions are far from the truth. Like some other people, I know how to make up for my weak points. Have a beautiful laugh, warms every listener's heart when I get going. Even my mother agrees, the poor old dear, and giggles along with me, you can count on it. Also in my defense it must be said that I belong to the human species — a particular, most complex organism, with a body, a personality, and a thirst.

You do not believe in the saving grace of my laughter, want to hear a more convincing answer. Thirst, you retort, has yet to save a man.

You do not need background information, I should respond only to the questions you ask. My comments are irrelevant, confuse the matter, as there is nowhere for them to be filed. Fine, I shall adhere to the given columns. A short yes, a short no, and what lies in between is not of interest. But what happens in the case of my life not fitting into one of their columns, if the given answers distort my meaning, what do I do then? Mother, you do it, and do it quickly. Was once young, was once handsome. Also loyal, devout, and humble — I was all these once. Should I not be able to decide myself, I ask that you protect me. Should it not be looked into again to save money and time, I ask that you do so.

You do it. Or else I'll hang myself. I'll swallow a couple of tablets. Then I'll have my peace. Or you could slash open my wrists. My warm blood on the cool sheet. My blood, "enemy to the national community," on the freshly washed sheet. My inherited inferior blood, what would it matter, after all. The evaluation of my questionnaire shows that no tears will be shed on my account.

Herr Office Manager, sir, highly valued Union of General Practitioners, your Highness the Local Health Authority. I refuse to surrender. A doctor is not an oracle and cannot explain what turns the future may take. I will not hand myself over. Not even you can be so farsighted. I will bite your hand. You will have to come and get me. I will spit in your face. I — a bothersome psychopath — dismiss all your reproaches. I have been selected in an inadmissible way. I do not follow the legal connection between my thirst and my genetic makeup, and therefore ask that you reconsider your decision.

The hunter pursues the hare in the field. The soldier goes to war for his Fatherland. In spring the meadows flower: yellow blossoms. The education that equips one for life is not that learned in school. A mistake is not a lie. To lend is not to give. If one scrimps on sympathy, one is a thrifty person. Why and for whom is one stinting?

I have resolved to respect the will of the person concerned. The subject of examination is rebelling. Am I to be left no dignity? Admittedly there is a problem. But will it disappear if my ardor is stamped out? Would it not be possible to think up something else? A little punishment, a good measure of torture.

I admit there are friendlier people around. It is not nice that I soil my bed at night. And I would have run my father's bakery into the ground had my brother not taken over. But surely there is a more human way to punish me for no longer being operational. That is something you can learn, to be operational. Show me where economics is lurking, and I'll study the basics and come to love it. I am not too old for love. Or I could go to a re-education center. Send me to a house of correction. I will cut leather, chop wood, wash dishes. Let me still be useful.

Help me, Mother. My morals are impeccable, my grasp of ethics very, very beautiful. As far as what I learned at school, you can judge for yourself:

$$7 \times 9 \ = 63$$
$$17 + 32 = 49$$
$$51 - 16 = 35$$

Who was Bismarck? An old fool.

Who was Luther? Son of a whore, perhaps an angel.

Holiest Union of General Practitioners. In case you were not already aware, I am no Lamb of God. I am not cut out for this role at all. I have always been self-pitying. A sniveling, bloated person. I am no penitent. I would not be a pretty sight: snotty, howling, pissing on the cross. You have got to understand. I do not possess the necessary qualities. Not even my mother would shed a tear.

One imagines the Savior to be handsome and noble. He must come from high above, so that those watching have time to follow his fall. A big cheese, a king's son if it can't be the Son of God. The chosen people, but not the son of a baker. Believe me, I do not fit the bill. I know what is good for you and I am not it.

You have managed to collect a rich array of victims. I suggest you pick someone else. I am perfectly willing to help you choose. Take him, or him, or him.

And then, dear Local Health Authority, I want to add, look at what you have left to catch up on. All the cases handed in.

So many women that have yet to be treated. So many women who are waiting to be taken into the city hospital, to the gynecology ward, so that a specialist can cut through their ovaries, so that no man, to the devil with them, so that no man can fertilize the sick egg of those sick whores.

Snip-snip, clip-clip. Snip-snip, clip-clip. The scalpel nimbly cuts through the plans of the Creator. Made us in his image. Wants us to multiply. Was a crude nature. An evil force.

Death is in his court. He holds death in his hand. Judge, executioner, blade, and gallows. Our death is a sacrifice to you. Our horror is your freedom. Our torture your memorial. With every cry I raise a monument made of air to you. That is my contribution. Do you hear me? Do you hear?

What would you do if you won the lottery, for example? There is a nice thought. Why can one not set fire to one's own house? Why does the sun rise? Why do children go to school? What does the boiling of water mean? What is the opposite of courage? What is faithfulness? What is piety? Why do we have courts of law?

The examination being performed on me is pointless. You are just wasting your time with me. I am nothing. Ask my mother. She scolds me. She knows it and can confirm it whenever: *masturbator sum*. A poor sinner. My hand is my loyal friend. Between my legs I turn it into a tugging predator and pull until the bed rocks. But, my good men, the act requires the whole person, not just the hand.

Of course, I like looking at beautiful women. Even the backside of the concierge sets my fantasy in motion. But I no longer find my way to unknown beds. And even if I did, I would only collapse on them groaning. An old snoring colossus. A bit of skin, a bit of fat, and all that alcohol in my blood. Believe me when I say I will not be fertilizing any eggs now. Those who lead idle comfortable lives, they could do it, but I am not up to anything anymore, restricted as I am by my manifold activities, drinking, sleeping, and eating.

What you call life is closed to me. The tangible beating of the heart as a sign of love is alien to me. Fear, greed, a little cheerfulness, these I can identify. A little glass here, a little glass there, cannot hurt anyone.

My gentlemen, you have to understand: the sick seed drips on the bedsheet. It dries there. A little stain is no crime. The concierge comes and takes my secretion away. It is cleaned, for goodness' sake. The concierge washes it all out.

From the room I can see down to the courtyard. I pull up the blind and see the bedsheet, billowing in the wind. My white sheet, set at half-mast. The flapping symbol of my surrender:

damp flag against the gray wall. Damp flag waving in the wind. Back and forth, back and forth. I hum a song in time to it. Should be your lullaby.

3.

Let us try to put it clearly. In one simple sentence: I do not want to.

No, I do not want to. *I* am no less thirsty than some of the German emperors. *My* will is the essential force for my soul and my universe. Taking measures to preserve my kind, I flee beneath the bed. In spite of my pitiful state I raise my legs, fart, fall to the ground, and crawl on all fours around my room. My mother screams for the concierge and hauls me back onto the bed. I sit there and cry. A wretched picture. I know the work has to be carried out, it is in the interest of everybody. It will make for a nicer future.

I can already hear the lark's song, the babbling of the stream, the chirping of the crickets, and all that goes with it. I can already see the shadowy lindens, winding paths, and a carpet of yellow moss there. Poor old me. Me, the old sinner. The future is ghastly. It has nothing to offer me. To the victor the laurel. And what do I get? I get to lie in the dust, and kiss the boots of the murderer. There I lie, poor old fool, hoping to melt a stony heart.

Hoping that someone will have mercy on me. That someone at least will feel for me. I have left all pride behind. I come to you. The journey is a difficult one, but here I am and I ask you to take me. The country does not only need young men. The country also needs someone like me.

I will sit in a cage and eat nuts for you. I will scratch my head and leap from branch to branch. As a fearful example, I'll serve as a warning. Repellent leper, pitiful wreck of a human. Then they could see what you have saved them from, these naturally healthy descendants of your naturally healthy ancestors. There they'll have a live example and will be afraid.

Take me. I wipe the tears from my face. I will give you everything I have. Here is my silver ring, here is a little glass — brother, drink.

When everything is over, when everything has been conquered, when everyone is dead, then you will have no one left to destroy. The Jew will be gone, the communist, the gay pig, the tramp, the stinking Gypsy, Negro, Asiatic, the German whore floundering in foreign semen, the Pole, the sidewalk poet, Bolshevik, traitor: I want to replace all of them for you, want to be your enemy. Mess me up and spit on me. I am degenerate. I am a dwindling percentage, the divine mistake, ethically and morally rotten, but I do not stem from those types: mother a northern tramp, father a northern drinker. Me: a piece of northern dirt that will drink itself into a state in which it cannot struggle.

Yes, I am having a drink in the interest of the Fatherland. Leave individuality behind and drink myself to sleep. For the sleeping enemy is preferable to the enemy awake, though it cannot replace the dead enemy.

Mother, you should have pushed him away, the father, who desecrated your temple. Smashed our shrine. You should not have let him penetrate. It would have remained a wish, a desire consuming you in quiet moments.

Mommy, one should not give in to every desire. You had me. And that was it. Or did he use devious means to sleep with you? Old rascal, I have to reap what you sowed. I ask the question: Why should the son be made responsible for the behavior of his father? I ask the question: Who, in these times of progress, believes in inherited sin?

Just a watch, a worn-out suit, and a master craftsman's diploma, that is the sum of the estate of the baker whose son I am. Oh, and this thirst, this exaggerated thirst.

I, chained to my body, vulnerable and lazy, have little hope as far as my person is concerned. My provisions consumed, I am out in the cold. Boozing has driven me into the ground. What more do you wish for? My features are already melting, my body freezing, my breath rattling. Is this death? Am I upon my deathbed?

Ave, pia anima.

Ave, and shut your trap.

The gate is locked. I go back. I am not waiting for Peter anymore. Who wants the mission? I will give my task to another. He can pay what I still owe. Here is my authorization. Angels, heaven, that is nothing for me. No, my lot is another one.

I am damned to stew in my own juice. I will happily cook in my own secretion, singing all the while at the top of my voice a song to the devil. Take heed, I do not accept your message. It ricochets off my body, and however often it strikes me I will not weaken.

Take heed, I will not have the devil driven out of me. Because your cruel angels have been struck down by decay. Solemnly I raise my arm. Here you have my German salutation:

Hail, you betrayers!

Hail, you murderers!

Good health and happiness to the angels of death!

Night is spreading over the land. Man is delivered into the hands of others. They mock him, they flagellate him, they kill him. And you stay silent, and no one talks about what they have seen.

And the father hands over his son, and the son betrays his mother, and the mother lives in indecency. Houses are torn apart. And the compassion one was taught is thrown out to be gobbled up by dogs.

They urge the hounds onward. They round up the hounds with whistles. So that they set upon the human. They rip his tongue from his mouth, they gulp down his testicles, and you say nothing.

Floundering along all the paths of your making, you sacrifice him who rejects your words. And abandon him in his time of need. You believe you have heard his voice, he who reveals himself from heaven. He shall grant you the promise. I tremble with fear. He wants to redeem you and to carry the sin.

Ah, you are easy prey. Your hearts heavy with theft and evil, you stand eagerly on the threshold and divide up the property of your brother, whose blood is still warm. Hatred, contempt, and murder is your trinity. Hatred, contempt, and murder your creed.

I stand here and proclaim my own sentence.

I stand here and wait for you to rid your circle of me.

4.

Let's finish what we have begun: I have been chosen to realize the racial biological points of the program. And to help the doctor perform his duty.

The doctor is a conscientious fellow, he will take all this to great heights. He knows what an important role he has to play. With his aid the world will become more beautiful some day. He is doing it for his children. Things should be better for them. And the few worries that come to him at night — could it be the case that the gentlemen from the Authority on Racial Biology have erred? — they will be overcome by a raise in salary.

I am racially an extremely unfavorable manifestation. Father, hereditary disease. Seventy-year-old mother, hereditary disease, and me: a pitiful bastard. Who would want to marry me?

Ladies and gentlemen, with this piece of meat, myself I mean, I will try to entice you. Grant me your queasiness if sympathy is out of the question. Three more days, I hold the summons in my hand, then I have to report. And if I do not report, the police will come for me. They want to take my secretion, my milk from me. Is that fair?

Ladies and gentlemen, my scrotum: although it neglected its duty, I am most fond of it. Garnered no respect from women. It did not serve the Fatherland. And never compensated for its limited capacities with particular ardor. But nonetheless I like it. There are more handsome ones, bigger ones, younger ones, but I am content with it.

May it not be left to me for my further use? To soothe my distress? To while away the idle hours? What else is left to me? It does not harm anyone, after all. I cannot help it, I have grown very attached to it.

Dear old friend, we have not done great business. You were thrifty with my secretion. And now? We have spent years together, and it is to end like this?

Ladies and gentlemen, please forgive me for placing myself and my sexual organ so much in the foreground. I know that as I speak sad things are happening. It is hardly a time for complaining, when murder is rife. I know that I am a self-pitying oaf. Believe me, I am a moral person, wary of attracting attention, and I avoid talking of things that could offend my fellow human beings. But I must stress once more, my scrotum is not an unnecessary organ.

You have heard enough. Your patience is running thin. Just try for a moment to put yourself in my place. Would you not do the same thing? Struggle with the same zeal to preserve your best friend? True enough, convention prevents dedicating too much time to the scrotum. There is so much to discuss, that one must not get caught up in unimportant details. And yet, I cannot so meekly hand a friend over to the hangman. Nor do I want to play down its worth. It is at the top of my list of sight-seeing attractions. Therefore I suggest you take my sphincter instead. I would also sacrifice my urethra without batting an eyelid.

Ladies and gentlemen, I am unwilling to part with it. I will lock myself in the pantry. No one will find me there. And if you do find me, then I will scream. Come on, gag me. The neighbors are looking out of their windows. In its place I will give you my colon, my appendix, my kidney. The neighbors are whispering to one another. Now the old boozer is getting what he deserves. My mother is ashamed. She has asked the priest to be with her, and he makes the sign of the cross over me. The trial is heaven-sent. In a letter it was declared that I should be redeemed. Now here is my salvation. My mother is weeping, the old whore. A little snip, it cannot be so bad. I should behave myself. Should think about the family's reputation. I should be sensible and take it like a man. Does he also know fear? Can he not sleep at night either? I start to whimper. The policeman hits the son of the bitch, that is me, encouragingly on the back. It can't be that bad. In my distress, I even shit in my pants. Then, it drips onto the floor. Now he starts beating me in earnest. I fall at his feet. He kicks me in the spleen. I shout out: Why can't you love me? Why can't you love yourself? Why can't you love me within yourself? Why can't you love yourself within me?

Does he not see the similarities? My life line goes right down to my wrist. My heart line is cut through — no luck with women — my head line is pronounced. Do I not have any right to dream? No right at all?

With animals, castration happens for economic reasons. To tame them and to fatten them up. I am washed. The sponge is cold. Soon I will get something warm to eat everyday. The doctor comforts me. It won't hurt in the least. I will also get a few cigarettes afterward if I want. I want to talk, but I have to be quiet. He is busy. He will be happy to listen to me later. What good is his understanding to me afterward? I start to cry. A pitiful human being. A nurse pats my head. I will sleep in a moment. I have so much to say. So many words — have I used them all up? She takes the sheet. Give me speech. She pulls the sheet up over my head. Now I mustn't move anymore, and if I am not quiet they'll remove my heart. I won't be distracted. Let me speak about the Fatherland. I'm singing. Soon I'll be in the choir of the Holy Ghost, and its representatives on earth. I sing a song.

A hymn to my testicles
And to my children:
You have cast out love
Now it must roam.
Does no one want it?
It's my turn to talk.
Will no one listen to me?
Death will lend me his ear.
He caressed my head.
He was godfather to my children.
Then he had to go.
He leaned against my bed.
He held the white sheet.
Death sings me a song.
Mother, is there really something horrific,
Something horrific going on inside me?
Am I the vessel,
Am I the vessel of illness?
Does danger lurk within me?
Mother,
With the knife,
With the hunting knife,
The man rips me open.
Here I lie and listen to Death.
He sings a song to my testicles.
It is my turn to pronounce Fatherland.
It holds the sheet over me.
Will no one listen to me?
Then I must wander.
And listen to Death.

The Lighter

1.

It came at about eight o'clock. We had just finished eating and my mother was clearing the table. I was sitting next to my father, who was drinking schnapps. Because I have impeccable hearing, I heard the knock first. It was more of a scratching, like a cat weakened by hunger trying to claw through the bars of a cage. I told my father that someone had knocked, and followed him out to the hall in spite of the fat stain on my right trouser leg, which had only spread during my attempt to clean it.

He ran past us, into the kitchen. He had buttoned his jacket up wrong. A brown corner hung lopsidedly over the waistband of his trousers.

"They are coming today," he said, taking no notice of the steaming cup of ersatz coffee placed in front of him, along with the sugar bowl, as is our family's custom. My father asked him how he knew.

"I can't tell you that."

"Know what?" I wanted to know, and looked up at my father. He motioned me to be quiet. I pulled Herr Rößner's coffee cup over to me, and listened attentively.

"Did anyone see you?"

The neighbor shook his head. I carefully took three sugar cubes out of the sugar bowl and dropped one of them into my cup.

"But you can never know for sure," he said.

With a muffled plop it disappeared into the brown liquid. I fished it out with my spoon and sucked it with a slurping noise.

My father got out his pipe case. Either he will drink his schnapps now, or things are really serious, I thought. When I saw his face I decided that now was not the hour of repose: he would clean the pipe, and fill it, but not smoke it.

"We can't take any risks," said Father.

I dropped my second sugar cube into the cup. The coffee slopped over the side, leaving a ring on the saucer.

"You'll bring her here."

Mother looked at me with disapproval and removed the sugar bowl from the table. That did not bother me in the least, for I still had another cube hidden in my fist. The sugar had started to melt, becoming sticky.

My father scraped out his pipe, knocked it twice against his hand, opened the pouch, and started to fill it.

"Just for a couple of nights," the neighbor said, "until I have got everything ready."

"As long as you like," said my father and closed the pouch again, "you can count on me one hundred percent."

I stood up and went over to the shelf where the cigarette lighter was. I had just filled it up yesterday. I had also changed the wick and polished the silver.

Herr Rößner held out his hand to my father.

"I will never forget this, Gerhard," he said, "as long as I live, I will never forget this."

My father shook his head.

"Not at all, not at all," he said, feeling in his pocket for the lighter. I eventually fished it out from underneath the fruit bowl.

After shutting the door behind our neighbor, who went racing down the stairs, I sat back down, finished the coffee, now lukewarm and bitter, and asked my mother for a piece of cake. She had baked it for tomorrow's guests, but we would have to cancel them now that my father had decided to help our neighbor out of his fix.

"You may as well cut it now, rather than leave it in the oven," I said.

My mother shook her head like a disgruntled cat.

"You will not get any cake," she said, "nor will your father, and as for celebrating, there has been no reason for that in a long time," she added, furiously jabbing at the pot in which the potatoes from dinner had burned: nothing good would come of it, my father was leading us to ruin, the household could consider asking her opinion once in a while, for besides just doing all the cleaning and cooking she did in fact bring in a third of the household money. . . .

I quietly slipped away to my room.

I had just washed my sticky hands and was lying back refreshed on my bed when my father came in. I shifted a little to the side to make room for him. He sat down on the edge of my bed and puffed his pipe.

"We are having a visitor," he said.

I nodded, and stared at the end of his pipe.

"Just for a few days," he said.

"Yes, yes," I said, "I already know that." I was not stupid or anything. Why was he repeating what I had just heard with my own ears in the kitchen?

He took another draw on his pipe and blew the bluish smoke over to the shelves he had attached securely to the wall over my desk. They housed my model airplanes. I had built them with him and, following a diagram, had painted them true to life.

"Your mother does not want her in the living room. . . ."

"No no," I said, "Oh, no."

"So her fate is in your hands," said Father. And although I knew that he just wanted to flatter me by saying that, that this was a cheap trick to garner my approval — a trick that I would not fall for — I was flattered in spite of myself, and agreed to it.

"Just a few days?" I asked.

"I give you my word," said Father.

Then together we poured over a brochure that I happened to have in my pocket. It had pictures of an airplane used for businesspeople and tourists, with two motors. Its parts were available from the model shop.

I carried my bedclothes into the living room. The wool blanket slid out of my grasp and landed in the hallway, looking like a small flowery knoll. Mother, who had been watching my industrious activity from the kitchen doorway, shouted to me that I should not make a mess when we were expecting guests any minute.

"If they were not coming," I retorted, "I would not have to vacate my room, and my blanket would not be lying on the floor."

"For goodness' sake!" said Mother, shrugging her shoulders, and went back to her pot, which she was now rubbing dry with a cloth.

I was proud to have used a sentence with three conditionals in it, done correctly. I fetched my exercise book from the desk drawer, and was about to write it down, then stopped. I remembered I had promised to be as silent as the grave. That sentence contained everything that would ignite my classmates' curiosity. I certainly would have been asked who was coming, and which blanket we were talking about.

You win some, you lose some, I thought, and read through the fifteen sentences again that I had already noted down. I rubbed out the last one with my special eraser, now quite round from being rubbed so vigorously against the wooden bench, and shutting the book decided to bravely face the punishment exercise that was hanging over my head like a sword of Damocles. I would not have time to construct the thirty-five other conditional sentences tonight, for the night promised to be an exciting one. Nor did I have a good excuse at hand for this deficiency. As was often the case, the truth would have made the best excuse, but I could not betray my father, for I was tough, silent, and loyal.

There was a knock at the door.

"Shut the curtains," said Father, and hurried through the hall.

There was a grumbling from the kitchen. I pulled together my mother's pride and joy. They were actually only meant as decoration, and so they did not shut completely.

"There is a gap in the middle," I measured it with my fingers, "about fifteen centimeters wide."

My father took the guests into the living room.

"Sit down," he said to the neighbor's daughter. She stared at him stupidly.

"Perhaps it is better if you stay for a little while, until she gets used to us."

Herr Rößner nodded. "Do you see, Anna," he said, "these are Daddy's friends, and you are going to stay with them for a few days, so that Daddy can prepare everything for the holiday."

She clapped her hands. "Pony, pony."

"That's right," said Herr Rößner, "what does a pony say?"

"Yippee, yippee."

"Anna says yippee," said the neighbor, stroking his daughter's hair, "because she is sitting on the pony. The pony whinnies." He whinnied.

"Do you think it is safe in the country?" asked Father, while Anna pulled at the neighbor's sleeve.

"Brr, brr," he said and tried once again to imitate what he took to be the whinnying of a horse. "Safer than in the city."

Anna laughed and clapped her hands. "Brr, brr," she said now too, "brr, brr."

Now my mother came out of the kitchen. She had taken off her apron. At last, I thought, for I could not take any more. Now she will read them the riot act.

Mother rolled down her sleeves, buttoned the cuffs, and looked at my father and at the neighbor with her "everything is under control" look that she always had after baking a particularly good apple strudel. She smilingly turned to the neighbor's daughter.

"They also have ducklings there," she said, "quack, quack, and cows, moo, moo. . . ."

Had everyone gone crazy? I dropped down on the sofa, and stared at my parents in distress.

"That is Peter," said Father, pointing his pipe at me.

Anna nodded over at me. She had big, heavy breasts that bounced up and down as she pretended to ride a horse. I nodded back.

"Peter," said my father, "show Anna her room."

Mine, I thought, not hers, mine, mine, and mine again. I took the hand she stretched out to me: it was soft and warm and made me think of a pot of vanilla pudding that had been put on the windowsill to cool with a skin forming on its surface. I led Anna into the room.

"Oh, nice," she said, blinking.

"If you touch those," I said pointing to my model airplanes, "I will beat you to a pulp."

"Anna, Aannaa," came a voice from the living room. She let go my hand and stomped off. More like a raccoon, I thought, looking at her buttocks, which were leading an active life of their own beneath her skirt. I slowly followed.

Anna was crying.

"My little girl," said the neighbor, and looked helplessly at my mother, who was trying to loosen the girl's hold on the collar of her father's coat, "I will be back tomorrow, and then I will take you with me to the farm, and you will ride the little pony."

"Come," said Mother, giving me a warning look, "Peter will show you his airplanes."

I tapped my finger against my forehead. Anna sobbed. I realized to my relief that she had not heard my mother's suggestion.

My neighbor hugged her tight. "My dear little girl," he said. "Daddy will look after you."

Now my mother had tears in her eyes, too. Those crybabies, I thought, referring to womankind in general.

"It's fine, it's fine."

Father patted Herr Rößner reassuringly on the shoulder, and said he had nothing to worry about. He had better leave, for any minute now that interfering Dr. Heillein from the first floor would return, and it was necessary that he not see Mr. Rößner leaving our apartment.

The neighbor nodded, and took my father's hand.

"I will never forget what you have done."

"It's fine."

My father swung his pipe in a circle through the air. It had gone out in the meantime. Some ash and strands of tobacco landed on the hall floor. This would have made Mother furious if she had not at that moment made for the kitchen. She opened the oven door, which emitted a wail of despair: Father had forgotten to oil it again. When the door had closed behind the neighbor, Mother entered the living room holding a tray, and on the tray were plates, forks, and napkins, and next to them on a round metal base was the apple tart. Our attention was drawn to its sweet aroma.

"Oh well, at least something good has come of the visit," I said, and took my place next to Anna as Mother shot me an angry look.

We made up the bed together. Mother had gotten out a fresh sheet that smelled of lavender. Conceding that we could not spend the whole evening looking at the bedcover, I did up the buttons. Then I showed Anna my books, but she did not seem that interested. She fell back on the bed, squashing the pillow, and stared sadly at my fleecy bedside rug made of wool. I told her she would see her father again in the morning and I knew how she was feeling. Two years before I had had my appendix removed. You could still see the five-centimeter-long scar.

"Here," I said, pulling my underwear down a little. "A whole week all alone, and the pain on top of that."

Anna was impressed.

"It doesn't hurt anymore at all." I took my finger down the length of the scar. It gleamed, a translucent pink.

"You can even pinch me there. I don't feel a thing. The skin is thinner, but not sensitive."

She touched the scar, but pulled her hand quickly back. Instead of protruding knuckles she had five little hollows.

My father came into the room.

"I see you are getting to know one another," he said, making me feel embarrassed.

I pulled my underwear back up, and fastened my trousers, resplendent with the large round fat stain on the right leg.

Now my mother came in too.

"Well, Anna," she asked, "do you like it here with us?"

Anna looked at me. I nodded. My mother yawned, and scratched her arm with rapid circling movements. A content domestic cat, I thought.

"I am going to lie down then," she said, and after wishing us all good night, she padded down to the bathroom. Soon we heard the rushing of water in the pipes. The insulation being so bad, it always sounded like Niagara Falls. A few seconds later my mother's own gurgling merged with it.

"How about hot chocolate?" asked Father with a conspiratorial wink to reassure us. I leaped up joyously, and my obvious glee was infectious. Anna trampled her feet on the wool rug. We softly made our way to the kitchen. Mother switched on her bedside lamp. I heard her picking up the newspaper from the table.

"She's reading," I said to Father. He nodded and got out a pan.

I brought over the milk. Father poured the whole contents of the bottle into the pan. Mother would have diluted it with water, I thought, and handed Anna the cocoa. She passed it to my Father. I fetched the lighter from the shelf and flicked on the flame. In the darkness of the kitchen it glowed like a comet.

"No," I said. "That is not for you."

Anna jostled me and reached for the lighter again.

"Go on, give it to her," said my father.

"But she jabbed me in the ribs."

It really did hurt. Grudgingly, I passed her the lighter.

The neighbor's daughter lighted the stove. The three of us waited until the milk boiled up and reached the edge of the pan. We warmed our hands over the stove.

My father had gotten candles out of the cupboard in the living room. They were now burning on a wooden board on the kitchen table. He had also put the cookie jar on the table. The contents were steadily going down.

"Tell us about your bullet," I said, meaning the shot that had grazed my father's leg during the war.

"Another time," he replied.

I shook the last crumbs from the jar into my hand, and sucked them up.

"Or the story of the theft."

Father took out his tobacco pouch and filled his pipe.

"It's late already," he said, "it's time for bed. Take Anna to her room."

I took her hand and went into my room. She wanted to see my scar again, and tore at my waistband.

"Go to sleep," I said, "slee-ep." When she appeared not to understand what I was talking about, or pretended not to, I put my head on the fresh pillowcase and snored a couple of times.

Anna laughed.

"No," I said, "do not laugh." I looked at her breasts that were swinging back and forth in time. They struck me as being a real hindrance. How unpleasant it must be to have two swings attached to your rib cage.

"Do not laugh, sleep."

I left the room and lay down on the living-room sofa. Your teeth, I thought, you can brush them in the morning. I kicked myself free of the woolen blanket, which my father and I referred to as Bernhard, for the sheep that had been shorn to make the blanket must have had bristles rather than hair, just like my aunt's boyfriend, Bernhard. He was a real estate broker and wore a toupee that looked like a colored cow pattie that had sprouted bristles overnight. It was scratching even through the sheet. I discarded the blanket and thought about my new model airplane. Then I dozed off.

I must have been asleep for about half an hour, when a hand stroked my face.

"Five more minutes."

At first I had thought it was already time to get up. Then I saw that I was not in my room, that it was dark, and I was scared. Anna sat down next to me on the sofa. I picked up the alarm clock, which I had set and put on the table. The clock face glowed back at me. Half past eleven.

"You stupid cow," I said, "do you have any idea what time it is?"

Anna tore the alarm clock out of my grip and threw it to the ground. It landed on the carpet and the alarm went off.

"Show," said Anna, tapping my tummy.

"You stupid ass." I bent down to shut off the alarm clock, which was spinning around the table leg. Its two thin steel legs pointed tremblingly upward. It looked like a helpless beetle.

"Shh," I said, "if you wake up the cat, we'll be in real trouble."

I went over to the window and pulled the blind up a good ten centimeters.

"But just once, and then it's back to bed."

Anna nodded. She was wearing a striped nightgown. The top buttons were undone. I told her to move, lay down flat on my back, and pulled the elastic waist of my pajama bottoms down a little. Anna had cold hands. I let the elastic slip back up.

"That's enough." I turned onto my side, pulled the blanket up over my ears, and waited.

"What's wrong now?" I asked after a while. She had not budged and I could feel her backside, taking up space so that I had to press myself against the back of the sofa and almost suffocated in the stuffiness.

"What do you want?" I sat up and looked at her. She was crying.

Just what I needed. I peered at the big hand of the clock, which was mercilessly moving round. There was no chance with Mother. I would have to get to work on my father before he came to the breakfast table, to talk him into giving me a note for school, to explain why I was late.

I got up and went into the kitchen. I could not stand the sound of her horrible sniffling.

"Here." I passed her a napkin.

She blew her nose several times, then handed it back to me. Disgusting, I thought, taking the snot-filled napkin with two fingers and dropping it on the table.

"So," I said, "now you are going back to bed."

I led her back to my room, pulled back the cover, and patted the mattress twice invitingly. She lay down, pulled up the cover, and stared at me with her big sad dog eyes.

"All right, then, but only for a short time."

I sat down next to her, held her hand, and looked at my fifteen model airplanes, which I would soon push together to make room for a business and tourist plane.

At dawn, I woke up. My body was aching. I stood up and stamped my left foot on the woolly rug. It had gone to sleep because Anna had lain on top of it. It felt like a pincushion. Anna was snoring. I went to the bathroom. Sleep was out of the question now.

When I came out, all washed, my father came shuffling toward me. He asked me if I had slept well. I laughed derisively and went into the kitchen. Mother was bent over the oven. I passed her my cup and spread a biscuit with butter, dripped some honey on it, and swallowed it in two bites.

Father cleared his throat and sat down next to me on the bench. I told him I had not slept a wink because I had had to spend the night with Anna, who was suffering from homesickness. That I could have understood, had it not deprived me of my sleep, which would have been less than excellent anyway in the strange bed. Another conditional sentence of the highest order I thought proudly, happy to have used a perfect form, though quite which one I was not sure. I reached into the breadbasket, and took out the last biscuit. It had been nibbled at in the corner. Disgusting, I thought, but bit into it anyway.

She was standing in the doorway, verb of place. Or she had planted herself in the doorway, verb of movement, for now the doorway did not signify a position but a movement. I was slowly picking it up.

My mother saw her, who or what, accusative, first and called her over. Anna stood there as though rooted to the spot. I stood up, fetched her, and sat her down next to me, which made two accusatives, sitting side by side. I gave her my biscuit, which she crumbled immediately. My mother refilled the breadbasket. As we were on our fourth biscuit and my angry stomach was beginning to settle down, the doorbell rang.

"Who can that be ringing so early?" asked my mother, and cast a worried glance at the oven.

"Take her into the bedroom, and not a word," said Father, making his way slowly to the apartment door.

I took Anna's hand and hurried her into my room. I rapidly looked around me. Suddenly it all seemed too small.

"Under there," I whispered, holding up the cover a little and pointing under the bed.

She got down on her knees.

"Come on, do it," I hissed, giving a helpful prod with my foot. Laboriously she pushed herself under the bed. I lay down on the mattress and pulled the cover up to my chin so that no one would see I was already dressed.

The door opened, and my father came in. I could not tell

from his face what was going on. Behind him, I could hear a man's voice. Whatever will be, will be, I thought, and swallowed. My heart was beating wildly. Father stepped to the side. I could feel the biscuit rising in my throat, shut my eyes, but then opened them wide again immediately. In the frame of the door a man's hand appeared. You fool, I thought, you have chosen the silliest hiding place imaginable. Under the bed is the first place anyone would look. I gave my father a sign. And then I saw the neighbor and started to cry.

After we had extracted Anna from under the bed in a combined effort, we went back to the kitchen. Father stroked my head and said he was proud of me. I was ashamed for crying.

The neighbor turned down my mother's coffee for a second time; there was no time to lose, he said, and asked my mother to help Anna get dressed. They went to the bathroom together and came back ten minutes later. Mother had dressed her in a clean dress with a white, starched collar and combed her hair back into a ponytail.

"Since her death," said the neighbor, talking about his wife, who had died the previous year, "no one has done her hair like that."

He thanked my mother and father and then came to me.

"That was very decent of you."

He got out his wallet and pulled out a banknote.

Four model-airplanes, I thought, first rate, and shook my head.

"I would rather buy you something," said the neighbor, "but there is no time."

I took the banknote, looked at the watermark, folded the note in the middle, and thanked him. Herr Rößner smiled.

"Good," he said.

He picked up his bag and slipped the strap over his shoulder.

"We had better go."

Anna was still standing next to the oven, and would not move.

"She wants to have the lighter," I pointed to the shelf. "Because we had hot chocolate last night."

I looked at my father; he nodded. I went to the shelf, took the lighter, which I had cleaned and filled only the day before yesterday because my father always forgets things like that, and passed it to Anna. She smiled at me, lit it a few times, and then popped it into her jacket pocket.

2.

My parents had made an exception and said I could stay home from school. So I had taken over the clearing up of the breakfast things, which was fine by me. Particularly as I planned to swipe the biscuit that the neighbor's daughter had left half eaten as a kind of souvenir. Hard times necessitate hard measures.

I was daydreaming a bit, but tidied up quickly when I saw how late it already was. I did the dishes and left them to dry on the dishcloth — even though my mother did not like that because it left stains on the dishes, she thought — and took off before my mother came back from shopping and could give me other household chores. I had the banknote in my pocket and set off for the model shop.

They were standing at the traffic lights. I recognized Anna's dress, its white collar dazzling in the morning sun. Ah-huh, I thought, and they were in such a rush at our house. I went toward the small group made up of Herr Rößner, his daughter, two men, and a woman.

I was almost next to them before I noticed that Herr Rößner's lip was bleeding. He was weeping and trying to break loose from the grip of one of the men. Anna was holding the lighter I had given her, looking at it indifferently.

I went past them. When I had reached the street corner, I turned around. The lady, wearing a blue suit that hung loosely from her body, had one arm around Anna's shoulder and was leading her to a car that was parked at the edge of the street, speaking soft words of encouragement. Don't go with her, I wanted to scream, don't go, and I stumbled over a bag full of apples that someone had left in the middle of the pavement. Please, please, please, I thought, don't go, every idiot knows, every silly ass knows, that they do away with people like you there, because they are stupid like you, that they lay the idiots out cold, everyone knows that, my father told me, and he had learned it from yours, you silly pig, you stupid ass, don't go with them, I thought. And as I was picking up the apples that had rolled over the street, Anna reached the woman whose arms were circling excitedly in the air like the propeller of an airplane, and got into the car.

Three Penknives

Allow me to briefly introduce myself. I am a housewife and mother of four strapping lads who, for the sake of the Führer, the People, and the Fatherland, I am trying to bring up following good principles: by that I mean, strictly German. I am devoting myself to this task with body and soul.

Both my husband, an employee of middle income with the Altona Insurance Company, and I joined the Party in 1933: we have been active members for seven years now. Aside from my housewife duties, made difficult by the daily hurdles that lie in the path of a mother of three growing boys and one grown-up son, I work four times a week as a volunteer at the Service of German Mothers section of the Women's Organization of the National Socialist Party. There I give courses to unmarried women on the noble duty of childbearing, or as Strammerle, our local propaganda leader, so nicely put it at the monthly Mothers' meeting, "on the necessity of an abundance of children for the future security of the great works of the Führer."

For this, as well as of course for our being blessed with children, I was last year awarded the bronze cross for Motherhood.

I have learned from my neighbor, Herr Krause, that soldiers or those that have been drafted can apply for confiscated goods at reduced prices. Herr Krause asked the Ghetto Administration for a watch for his son about two weeks ago, and received it eight days later by insured package.

My oldest boy will be drafted next week. He is joining the air force. He has already gotten through the entrance exams in Munich, Frankfurt, and Wiesbaden, rather successfully I have been told by some trustworthy sources.

However, he already has a watch. My husband and I gave him one for Christmas. It being an example of German quality, I do not imagine it will stop working in the foreseeable future.

Would it be possible to make an exception and instead of the watch to send three penknives? Under the condition, of course, that the responsible authorities have seen fit to confiscate these objects.

I trouble you with what must seem a minor request, as it is not possible at the moment to acquire reasonably priced items of quality in the Reich. I can assure you that I have looked for several weeks. In order to do this, I had to sacrifice some afternoons that could have been put to better use, at the Service for German Mothers, for example.

I would be very grateful if you could help me. You would be fulfilling the dreams of a mother and her three boys.

I would be much obliged for your swift response, and send my best wishes.

Heil Hitler!
Helga Pfeifer

The Golden Necklace

1.

"Later, later," he said. "Always later."

Ludwig sat up and looked under the bed for his shoes.

"In two days I'm off to the front. Some never come back, or come back in such a state they wish they had not come back."

"Quiet," said Marianne, pulling him back down to her.

He shook her off, stood up, and clasped his hands to his breast.

"Hello, Mr. Pfeifer. Hello, Mr. Brackmann. Would you not agree, Mr. Pfeifer, music is something quite wonderful. Yes, Mr. Brackmann."

"Leave my father out of this."

"Now, you will have my Marianne back home in good time for the concert on the radio. . . ."

"He has nothing to do with this."

"There was a time when we went to concerts."

She got up and tried to grab him, but instead clutched only air.

"I told you to stop."

"But today, you see, in these difficult times . . ."

"Stop it, I said." She hit him.

"Don't ever do that again." Ludwig twisted her arm.

"You're hurting me."

He let her go, sat down in the armchair in the corner of the room, and impatiently tugged at his shoelaces.

"Damn it . . ." He hurled the broken shoelace on the floor.

She sat next to him on the arm of the chair.

"Why are you always so angry?"

She ran her fingers through his hair.

"You should give me a lock of your hair when they cut it short."

Ludwig rubbed his head against her upper body.

"I will look after it, and then when you come back we can burn it together."

He undid the first button on her blouse and slipped his hand in. Marianne drew back.

"Come on," he said, opening the other buttons. She looked over to the door.

"He won't come in. He's listening to music."

Marianne shook her head.

"Come on," he said, "come on."

She twisted her torso away from him, did up her buttons, and went to the door.

"Listen," Ludwig said, dropping down on the bed. "Even Erna has done it already."

She stood still and looked at him in disbelief.

"Eckstein told me."

Marianne frowned, as if in deep concentration for a long moment, then smiled at him.

"Werner didn't have time to tell you."

She opened the door.

"When you were on the Ferris wheel with Erna, when you were up at the top and waved down at us and we were buying a bottle of beer. Right after the old acrobat and her husband."

Ludwig clasped his hands behind his head.

"Afterward they washed the sheets, which his mother saw. Because she came back early, she immediately knew everything."

"You're lying."

Marianne went into the living room where her father was sitting next to the radio. As she started to embrace him, he motioned her to be still.

Ludwig grumpily tucked his shirt into his trousers — it had traveled up over his flat stomach — then followed Marianne and sat down next to her father on the sofa.

2.

I'll give it to her right away, thought Ludwig, I'll give it to her right away, and then I still have two hours and she won't be able to refuse. One hour is enough, he thought, and then if I go directly to the club I'll still be in time for bowling. Or I'll take her home and join them later to say good-bye when they're having their beer. He passed Marianne the small box made of black cardboard.

"Here you are," he said, his eyes on her breasts as she took off the lid and carefully unfolded the tissue paper.

"Oh," Marianne went up on her tiptoes, "that is so sweet of you." She gave him a kiss.

"Look, P. L." Ludwig pointed at the heart. "My initials."

She held the pendant in her hands and kissed it.

"So that you never forget me." Ludwig smiled bashfully, then put his hands behind his back.

She turned around and held her hair up. Ludwig took the chain and held it round her neck.

He had bought it off one of his old classmates who had brought it back with some other items of jewelry from the front. You could get everything cheaper there, his friend had told him, you simply went to the Ghetto Administration and handed in your order. It seemed like the land of milk and honey to him, so many beautiful things and so cheap.

Actually, Ludwig had been looking for something more reasonably priced, something silver or nickel — it was not an engagement present, after all, he did not want the girl to have false hopes — but then because of the letters engraved on the flat surface of the heart, he had opted for it.

He fumbled at the tiny golden catch. It slipped from his fingers and he cursed under his breath. On the third attempt he managed. Marianne turned around and showed him the necklace. He nodded with satisfaction. The heart lay nestled at the base of her neck.

"Beautiful," he said. "It looks good on you."

Ludwig circled Marianne's hips and led her up a narrow path to the clearing. No one ever comes here, he thought, and pressing her against him, he looked at his watch.

When they got there, he settled down on the damp earth, covered in leaves. On the right-hand side, low conifers edged the clearing. Behind him lay long dark tree trunks. Ludwig pushed himself back and leaned against them. He tapped the ground.

"Come here," he said, "sit next to me."

He took off his jacket and spread it on the ground.

"Come here, I won't touch you."

Marianne giggled, then sat down next to him, fingering the heart. It hung cool against her neck.

"Seventeen," said Ludwig, pointing to the figure the loggers had written on the trunk.

"Will you write to me?"

"Yes." Ludwig kissed her ear.

"Every day?"

"Yes."

He looked at her knee. He would really have to hurry things along to make the bowling evening. He embraced Marianne and as she was talking inched her skirt up.

"Yes," he said, "yes, indeed, every Saturday." He clasped her knee.

Not a bad knee, he thought, and left his hand there. If I go too quickly, he thought, she won't let me do it. Carefully his fingers reached her thigh and he felt himself grow hard between his legs.

"My heart," he said, "belongs to you now."

"I will write to you, too, then we will be close and can share everything, and when you come back . . ."

Ludwig slipped down until his back touched the ground, turned on his side, and lay on top of Marianne.

"And when I come back," he said, rubbing his lower body against her thighs, "then we'll get married."

"Yes," said Marianne and pushed his hand away, because he was holding on to her breast so tightly that it hurt.

3.

Now he is taking me up the path, thought Marianne, so that he can try again. There's never anyone there, now I'll have to let him. Everyone in the class has done it already, Erna too, and now it's my turn. She gave him a kiss.

"That's very sweet of you," she said, and made him fasten the necklace.

Now she was really someone. She, too, had her man whom she could worry about — he was going off to war, after all — and whom she could bring cakes to, for they never ate enough in the army. She would watch him compassionately as he wolfed it down. That was the best compliment that could be made about a cake.

She fingered the necklace. A beautiful necklace. Tomorrow she would show it to her classmates, while he was receiving his first orders. And of course I'll show it to Erna, she thought. Erna had been given a bright blue stuffed animal, and a gingerbread heart, which seemed ridiculous compared to her farewell gift, and Erna was bound to think so, too.

"Come here," he said, tapping the ground.

She had heard that the hymen could be broken by doing gymnastics, performing a cartwheel. She had tried, but did not believe it had worked, since you were meant to feel pain afterward.

Even if it hurts, she thought, it's not serious. At least I'll have it out of the way at last.

"Come on," he said, and spread his jacket out.

She sat down next to him on the ground and regarded his profile. A little nose, with an upward tilt. Like a pig, thought Marianne. She laughed.

He will do it any minute now. She fiddled with a dry leaf. I hope he doesn't crease my skirt. Perhaps I should take it off? No, then I would be stark naked.

"Aha," she said, and looked down at her skirt, which was crumpled now anyway because he was leaning over her to point out the number on the tree trunk. Rotten luck, she thought. It was out of the question now. She had intended to wear the skirt tomorrow along with the same blouse and woolen jacket, so that her classmates in the morning and Erna in the afternoon could see what she had worn. They should know every detail.

"Will you write to me?"

"Yes."

"Every day?"

"Of course . . ."

Or, she thought as he caressed her knee, I could hang the skirt in the bathroom this evening, perhaps the steam will get out the creases.

"I'll even write to you tomorrow from the barracks, and on Saturday you can come and visit me."

Now he's going to lie down on top of me. Marianne saw a drop of sweat on his top lip. Why is he sweating like that, she thought, it's happening too fast, and she asked him whether he had seen the film set in Tivoli.

"It's a tragedy about the farmers in the mountains."

She told him about Lona, the heroine, who was twenty years younger than her husband Thomas, who had a farm far from the beaten trail and a farmhand by the name of Martin whom Lona was in love with.

"This disastrous passion brings about her ruin," said Marianne and quietly repeated her sentence as he was rubbing his lower body against her knee.

Like a dog gone wild, she thought, and wriggled straight underneath him.

"My heart," he said, "my heart." She felt his heart pounding against her stomach.

He reached under her skirt and with one tug pulled down her panties. She had chosen them especially for this occasion — panties with a flower pattern that matched her bra, which now hung crookedly over her breasts. He did not notice the pattern, simply tore them down and threw them in a wide arc through the air to the side.

Now I am his woman, she thought, looking at a tree trunk with crumbling bark. She fingered the heart. If he were to fall in war, she would keep it as an eternal reminder of this day. She would also show it to the child that they were perhaps even now creating. It is a noble souvenir, she thought, one that could be shown to a child without any second thought, even if the father had fallen on the front. She sighed. She would also keep the medal. On his thirteenth birthday she would solemnly give it to her son.

"Now," he said, "now, and now, and now."

And then it was over. He rolled off her, sat up, wiped his sweaty forehead with the back of his hand, pulled up his trousers, which hung about his knees, and looked at his watch.

Yes, now I am his woman, she thought, and dabbed at her leg with her panties, while he was doing up his trousers, to stop the trickle of the sticky white liquid.

4.

They went down the small path together. They waited at the tram stop. Ludwig paid and sat down next to her. They passed the football stadium, which was empty now. At the second stop an old man and a lady with three children got on. The children raced around the empty car. Marianne offered them a bag of sweets. Slowly the tram filled up.

When they got there, Ludwig let Marianne get down first, then he leaped down the three steps. He had actually intended to take her only as far as the street corner, but took her right up to her door and, although she had not asked him to, went upstairs with her too.

Marianne's mother was waiting. She had just put water on to boil for coffee and there was apple cake.

At five o'clock Ludwig was still at Marianne's, at six o'clock too, but he had stopped looking at his watch. At seven o'clock he got up to leave. Marianne went with him to the door, and it quietly shut behind them. They stood for a while in the corridor. A man carrying a coal bucket went past them and up to the third floor. They heard him unlocking his apartment door, pushing the coal bucket through with his foot, and the sound of the door closing. Then all was quiet again. They sat on the stone steps. He embraced her. She laid her head on his shoulder. The streetlights went on outside.

5.

The following day she showed Erna her gold necklace — it was much admired — and looked up the medical encyclopedia. It had a place of honor in the bookshelves next to the atlas, the dictionary, *Mein Kampf*, the Bible, and the color picture book of plants and trees of Germany. Erna had gotten it from her godmother for Christmas, since she had found it more properly educational than the dress that had been requested, complete with a deep scooped neckline designed for nothing but manhunting. Erna did that anyway, even without the dress or the neckline, and captured her first man, called Ecki, one Saturday afternoon at the Bowling Club. His real name was Werner and he was half a year older than she.

There it was in black and white:

There had been a stiffening, engendered by the congestion of blood, of the part of the body equipped with erectile tissue and residing between the curves of the groin — known in brief as the male sexual organ — which she could now admire in both cross and longitudinal sections. The stiffening was a tensing up that began in the cerebral cortex, proceeded down through the diencephalon and the spinal cord, finally reaching the nether regions, and was occasioned by the touching of the pair of hemispherical glandular organs on the front of the female upper body, which were winking up at the sky because the flowery bra had slipped up, and which he first fondled with his fingers before suckling on them with the fleshy upper and lower rim of the opening of his digestive canal.

Ah-huh, she thought, and looked at the erectile tissue, the glans, the urethra, and the scrotum, marked in red, which if she was not mistaken she had felt against her perineum or sphincter, when the male sexual organ had penetrated the female sexual organ. Ah-huh, she thought, and she also looked at the female sexual organ, of which there was a diagram too, made up of a vagina, a uterine orifice, two ovaries, an ovum, and a uterus, in which perhaps even now the fruit of her love was ripening. She read through everything with exactitude, then looked up frightened.

"Listen," she said, "I don't think he has that."

"Doesn't have what?"

"You know, he didn't push anything up."

"Didn't push what up?"

"You know, the foreskin."

"That's not possible."

"I certainly didn't see it."

"Maybe you looked away at that moment."

"I did not."

"Then you just weren't paying attention."

"Believe me, I was."

"Well then, he must have a Jewish willy."

"He does not."

"Well, then, you just didn't see it. I definitely would be surprised if he did have one."

"If he had a what?"

"A Jewish willy."

"He does not," she said, furious.

"That's what I mean," responded Erna.

"But how do you know that he doesn't?" asked Marianne.

"They wouldn't take him on then."

"Do you think so?"

"Yes, sure," replied Erna. "Do you think they want Jews in the Wehrmacht?"

She shook her head. Ah, the Wehrmacht, she thought, that makes our men men, and protects our homeland, and will conquer the world victoriously, thank goodness we have it.

Proudly she grasped the heart with his initials engraved on it. It bounced against her throat and would remind her of him until he came back to marry her. She would bake cakes for him and iron his shirts and darn his socks and make roasts and have lots of sons. She would bear sons for him and for the Führer, for the will for a child was there, and where there is a will there is a way.

And all of a sudden that poem about the Wehrmacht came to mind that she had learned by heart: "He who runs to the flag, he who burns for the flag, he who knows the flag, will be steel," a poem that she now for the first time fully and completely understood. And with one hand she cradled the heart, which was not made of steel but of gold-plated silver, and with the other hand her belly, in which perhaps even now the fruit of her love was ripening.

Statement of the Officer for Accounts

(The Stamp Collection)

O<small>N OUR DAY OF ARRIVAL, TOWARD ONE O'CLOCK</small> — I had just taken up my quarters and had almost finished unpacking — Vogt, a member of our unit, came into the room and announced that a convoy of Jews was approaching.

"They have come from Wilna," he said and added that we would be able to see them pass through if we left that minute.

We had chosen the school for our living quarters, since it had central heating and space enough.

Although the civil population certainly would not have objected — their impeccable attitude had been picked out for special praise several times in the circular that we received once a week — I did not believe that the Jews would be driven into the village.

Vogt, well known for his opinion, asked me if I wanted to watch the convoy.

His exact words were: "We should not miss this piece of theater."

Since I didn't have any urge to write the letter I owed my mother, I took my jacket down from its hook and went with him. Corporal Zink joined us.

We took a shortcut over the field, crossed a stream that was already freezing at the banks, and thanks to Vogt's spurring us on we reached the country road after a good quarter of an hour. They would have to come by this way, approaching, as they were, from the north.

We got there in the nick of time. We only just managed to group loosely around the boundary stone that marked the field when we already saw the convoy in the distance, rapidly approaching.

Roughly estimating, there were around three hundred people. They walked in rows of four. On every coat and jacket the yellow star was attached.

"A model convoy of Jews," said Vogt.

I nodded, for he was right. The convoy, comprising only Jews, was divided up conventionally, children at the front, then women, some with small children in their arms, their husbands of all ages taking up the rear. Almost all the Jews were reasonably well dressed, had shoes and coats, and carried small suitcases or bundles.

The convoy was supervised by SS men who walked in intervals of four, five, or perhaps six rows alongside the group. I can remember it distinctly, since there was undeniably a certain competence that would have saved me much work had it appeared in our unit.

At the rear of the convoy were four SS men who greeted us with a nod of the head, and Vogt shouted over a risqué joke about the BDM,* whom he referred to as the "Baby Distract Me," and they guffawed with laughter.

That was just Vogt's way. His big mouth had gotten him into trouble in the past and he would have long since been sent packing if he were not considered an excellent soldier in every other way.

Out of curiosity, and to discover whether there was a camp in the vicinity — we had not heard of any but were aware that they were popping up like mushrooms all over the place — we followed them at a distance of thirty meters. After ten minutes they swung off the country road and turned left onto a small path.

---

*Bund Deutscher Mädel: League of German Girls.

Before we had gone a full kilometer we reached a deciduous forest. Vogt said it could not have anything to do with a camp: the escape possibilities were too great in this terrain, where it was hard to see what was going on and therefore impossible to control.

"You can't go putting ideas in their heads."

This sort of terrain, Vogt continued, would be asking for trouble. That was why a camp should be set up only on even ground, and then only if the area had been cleared of trees.

"If one of them rebels," said Vogt, "you'll soon have the whole rabble at your throat, and then you can kiss it all good-bye."

We came to a clearing, which resembled a building site. A companion from the SS standing over to one side and smoking a cigarette told us it was a petrol storage area that the Russians had built and kindly handed over. We laughed. He held out a package of cigarettes. We refused: we knew how difficult it was to get hold of cigarettes. The SS man told us not to be shy.

"Like the 'Baby Distract Me,' " he said to Vogt, and told us to help ourselves. He got a special ration for the job he was about to perform.

Corporal Zink asked what was going on here.

"Feel free to look around," encouraged the SS man, which we immediately did.

We crossed over the area. In the middle of the clearing a ditch had been dug. The convoy of Jews stood somewhat to the side of it. They had been ordered to drop their luggage and stand in groups of ten. The Jewish women and children were led into the forest. This resulted in some shouting from the families who were split up in this way — the men remained, as I said, standing in groups of ten.

"If they don't see it," the SS man confided to us, "it all goes more smoothly."

He was referring to the women and children.

Vogt, who had taken a camera with him, went to the edge of the hole and took a photograph looking into it at the corpses already there, and joining us again asked the SS man when they completed that lot.

"We shot them just yesterday," he said, adding that it had gone without a hitch and that he hoped today would continue without any unexpected incidents. He thought this was unlikely, however.

"Today there are also children and women," he said. "They turn wild as soon as they hear the first shot and start screaming. The mothers in particular," he went on, "can turn quite aggressive."

That's why, the SS man explained, having smoked his cigarette to the end, as he went to the ditch, they were led into the forest, so that they did not see it happening. The first ten men were led to the edge of the ditch. As they had tied their shirts around their heads and could not see anything, they advanced slowly. The first man held onto the truncheon held out to him by an SS man. The other nine — old ones were mixed in with younger ones — held on to the man in front of them.

When the first one reached the edge, the chain stopped. The SS man pushed the second Jew next to the first one. And so it went until they were all lined up next to one another.

Vogt said he thought this method was a time-waster — by the second line-up at the very latest the Jews would realize they were going to be bumped off, so they could forget that blindfolding business.

"You may be right," responded Corporal Zink, "but a glimmer of hope always remains. That's human nature. They think it can't happen to them, so the method is not unrefined."

I didn't have an opinion on all this, and listened attentively.

The first group of Jews was shot. The shots came in a volley of fire from ten SS men standing about twenty meters behind the row. The Jews fell into the pit. An SS man stepped forward, checked if there was anyone still moving in the pit, and in some cases gave an extra shot in the head.

The second row was set up at the edge of the pit. Vogt took

a photograph of them, taking a step backward so that he could fit in all ten Jews. Five minutes later that group was shot dead and the third row stepped forward.

I was starting to get cold, and as I thought we had seen enough now, I asked if we shouldn't be getting back. Vogt replied that I could go if I wanted to, Zink too, but that he wanted to watch the women and was thinking of photographing them. Since Zink wanted to stay too, I stayed with my companions and lit my cigarette.

It must have the fourth or fifth group, when a man broke out of the line, tearing the shirt from his head, and ran toward us. It was an elderly Jew. He stood in front of us. In immaculate German, he rolled his *r* a little but that was it, he asked us what we wanted from them.

"I am just a watchmaker," said the Jew. He was trembling all over.

Vogt took a photograph of him.

"Jew facing death," he said, and took another photograph of the SS man beating him with his truncheon to the pit.

The Jew fell headfirst into the pit. Vogt asked if he could take a photograph.

"Yes," someone told him. "If you are quick."

They were already behind time, and wanted to do the whole convoy, including women and children, before it got dark. They did not have any searchlights to keep watch or to aim.

"Now I have him dead too," said Vogt when he came back.

Naturally things did not proceed as smoothly as the SS man had hoped. Some Jews had to be beaten up to get them to the pit. Others tried to escape and were shot on the spot. Lots of Jews hung white cloths around their shoulders and went praying to the pit. Those that were praying refused to blindfold themselves. The officer in charge permitted this, for they went without a peep to the edge of the pit. This was a sign of his ability to adapt to situations, invaluable in such an operation.

A middle-aged Jew threw himself at an SS man who, after

the Jew had been beaten back into his row by two other SS men with truncheons, shot him in the arms and legs that had touched the officer: when he collapsed he was shot in the stomach and thrown into the pit alive.

"Now he will die a wretched death," said Vogt.

Corporal Zink agreed with him and added that he had been a fool, as he had to die anyway.

"Surely it is smarter to die as quickly and as painlessly as possible, which can be the case only if the men have a chance to aim."

"Logic," answered Vogt, who had also photographed this incident, "is not their strength."

We stayed at the place of execution for two hours in all. I could no longer say how many groups were led to the pit's rim. In any case, the pit was filled almost to the top with piles of corpses.

The children had their turn before the women. They were allowed to stay dressed and also did not have to be blindfolded.

"There is no point," said the SS man, who was taking a break and had joined them. "They are afraid of the dark. We've tried it before, but it had the exact opposite of the desired effect. The children sank to the ground crying, and we had to polish them off there. A messy business."

Corporal Zink said that he felt sorry for the children. You could see the fear in their eyes as they cautiously stepped to the edge of the pit.

"Jews' children," responded Vogt. He was renowned for his candid opinions.

A boy around age eleven or twelve clung to a stamp album so tightly with both hands that it looked as though it was helping him stand up. He did not want to go and was prodded forward by an SS man holding a stick. The boy kept looking around him and shouting something I did not understand. Probably his special name for his mother, as the letter *M* was in it.

Lots of small children between the ages of five and ten had dolls or cuddly animals with them that they pressed to their thin bodies.

"They are simply allowed to take them with them?" asked Vogt.

"You try getting them to let go," replied the SS man.

"That is their obsession with possessions," said Vogt, thereby earning a disapproving look from Corporal Zink and myself.

The children really flew into the pit, the impact of the shot throwing their light bodies in the air. I had had enough and said I didn't want to wait for the Jewish women. Corporal Zink joined me. Vogt would not have found his way back by himself, so he had to leave too.

An hour later we reached the school. The way back had been longer, since we had lost our way several times. Night had fallen unexpectedly quickly.

I took leave of my comrades and found a restaurant where I was served right away and sat myself next to four fellow soldiers, who were just back from home leave. They had lots to tell. I drank two glasses of a brown bitter-tasting beer that was brewed in the area. After three hours or thereabouts, I returned to my room and hung up the rest of my clothing in the steel cupboard that I had been allocated.

Costume Jewelry

. . . for the criminal
as well as for the best of men
shine the moon and the stars.
— *Goethe*

"Run," the soldier said.

He looked at him incredulously.

The soldier pushed the black barrel of his gun into his belly.

"What are you waiting for? Go on, before I change my mind."

He wiped his forehead with the back of his hand. It was an unusually hot day. The air was shimmering restlessly and made the dark red roofs of the village between the pine trees and olive trees seem as if they had been painted by a shaky hand. The soldier took off his cap and held it as a sunscreen in front of his screwed-up eyes. He had hair the color of corn, cut short thus emphasizing the squareness of his skull, and pale freckly skin. His nose and the top curve of his protruding ears were glaring red.

They had all been caught. Even the fat one, although he had run as far as the wood, where the hill began. He knew the paths on the hillside, for his grandfather and father had been shepherds.

He shook his head. He did not consider making a run for it. He knew what would happen as soon as his back was turned.

"You look in the eye of man when you . . ." He imitated the pulling of a trigger with his thumb and forefinger.

They had fought until they ran out of ammunition. He had

torn open the last boxful and distributed the bullets. They had lost because they were fishermen, a few farmers too, but not soldiers.

They had held their position for barely half an hour, and had been forced back closer and closer to the village where, as they approached, the wooden shutters were pulled shut so that they did not have to see the terrified faces of their wives and children and their wives did not have to watch their defeat.

If only he had not listened to Luca, who had called him a coward and who was now standing alongside the others in the country lane. He turned his head to the side and looked over at the small group. He recognized the old man by his limp. Ludvig held his arm tight. He was the eldest son and had not married. A few months ago he had taken over the bar. He had had the place whitewashed and taken his father's place in front of the gleaming yellow and bronze bottles, for his father, known to all simply as "the old man," suffered from backache.

He had hoped to turn the bar into a restaurant, where the better families of the village would come to dine on Sundays, and as time went on families from the neighboring villages would come and, who knows, perhaps even townfolk. But the locals simply ignored the menu and the other novelties, and even the walls disobeyed his dreams — a few months later the fatty smell of cooking and tobacco smoke had turned them gray again.

The soldier followed his gaze. "They will be shot."

Anton shrugged his shoulders. Now we need him back here, he thought, remembering Ludvig's brother, his childhood friend, who had taught him how to read when the priest wanted to throw him out of school. He had escaped from the village, for he neither wanted to be a fisherman nor run a bar or restaurant, and the village was too small for him. He had married a city girl, and they now lived with her parents.

"You are probably afraid that I am going to sink that little black fellow in your back?" asked the soldier. "Or are you hoping to put down roots here?"

It was one and the same thing. He turned around. In front of him the deep blue sea was shimmering. If only I had not listened to Luca, he thought, then I would be waiting for evening in the shade of the boats, passing around the bottle. No, he considered, the bottle would be for me alone, because everyone is here. And he reflected upon how strange fate could be, that they were now to die in this dusty country lane.

He knew the way inside out, they had been here countless times, it being the quickest route to the sea. But he had never taken much notice of the lane, his eyes had always been fixed on the sea, which from this elevation lay there in all its glory. He had never had any reason to. In this country lane, then, not like the unfortunate victims of the waves out at sea.

This is not a nice death for a fisherman, he thought, but then found this ridiculous, for no form of death was nice.

Oh, why not, then, he thought. He waited. Any second now he will aim at my head. He tried to listen for the pulling of the trigger, but could hear only the crickets rubbing their front wings together. He slowly made his way toward the hill and stared at the sea.

He wanted to be in the water and submerge his hot head and hot body, which seemed too bulky to him, too large a mass to target, in the salt waves, to swim so far out that everything around him was dark blue and cool, and the coast, the beach, the country lane, and the village were merely thin ocher-colored strips in the distance.

He took another step and passed the tree that the old women in the village believed was cursed, for hardly any leaves ever grew on it. If he lets me get as far as the scrub then I'm free. Then he would have to search for me. Three more steps and then I'm free.

"Holy, holy mother Mary."

He broke into a run. Thorns ripped his hands and legs. He thrashed his way through the thicket and tripped.

He lay motionless on the ground, for how long he could not say, and listened to his ragged breathing. Then he crawled further on all fours and sat crouched. The yellow grass was high. It cast long, thin shadows, that looked like the silhouette of a virgin. His thoughts turned to the women in the village, who would be staring petrified at the doors through which their men should return.

By now they would be starting to realize that their men were not coming back. But nonetheless they would prepare the meal, set the table, put a glass and a bottle of wine next to the plate. He licked his wounds, they tasted salty. He had not heard any shots, just isolated screams. Perhaps they were asking each person individually, to be able to get others too, or they were letting them go free. No, that was unlikely.

He would have liked to have stood up, to stretch his legs, but instead he went on his hands and knees to the slope and carefully climbed down. Although he offered an easy target, he stood at the foot for a moment and looked out to sea, a deep luminosity. Then he raced to the boat and scrambled beneath the nets.

He had had to mend the nets for three whole years before he was allowed to sail out and throw the nets out and pull them in. It was only after that first night alone at sea that he understood what they were talking about as they sat at the old man's, and why they called the sea the origin of everything and the boundary to beyond.

What good did it do him? Did not even have his own boat, and those others who did have a boat of their own, what good was it to them? He pushed the net from his face because it was difficult to breathe, and although he did not want to, he fell into an uneasy sleep.

He woke up with a fright, because he thought he had forgotten to cast the net, looked around him, saw the black sea, and the deep dusky sky, and remembered where he was.

They had forgotten about him. The young soldier, who had

followed him, had let him run free, and the others, who had told him to catch the escaping prisoner, had forgotten him. His body ached all over. The soldier had randomly let him go. Why him and not one of the others, the little one with three children, or his brother, who was also married, or Alex, who was to be engaged in a month's time?

"One, two, three, four . . ."

He started to count. After the tenth shot he stopped. You swine, he thought, you accursed murderers are killing all the men in our goddamned village. He ran up to the hill and tried to scale it in one leap, but slipped and listened to the peculiar rhythm of volleys of firing. They came erratically, like the angry heartbeat of a fish thrashing in the net.

"You goddamned, goddamned . . ."

He raised his hand to the hill that had seemed so enormous to him as a child, let it drop again. Then he turned round, went to the surf and sat down in the wet sand. The salt water was pleasantly warm, and stung his grazed skin.

The sea, he thought, the sea is indifferent. It comes and goes, and does not care about the suffering of people.

At some point the shooting ceased, and when the noise of rattling motors disappeared into the night, all was still. Only the surf broke on the shore. He wiped away his tears with his sleeve, looked up, and saw the bright stars of Taurus and the constellation of Scorpio. They twinkled like costume jewelry, dim against the throat of heaven.

The Pearl Necklace

Two weeks have already passed since I received your letter, and I'm only getting the chance now to sit down and write.

Thomas, my boy, thank you for the drawing. It is hanging above my bed and is a source of great pleasure. I hope you are looking after Mommy and your sister. You are the man of the house now and have to supervise.

Nor are you allowed to be a nuisance to your mommy. In her letter she told me what happened at school. That is not good. Before undertaking anything you must always consider whether it is really worth it, otherwise you will never be your own boss. I am very proud that you passed the entrance test to the Hitler Youth, and I am sending a little present along with this letter.

My little Nette, that naughty boy pulls your pigtails, does he? Mommy has told me that you are very good, and quite the little housewife already. I'm glad to hear it. When I come home, you'll make me something to eat, all by yourself, and then we'll go cycling. We'll only take the boy if he leaves your pigtails alone. Do you hear, Thomas? Yesterday I saw a Russian girl, the same age as you. Then I was really homesick for my children.

I hope to be able to come home for Christmas. Perhaps I'll even bring a Christmas goose with me. Out in the yard, there are three hundred cackling geese at the moment, and with a bit of luck ours is among them. Even if they don't give me leave, I'll send it back to you with one of the boys.

Mommy, do also accept parcels that don't come directly from me. I only hand out our address to those I can trust one hundred percent. I have boys all over Greater Germany and always pass something along when one of them is on home leave. We are, as you will have gathered, a merry gang.

Just one thing, Nette, for you, too, Thomas, you mustn't draw attention to it and must be very quiet when you or Mommy receive a package from me. On our very street there are gossips. I'm thinking of Frau Eckstein, whom you yourself, Thomas, rightfully called a chatterbox. Should she find out, she would rather talk till her mouth fell off than keep her peace. So the Enemy, that's Frau Eckstein, is always listening!

You, too, dear Mommy, be silent for heaven's sake. Envy is simply too great a thing, and not every husband has such a privileged position as yours and is able to get their hands on the most beautiful things.

Yesterday, I sent off ten one-kilo parcels and two large packages, which should reach you soon. You won't be going hungry, and there are some nice goodies, too. A special present for Mommy is in the hands of one of the boys, Dieter Walter. I've told you about him already, my one true friend here, and he'll call in personally. It's too precious to simply send by post, so there is something to look forward to. Well, children, now Mommy will be all excited. It's her Christmas present and anniversary present all rolled into one. You see, I forget nothing!

Be nice to Dieter. He is a good fellow, and I am sure you will like him immediately. His ex-wife had been having an affair with a Jew. The poor devil went completely off his rocker, as the local group leader, before being called up. Now his career is at an end. I hope we get our hands on that Jewish pig sometime. Don't broach the subject. It's painful for him, and Dieter doesn't like talking about it.

Dieter will have some photos with him, so that you don't forget what your daddy looks like, and he'll fill you in on what our life here is like. It's a completely different thing to have someone made of flesh and blood telling you, although I think my letters capture some of it, too.

I have also asked him to look in on your parents in Reinick-endorf, and I have given him some blocks of butter for Granny — three kilos, altogether: what she doesn't need, she can sell — so she'll be able to bake a proper crumble for you again at last, with the nice fruit that she preserved in the summer. For Grandpa I have slipped in packages of cigarettes and tobacco, even though Granny disapproves. Men have to decide for themselves what they should do, can do, and want to do. The same goes for your father. You see, although I may not write often I do think of your parents.

My next words of wisdom are: be economical. Thomas, I am counting on you for this. Extravagance is in the nature of women.

Mommy, you should tell your parents this too. Winter is just around the corner, and it will be harder with parcels then. I'll send them to you nonetheless. When I can, that is. So do not open the sugar and the flour, since they do not spoil so quickly.

We got into a real mess here. We had two barrels filled with honey. The Russians had told us that the barrels had been properly disinfected and washed out. They were gasoline barrels and we had nothing else at hand. No such luck. Whatever the Russians do, it's as badly bungled as their warfare. The whole batch tasted like gas, and quite inedible. Dieter viewed it as sabotage and thought the saboteurs should be shot. I believe it was just the usual bungling up. If you could only see these people. . . .

Thomas asked me what our life is like here. Here is a description. Dieter will confirm all this and fill in the details.

I have just noticed that I have already filled a few pages: unbelievable, I was not aware of it at all. When you are writing to your loved ones, of course, your heart takes flight.

Well, I get up at six o'clock. I live in a house that looks like ours, only not so clean and tasteful, and with no front garden, hedge, or freshly mown lawn. We don't have a Thomas here, you see, to keep the weeds at bay, so everything is overgrown. I live on the first floor, Dieter and another man on the second.

I have already told you about the other man, a von so-and-so. He is the one who drinks himself silly. For the fourth time now he has made such a racket that Dieter and I have decided, although it is certainly preferable to deal with unpleasant things on one's own, to lay our complaint before the superior and make sure at long last that he is transferred. It is against our principles, but he spoils the harmony of the house.

Back to myself. I have three small rooms. One is my office. In one of them I sleep, and the third one, which I share with the other two, is the kitchen.

There is an oven in the kitchen. The other rooms are not heated, which is great fun at night if you need to go to the bathroom. But I won't go into those adventures. Dieter will show you a photo of the kitchen.

So I get up at six, wake up Dieter and von so-and-so, and go get washed. We have a housekeeper, who is not as perfect as little Nette. She brings the wood that the prisoners have chopped up into small bits, and makes our breakfast. She is a political one, a Pole, and speaks a little German, albeit broken German.

At seven o'clock there is coffee. By then Daddy is already dressed, shaved, washed, and ready to start his day.

There is bread, as much as you like, a bit of butter, about sixty grams of it, sometimes artificial honey. The real stuff was ruined, of course. I always eat four slices of bread and drink two cups of coffee with milk and two lumps of sugar.

Then I work in the office. I have lots of files to read through and my eyes get tired. It is no work for a man, but that is the way it is. Thomas, it's just like school is for you. You see, your father has to buckle down too, and grin and bear it. You have to learn to be patient, and get rid of your bad habits.

At twelve-thirty we head to the canteen for lunch. That is always good. Plenty of meat and fat. We have our own animals: pigs, sheep, calves, and cows and now geese, too. Ah, Mommy, I can picture your dumplings, and start drooling. At Christmas I will be with you!

There are potatoes to go with it. As many as we like. That's no problem here at all. We have them in abundance. And, believe it or not, preserved cucumbers and tomatoes. The cook runs a delicatessen back home. His wife now manages the shop. He knows his profession and makes delicious things for us. It is a matter of luck.

In another unit the cook was a plumber before coming to the front. Our cook told us this. Well, you can imagine what his things tasted like. I wonder why they took him on, for normally they try to employ qualified staff. We have already spent some merry evenings, laughing up a storm as we tried to imagine the menus he must have put together. Soldering water soup, chops à la workbench, crêpes of hammer with a smattering of nails, and preserved drill. Bon appétit, is all I can say.

Depending on my mood and how hungry I am, I can eat up to three platefuls. It is not rationed.

Then we work on until six o'clock in the evening. For supper we get something warm to eat again, fried potatoes, for example, in a bowl with fat and scrambled egg, or something cold, like bread and cold meat. The Russians have a type of garlic sausage that tastes almost as good as our cold cut, just a bit spicier. But there is no one to kiss here, so it is all the same, right, Mommy?

You see, my body is well catered for, so Mommy, who believes I am bound to catch something or other here, can put her mind at rest.

By the way, I have also taken a photo of our cook. I will pass it along with Dieter. He is a squat, not to say approaching fat, sort of a fellow and the war seems to agree with him.

In the evening we either play cards or booze or visit the boss. There is no saying no on that front. If the boss wants to have coffee or schnapps, we have to go, for he likes to have a few of us around him. I believe I have made a pretty good impression on him and, all being well, can count on my promotion to . . . by Christmas. Well, Thomas, tell them, you are the only one who knows about this sort of thing. Then you'll all be proud of me.

I will come home with my new insignia, and I'll put on my uniform on Christmas morning, and we will go out for a walk together, and the neighbors will stare, especially Frau . . . I've drawn a sudden blank, what's happening to your Daddy?

I would naturally far prefer to have my peace and quiet alone with Dieter. We even have a bowling club here, but the boss doesn't enjoy bowling, so I have to pass it up, too.

By the way: there is beer, as much as we want, at lunch, and after dinner. At the boss's we drink schnapps because he does not care for beer, nor does he like to see his men drinking it, being of the opinion that it makes a person fat, and a fat belly in uniform is an insult to the SS.

I have a little glass when I am within my own four walls, because I cannot share the boss's views on everything.

He is completely different from the last one and, after the first few months that it took to get used to his mannerisms, I don't find him too bad at all. He is tougher, not as self-pitying as the last one. And now we really have iron discipline. Complaining is taboo, of course. As is shirking any duty. One man who was chickening out — he didn't want to shoot anymore — had to do it every day for a week. That was his punishment. Don't worry, Mommy, Daddy does not often go to the forest to shoot, only when he really has to.

Mommy, if the pearl necklace, whoops, out it popped, oh well, it doesn't matter, if the pearl necklace is not your style, I can get hold of something different for you. But I know that you always wanted one, and now Daddy has gotten one for you. It wasn't even that expensive. So don't worry about that. If it is too short, it can be lengthened. Dieter will present it to you most solemnly, along with a letter that is for your eyes only.

So, my dear ones. Nette, what I wanted to say to you: you shouldn't wet your bed anymore, and must sit up straight without leaning on your elbows. When you are a big German girl, you'll travel round the world so much that you will have to comport yourself with dignity since everyone will gawk at you. You mustn't make us ashamed of you, and must start this very day to keep a tight rein on yourself.

Only he who has himself under control can judge others and rule! The same goes for you, Thomas. Take heed. It is important.

Now Mommy has to bring you up all by herself, and you must help her, because I can't keep an eye on you nor set you an example as long as I am at the front.

So, do not let us be ashamed of you, be good until I come home, and everything will be the same as before, only nicer, because peace will reign supreme again and we will be a proper family, strengthened by these trials.

How is Heinz? What is the garden like? Have you chosen seeds already? I'm not in favor of the sheep's sorrel, nor the weeping heart, even though Mommy likes the name. Buy something sensible, that flowers nicely, and is hardy. You can put the garden gnome next to them. He will keep watch over you until I return. Only joking, Thomas: I'm aware you are looking after the women.

By the way, you should pass on a pound of butter to the SS Sturmbannführer's wife with my best wishes, so that he does not forget me. Doesn't have to be right away, but soon. Not that I need him now. I have made the acquaintance of others who may prove helpful to us when I come home, not to mention the excellent reputation I can claim. They only had nitwits before, and were no longer accustomed to having a real man.

Nonetheless I ask you to exchange a word with the woman, for her husband has always been so decent to me.

It is right that Heinz does not join us in the east. He is too soft for this place. He would start sobbing like a girl if he ever had to polish someone off. That's either a result of his illness or to do with that Jew, that furrier, I forget his name, he worked for. He did not have the right attitude, never did. It's his mother's fault too, she wants to make all the decisions in the house. She tried to do the same with me, but no way.

Good that he has been sent to France. He'll have it easy there, although even the softest man changes here in three weeks. It is a matter of getting used to things. Soon you can see blood, although black pudding remains unpopular.

I know that, regarding my opinion of your brother, you cannot agree with everything I say. All I can say to you is that in these difficult times we need men who are tough, not momma's boys, like little Heinz Schröder is. Otherwise nothing would work.

So, my loved ones, there I'll stop. I miss you all terribly, especially on Sundays. We don't often leave the base, and I want to be with you again.

I will do everything within my power to be with you at Christmastime. I will try today already to work on the boss — he has family and children, too.

Thomas, I hereby officially hand over to you the task of choosing a Christmas tree, worthy of our family. One that won't be losing its needles already on New Year's Eve. Got it! I have shown you how to see to that.

The chocolate, French and apparently particularly good, is for my two little sweet-toothed ones, Thomas and Nette. It is not to be sold.

So, now I am really going to call it a day, because I am being called to yet another operation.

For my children, kisses and a big hug.
For darling Mommy, a long intimate kiss.
You are my happiness and my life.
Your Daddy

P.S. Write to tell me if you like the pearl necklace.

The Camera

1.

Sometimes she woke up at night for no reason. Then she would lie in bed, listening, until the pounding of her heart gave way to the soft crunch of car wheels on the asphalt: it came from far off, rose to a threatening crescendo beneath her window, and faded away a brief moment later.

Still in the dark she would reach out to the bedside table, so that when the headlights hit it she would find her glasses immediately. Without them she felt helpless. Instead of waiting for the thin stream of light, she could have switched on the bedside lamp. Before going to sleep she positioned the switch in such a way that she could turn it on without sitting up. But that, she knew, would not work. Even though she had spread a green cloth over the shade, the lamp was too bright and blinded her.

If she could not fall asleep again immediately, she sometimes drank a glass of water, or lit a cigarette. During such moments of fear she would sit cross-legged in bed and follow the movements of the heart-shaped leaves of the tree, whose upper branches swayed in the wind in front of her window, until her eyelids grew heavy. It was a linden tree. She listened to the rhythm of the wind through it and hummed a song that fitted in. At night she created melodies forgotten by the next day.

After a sleepless night she could see everything more clearly. She was like someone coming back to their senses after being intoxicated for a long time, and was grateful for everything: for the dried-out yellow leaves of the plant that she put out in the hall every evening, the corner table with its basket of fresh fruit, the beige-colored cloth under the basket, even for the dust that had gathered in the holes of the crocheting with their flowerlike shapes, which she wiped away with her finger.

In the morning she brushed her hair with long swinging strokes until it gleamed silkily, and showered beneath cold and warm water. Afterward her skin was pink and tingly. She went into her room naked and looked at herself in the wardrobe mirror, before selecting an outfit that she laid out to consider on her bed. Sometimes she ate breakfast naked, too.

While the coffee was brewing she pulled on a jacket and stood close to the wall so that only her clothed upper half could be seen through the kitchen window. When she took her cup over to the table she took the jacket off again. She ate without a plate and crumbs fell into her belly button.

If she was eating naked, she would sit with her legs placed parallel to the table legs. It was a habit that was important to her. If she was eating dressed, then she did so quickly and nervously, standing up.

When she had finished eating she smoked another cigarette, which meant she had to brush her teeth again to get rid of the smell of tobacco, rather than just rinse her mouth.

She had bad teeth. Even as a child. She did not like her feet either. She looked at them in the mornings, while drinking, cursed them and called them names. She had her father's feet. When she had reproached him for them he had playfully replied that his ancestors had always enjoyed good standing.

She ate a generous amount in the mornings. She bought the bread rolls the night before and left them out uncovered on the kitchen table overnight, so that the crust grew hard. That would have bothered other people, but not her.

It made her think of the skin of a fruit and she pulled out the white soft dough inside and pressed it against the top of her mouth with her tongue before spreading the roll with butter.

Every other day, she soft-boiled an egg. When she had

eaten the inside, she turned it over in the egg cup and smashed the shell with her spoon. She bought eggs, cheese, milk, cucumber, tomatoes, apples, cabbage, and occasionally slices of sausage meat shot through with islands of fat. This lasted her for the week.

She sat for a long time in a world of her own at the kitchen table. When the little hairs on the back of her neck started to stand on end, she got up, put the dishes in the sink, and went back to her bedroom. That was her sign.

She also had her routine for getting dressed, which she stuck to, for she did not want to be startled by any sudden change. First of all, she fastened her bra and nestled her breasts into the cups, then she smoothed her cotton vest over it, sat down, slipped into her panties, rolled on the stockings, which ran smoothly over her freshly shaven legs, and, after stretching out one leg then the other, she fastened them with her bright green elastic garters. She bought only silk stockings and washed them carefully every night in lukewarm soapy water before putting them over the line in the bathroom to dry.

She shaved her underarms, and every morning after pulling on her vest she looked to see whether any stubble had appeared overnight, turning the armpits black. She shaved them almost daily, and the hairs had turned to bristles, turning the armpits from smooth to bumpy as though pitted with black craters.

She did not wear makeup, not even mascara, and instead just pinched her cheeks before leaving the apartment to look fresh. If she went for a few nights without sleep she dusted skin-colored blush on her cheeks, forehead, and eyelids, where blue veins were shining through. Otherwise nothing.

She was not fundamentally against makeup, choosing not to wear any because she only felt at ease when her face was anonymous.

Once she had bought dark red lipstick, which she practiced putting on in front of the bathroom mirror, and then sat down to eat dinner with painted lips. The red imprint of her mouth remained on the bread. She had been surprised by the bitter taste of the lipstick in contrast to its color of sweet cherries.

The first time the man molested her was on a Wednesday. He was a messenger and therefore a rank beneath her. That day, as usual, she had crossed over the play park of the still-empty nursery, and arrived too early.

She had beaten the dust from her coat and with the lining showing like the flesh of a fig pressed from its skin, hung it over her chair and was just about to sit down when she was asked to take the files of last month downstairs, as they were blocking access to the new lists.

"Right now?" she had asked, and then reluctantly pushed her chair to the side.

Even before she heard his steps, she could feel his gaze, and had already sensed him in the corridor as she opened the heavy wooden door with her foot. He was coming down the stairs with the light feathery tread that belies a muscular body. He was coming down from the third floor or even higher. When he was standing directly behind her, he slowed his pace. She wanted to turn around and let him pass but was afraid of losing her balance. Because of the files she could not even put a hand on the banister.

He did not offer to help her, instead followed her step by step down the stairs. She wanted to apologize for taking up the whole width of the staircase, but an inescapable heaviness took control of her mouth, lips, and tongue and made breathing difficult.

She could feel his eyes clinging to her body and felt drops of sweat running from the hollow between her breasts down to the edge of her bra, where they were caught.

When she reached the bottom she dropped the files on the stone floor and grabbed hold of the banister. Outside she heard the shrill whine of a saw cutting through metal. He slowly came up to her. She wanted to throw open the door and flee into the storeroom, but stood still. She could not leave the files, stamped with second-highest stamp of secrecy, with a man whom she knew only by sight, since he had once delivered a package to her office. Then she had hardly noticed him.

When the man had come so close that she could smell his breath and could tell he had been drinking, he stuck out his tongue, and made a smacking noise.

She stared at his tongue that seemed unusually long and thin. It repelled her. It was as though it wanted to crawl over to her. The man pushed past her to the door and rubbed his hips against her with a thrusting motion. She turned her head to the side and looked at the wall where the smoky gray paint was beginning to peel off.

When she had gathered herself together again, she picked up the files and smoothed her skirt. There, where the man had touched her body, she could still feel him. She ran a hand through her hair. Then she went into the storeroom and handed in the files.

2.

In the evening she stood under the shower for a long time and rubbed her body dry until it was red, to get rid of the man's cloying, rotten-smelling sweat. She rubbed herself with small, circling movements, rubbing particularly fiercely at the hollows of her body, and when she felt dry and clean again she spread the towel over the radiator. She liked her body smell, soaked into the material of the towel. It brought her back to something familiar.

She put the plug in the washbasin and filled it with cold water. She submerged her head, coming up only when she felt her lungs were about to burst. She took several deep breaths, then submerged her head a second time in the sink. Her blood hammered in her temples. She pulled out the black, rubber plug and watched the gurgling water as it was sucked into the dark hole. Her hair tried to follow suit. She reached for the guest's hand towel and tied it around her head.

The next morning, she went to work on foot as usual. From the empty playground of the nursery school she heard the distant cries of a boy being pulled along to the entrance by his mother. As she passed them she saw a thread of spittle that stretched from the boy's mouth to his woolen pullover. The same as him, she thought, not knowing exactly what she was referring to.

Shortly after lunch, she saw him again. He was delivering papers and had the stack firmly pinned against his body under his armpit. As he went by her she did not raise her head but noticed the mound by his groin, made by his balled fist in his trouser pocket. He stood still in the middle of the room, bent over, and put down his load on a stool. Paper, she thought, it's only paper. As he was straightening up and stretched she saw his back muscles through the material of his shirt.

"Here," he said, tapping with two fingers where he needed a signature.

He had a high voice that did not fit to his body, and against her will reminded her of a sunny day in late autumn. She shook her head to rid it of the image and started furiously to clean her typewriter. She could not concentrate, so there was no point in typing.

The messenger said thank you, and slowly turned around. When he came up to her table, he playfully put a straightened-out paper clip in his mouth and sucked on it. He had on the same blue overalls as the previous day and the same checked shirt, with sweat marks around the armpits that embarrassed her.

When the man had left the room, she sat a little longer, lost in thought. She had heard his name. He was called Oswald. She wrote it several times on a piece of blotting paper. It was not a nice name. The head secretary came to her desk. She bashfully crumpled up the paper and finished typing the report that she had been assigned and had spent the whole morning doing. Then she cleaned her desk and put the dustcover over the typewriter.

She was about to hand in the sheets of paper when she noticed a bloodstain on the label of the folder she had put the report in. Frightened, she reached to her forehead, but then saw she had hurt the skin of her ring finger on the sharp staple. She wiped the wet patch off the folder. Then she wrapped the bleeding finger in a tissue.

One week later, she met Oswald in the corridor. He was standing next to the door of the workroom, his upper body leaning against the wall. She was busy taking off her coat and did not notice him right away. As he slunk up to her she felt her heart start to pound. Oswald let his gaze scan her body. His eyes lingered on her breasts. She held her bag to her chest, took several steps forward, only to turn around and dash into the ladies' room.

She stood motionless behind the door. She wanted to cry, but pulled herself together and listened. Dragging his feet, or so it seemed to her, the man came up to the door, drew to a standstill, and scratched his nails down the wood that separated them, as though he wanted to hint at what she was missing through this scraping noise. After a while she heard him leave.

She took a look in the mirror at her red face, grown blotchy from the excitement. She loathed herself. She turned the yellow sticky bar of soap in her hands until it lathered, and scrubbed her face. It was burning. She gathered cold water in the hollows of her hands and washed away the soap. Then she tore open the window and let her skin dry in the morning breeze.

That evening she stood for a long time in front of the mirror, her nightgown in her hand, and looked at her naked white body. Then she went to bed, lay back with one arm under her head, fumbled in her gown with her other hand, and held her breast, which was warm and heavy. Her heart pounded, muffled like a night serenade. With her hand still in her gown, she dropped off to sleep.

Shortly before daybreak, she woke up bathed in sweat. She had dreamed that she was suffocating slowly and torturously in a dark green sea full of seaweed that squeezed her naked body more tightly the more furiously she tore at it. When the seaweed had completely overwhelmed her and dragged her to the sandy dark floor of the sea, she had surfaced from the dream and realized that she had pulled her nightgown over her head in her sleep.

She snatched the white gown from her body and threw it on the ground. Then she looked for her cigarettes and matches. She was trembling, but was too tired to fetch another nightgown from the closet. She wrapped herself in the cover and made the sulfur head flare up in the dark room. Greedily she dragged on her cigarette. The smoke hurt her lungs.

3.

The bus rounded the corner of the street. First of all, she saw its rectangular nose, and then through the front windshield the outline of the driver. Inside the people were tightly packed. From a distance they looked like one single twisting body. She felt for her change. She had counted it out and tossed it into her coat pocket. The bus stopped. She took a step forward and positioned herself behind a man holding tightly onto the arm of a child. The child had a satchel on his back that was too big for him. Laboriously, it clambered up the high step. The father followed with a jump. She lifted a leg to mount the step too, but froze, seized by a sudden feeling of apathy.

Later, she was wandering through the streets of shops. She stopped in front of a clothes shop and looked at the display. A red velvet dress was draped over a mannequin. One arm of the dress — the window dresser had stuffed it with tissue paper that poked through the buttonhole — was pinned to one side of the window display, covered with checked fabric. It seemed to her that the dress wanted to greet her or to entice her into the shop with an unspoken promise. A street cleaner was sweeping fliers into the gutter. He had a green band round his right arm. Many of the shops were still closed. Some had metal grates in front of the entrances. The market was almost deserted, too. She wanted to buy something, but didn't know what. When she saw a man opening the door of a photography shop she entered the shop behind him. It smelled of stale tobacco and male sweat. A few minutes later she left holding a camera that had been on a pedestal in the window. It was the offer of the week.

Then she went to a cake shop and bought a box of sweet liqueur candies. In the doorway she already had removed the red ribbon and the wrapping paper, scrunched it up and stuffed it into her coat pocket, embarrassed. She looked around searchingly and spotted a bench next to the pedestrian crossing. She gave her coat a hitch, sat down, tore off the cellophane, pushed back the greaseproof paper, and ate the candies, one after the other.

Town had started to fill up. She was now one of the women going into the shops with their shopping bags or stopping in front of shop windows. She took the empty candy box over to a trashcan. The opening was too small. She tried to tear up the box, but had to stop and draw in a breath, for she felt a sudden queasiness from the rapid movement, and stopped altogether when she saw that the eyes of two women coming out of the bakery were on her. She felt dizzy. She sat back down on the bench and unbuttoned her coat. The cold air calmed her stomach. Scraps of cloud floated by like boiled oat flakes. It would rain soon. She took several deep breaths, buttoned up her coat, picked up her camera, and went home.

4.

The head secretary did not pose any problems, simply nodded with compassion, for she too often suffered migraines, and handed her a report to type up. She promised to have the report handed in before lunchtime, went to her desk, and straightened up the cushion on her chair. She didn't need the cushion, but before settling down to work she did need her little routine. The plumping of the cushion and the sharpening of all the pencils were part of it.

She worked with concentration up to lunchtime. She glanced from the propped-up sheaf of paper to the white sheet that was gradually filling up with black letters and numbers, and in a rhythmic cycle of several minutes laid sheet after sheet in the red folder for completed and corrected reports.

During the first few months she had read what she wrote but had soon weaned herself from that because — distracted by the reading — she did not write quickly enough and could not keep up. She had made typing errors and thus had been the only one whose machine had not tapped away melodically in time. She had gathered all her willpower in order not to see sentences but only words.

At first, she had removed the dustcover most reluctantly from the machine in the mornings, as the constant contact with the keys had rubbed her fingertips raw; she had meticulously folded up the cover to delay as long as possible the moment when she would type the first word and send pain like an arrow from her fingertips directly to her head. Then she had learned to abandon herself to her pain, to lose herself in it, so that while the other parts of her body slowly grew numb, she felt only the pricking pain, which laid itself like a fine gleaming scaly skin over her finger pads. In the office it was referred to ironically as novice's pain. After a short while, she was to miss it as her hands, too, grew used to the cold smooth typing keys.

During the lunch break she rubbed some eucalyptus oil into her neck, ate a sandwich, drank a glass of milk, washed her hands and face in the ladies' restroom after smoking a quick cigarette that she threw into the toilet bowl, and went back to work.

5.

It had rained. She stood by the door and drew her coat tighter around her. The street's surface was glistening. Pools of water with bits of floating paper and leaves had formed in the gutter. She carefully crossed the road, taking care not to step in the puddles, for she hadn't yet taken her shoes with the thick crepe soles out of the suitcase where she kept her winter things. Next to her, people were hurrying home, all of them bent over in the same way. The streetlights will go on soon, she thought, and went over to the bus stop, for she was cold.

Just as the driver was shutting the doors, he leaped on at the last minute. She had sat down on a double seat at the very back of the bus and recognized him immediately. He wound his way through and stood in front of her. Smiling, he ran his hand over his rippling thigh. Up and down, up and down. She could not bear the soft rustling sound, turned her head aside, and looked out of the window.

"Marianne. Marianne Flinker."

She started. How did he know her name? Frightened, she looked at him. He smiled and touched his forehead as though in greeting. She wanted to get up, but that would have meant going past him. She shrank into herself and looked at her hands. They were trembling. A bead of sweat slid down her neck. She took a few deep breaths and decided to confront him. She sat up straight.

"What on earth . . ."

She scanned the overcrowded interior. He had gone.

Her hands folded in her lap, she let the general chat lull her. Only occasionally did scraps of words reach her; it sounded like a piece of polyphonic music and gradually flooded the interior of the bus traveling through the blood-red dusk.

6.

She stared into the black eye in which she was reflected, took off her glasses, folded the earpieces, and put them down on the kitchen table, the lenses looking up to the ceiling. Then she raised the camera to her face.

Carefully she pressed the little catch down with her index finger. The back sprang open wide.

She looked at the camera's insides. They glimmered blackly back at her. A big black hole, she thought, and nothing else, and she whirled the little cog. It purred like a contented cat.

She pulled the lever to the side and it swiftly clicked back in place, and she pressed the release button. For a moment the center of the lens lit up like a comet. She repeated the process until she was tired of it. Then she opened the drawer in the kitchen table, groped behind the cutlery, and took out a roll of film she had gotten long before buying the camera. She went into the bathroom just to be safe, for she had once heard that light damaged film.

Only a little light came in through the crack between the floor and the door. She perched on the rim of the toilet. A neighbor was running a bath and talking to someone. His voice was muffled. She traced the shape of the camera with her fingers. Her hands lingered for a moment on the protruding mound embedding the lens, then strokingly continued to the opening catch. With a stifled noise it sprang open. She took the film, which she had held between her lips, and tore off the packaging. After pushing up her skirt and opening her legs, she dropped the paper into the bowl of the toilet.

She touched the long cartridge. From a thin slit edged with downy material the tongue of film poked out, one side inlaid with a regular grooved pattern. With great care she pressed the cartridge into the appropriate hollow inside the camera, and stopped when she noticed the upper part was not sliding into place. She felt the chamber again and discovered the obstacle: a tooth that snapped back when she touched it. She pushed it up with her forefinger, so she could insert the film cartridge with no resistance.

She sat there motionless with the camera on her knee. The neighbor had turned off the tap. For a while all was still, then she heard him calling to his wife.

"Maria, Maria," echoed, distorted, up to her.

She went into the kitchen and took the cherry liqueur out of the cupboard. She filled a glass and drank it down in small gulps.

After the second glass, which she only half emptied, her gums had grown used to the sweetness. Slowly, she walked into her room, glass in hand, and sat down on the chair she had put next to the dresser. She put down her glass, taking care that the liqueur did not splash over onto the wood, picked up the camera, and looked at her room through the lens.

Table, chair, window, dresser, bed, wardrobe, lamp. Her gaze wandered over the pieces of furniture. After she had also looked at the ceiling and the floor, she got up and returned to the bathroom.

Her skirt slowly slid to the floor. She unbuttoned her blouse, removed her garters, undid the catch of her bra, and, after rolling off her stockings and slipping out of her panties, laid her clothes on the lid of the toilet. She turned on the light over the mirror. In the harsh lighting her skin looked gray. She turned the ridged ring enclosing the lens until focused and aimed it at her breast. The breast of an old girl, she thought, and imagining the tongue of the messenger, took her middle and forefinger and rubbed her hardening nipple.

7.

Tomorrow she would bring the report back. Why had she taken it in the first place? She put on her nightgown and went into the bedroom. It was only at the bus stop, as she had been feeling for her purse, lost in thought, and her fingers had touched the rolled-up sheets of paper that she comprehended what she had done, and was frightened. She sat down on the bed and took the sheets of paper out of her handbag. First thing tomorrow she would put the document back where it belonged. She would arrive earlier than normal and slip it into the folder while the others were quickly smoking a last cigarette by the open window. Then she would go to them, join the conversation, and forget all about it. She would also have to break off contact with the messenger.

"Oswald, Oswald, Oswald." She quietly whispered his name.

It had to be. She knew only too well. It wasn't worth it. Why, oh why, had she listened to him? Was he worth taking such a risk for? What had he given her, after all? She unfolded the report and gave it a cursory glance. It was the list of June 30 in which confiscated Jewish assets were reported. In spite of herself she started to read:

39, 917 kg	Brooches
7, 495 kg	Fountain Pens
18, 020 kg	Silver Rings
1 Case	Watch Parts
5 Baskets	Loose Stamps
44, 655 kg	Pieces of Gold
482, 900 kg	Silver Cutlery
98	Telescopes
20, 952 kg	Golden Wedding Rings
28, 200 kg	Powder Compacts — Silver or Metal
11, 730 kg	Dental Gold
35 Wagons	Furs
2,892 kg	Pocket Watches — Gold
3,133 kg	Pocket Watches — Silver
1,256 kg	Wristwatches — Gold
3, 425 kg	Wristwatches — Silver
1 Case	Lighters
97, 581 kg	Gold Coins
25, 580 kg	Copper Coins

53, 190 kg	Nickel Coins
167,740 kg	Silver Coins
20, 050 kg	Brass Coins
1 Case	Penknives
6, 640 kg	Necklaces — Gold
7	Complete Stamp Collections
100, 550 kg	Costume Jewelry
22,740 kg	Pearls
68	Cameras
82, 600 kg	Necklaces — Silver
20, 880 kg	Rings — Gold with Stones
4, 030 kg	Coral
343,100 kg	Cigarette Cases — Silver and Metal . . .

She thought of the messenger, folded the sheets of paper, and slid under the covers. Tomorrow, the day after tomorrow at the very latest, she would bring the inventory back. Why, oh why, had she listened to him? She couldn't risk everything. No one could ask that of her. She reached for the cigarettes, spilled the contents of the matchbox over her dressing table when she tried to take out one match, since her hands were shaking too much, and clumsily lit a cigarette. She inhaled the smoke quickly and coughed.

Tomorrow, the day after tomorrow at the very latest, she would put the report back in the folder. She would not be led astray. No, she would not. And all because of a messenger. Why on earth had she allowed herself to be drawn in? Why? Why she of all people? She would have to forget him and all the rest of it.

The holidays would be here soon. Only another three weeks. Only another twenty-one days. That was nice, wasn't it? She clicked off the lamp.

"Oswald. Oswald, Oswald."

She opened her nightgown, cradled her breast, and felt her heart beating. It hammered wildly against her hand.

The Louse

THE LOUSE IS A SMALL, WINGLESS INSECT that infests people and sucks blood. It is a parasite and for this reason must be wiped out.

A parasite is someone who resides in, on, or next to another person and feeds off him. The other person is home and food to the parasite and therefore valuable to it.

Killing the animal or person on which the louse has comfortably settled does not by a long shot mean the death of the louse. Instead it preys on another host with the speed for which it is renowned, and sets up a new home. The louse knows nothing of loyalty: it only knows the hard rules of survival.

To liquidate a louse, one first has to catch it and, because it is small and knows how to conceal itself, thoroughly comb through one's head from west to east, not forgetting the white parting. Once caught, it can either be squeezed between the nails, emitting a cracking noise as its last lament. Or it can be set on fire. This requires certain skill, but is rewarded by the sight of a burning, dancing louse.

The louse does not walk, it crawls. Like all pests, it multiplies quickly and has lots of children. The children like the warmth, and nestle into creases and dark places: they are called nits and are small potential lice, which should never be forgotten about. Therefore, after destroying a louse, one must deal with the children in the same careful manner, before they can become lice.

The louse never rests. It is cunning and adopts a friendly demeanor. It keeps its proboscis, located on the underside of its head, hidden away in a sheath, only taking it out when it knows no one is looking, to suck up its host's blood.

That is the louse: you do not see it, you do not hear it, and, while it is up to no good with its proboscis, you do not even feel it. It is only afterward that the unpleasant itching and scratching begin that can be traced back to the louse. It will not be around to get up to mischief for long.

Sometimes the louse fancies itself as a lobster or a crab because of its pincers. But it never ends up on a plate, and its legs are never sucked at with a touch of mayonnaise at ceremonious occasions.

The louse is denied such a pleasant end. It is too small and not nice to look at. It is simply a louse and is therefore polished off quietly and not spoken of afterward.

Yet, just because it is not a lobster does not mean a louse is always a louse. One has to differentiate between the different sorts that have come into being, as the louse knows how to adapt to its home.

If it lives in clothes, it is called a clothes louse. This louse eats its way into the material. Above all else it loves the rough cloth of men's trousers, and sweaters of fleecy wool.

If it takes up residency in pubic hair and in underarm hair, it is dark in color and called a crab louse.

If it builds its nest in head hair, it is called a head louse or *Pediculus capitis*. A head louse is gray, which is particularly helpful with old, weak, and gray-haired people. Ah yes, the louse is always adaptable and ready to assimilate.

The human louse has no proboscis. Instead, however, it has a triangle in various colors sewn on to the left side of the jacket and the right trouser leg and — in the case of the female human louse — on to the skirt.

The triangle is a piece of fabric with three sides of equal length. It is cut out of curtains, tablecloths, shirts, or whatever else. The color shows everyone — the guard, the commanding officer, and the other male and female human lice — why the human louse has been committed. This is known as the "reason for detention." It is more practical than lengthy explanations, and makes lying impossible for the lice.

If the human louse sports a blue triangle, it is an emigrant. An emigrant is an enemy who tried to escape and was caught in the act. When he is brought back accompanied by two or more policemen, he is taken to a place made for blue and other colored human lice.

The place is called KZ, or preventative detention camp, because there the human lice are protected from themselves, not that they appreciate it as they should.

If the human louse has a red triangle, it is a political detainee.

If the human louse has a pink triangle, one is dealing with a homosexual. A homosexual is a human louse who loves another human louse of its own sex.

If it has a black triangle, the human louse cowering behind it, as well as being a human louse, is also asocial; that is to say, lazy; that is to say, tramp; that is to say, Gypsy.

If the human louse is wearing two yellow triangles, one over the other, then it is a Jew. The question of who is Jewish is decided by the Law for the Protection of German Blood.

If the triangle is purple, then one is looking at a Bible-thumping human louse.

If it is sporting a green triangle, it is a criminal. That sort of louse is the subject of what is to follow.

Brief Sociology of Crime

(The Silver Amulet)

1.

Karl Streng entered the world of crime like a garishly made-up Lucifer in a low-budget theater production. Standing on a retractable platform, he was cranked up, to the accompaniment of some stage smoke and a bang or two, which did not however cover the asthmatic wheezing of the frail hydraulics, into the middle of the scene of the crime, to carry out the part — not the lead, but more than just an extra — that fate and his familial circumstances had allotted him. He was eighteen then and was two weeks out of the institution whose buildings had been bequeathed at the end of the century by a rich and benevolent family.

Streng had spent three years in the Sonnenfeld Institution. Arrested for pickpocketing, he was nonetheless judged "redeemable." His clumsiness — in the space of two months, to be viewed as his apprenticeship period, he was caught in the act ten times — had proven he was an inexperienced petty criminal.

And thus Streng's career as a pickpocket ended before he could take the final examinations.

So he had come to be at the Sonnenfeld Institution and after serving his sentence was delivered to freedom again with a few friendly words and his clothes, which he had outgrown in the meantime.

He did not have any illusions. Although he had quickly become Sonnenfeld's most skillful basket weaver and, besides the normal baskets that decorated the youth's cells along with wood carvings and clay pots, had made a wicker chair — painstakingly finicky work — for the director of the institution, he knew that this was no way to earn a living, of course. And even the dexterity gained through the weaving work that he tried to employ for illegal endeavors did not help him fill his growling stomach. Due to the present economic crisis, the pockets of his fellow civilians were as empty as his own. Something else would have to be thought up. Streng gave it some consideration.

With a friend he was staying with, later to disappear out of sight, he weighed several possibilities.

He was despairing, when the name of a certain type of weaving gave him a brilliant idea. It was a kind of weaving that Streng had shown a particular aptitude for at Sonnenfeld, because he was very good at drawing the weft round the stake. Because of this tight weaving of the switches of willow, one on top of the other, it was called body wickerwork.

Streng decided to start his own business and to try his luck with commercial prostitution.

That same month he signed on two girls he picked up at the railway station, who went with him for the price of a cup of coffee and an asymmetrical smile — he had lost a canine tooth in a fight.

To reduce expenses, unnecessarily high from the renting of hotel rooms by the hour, the little threesome moved into a rented apartment. Streng possessed all the qualities of a good manager. He treated the girls considerately, never forced them to do overtime, and gave them almost anything they wanted.

He was altogether satisfied with his modest life in the three rooms, which one of the girls had managed to make quite homey, and with the simple country cooking that gave him that satisfied feeling he had bitterly missed in his youth. And he said to himself — not through any lack of ambition, but because all in all he had a clear, circumspect mind, and knew how to value what he had — that if it were up to him, things could happily continue thus forever.

Things turned out differently, however. One of the neighbors, unsettled by the relatively high number of men who had been coming and going by way of her staircase since the new tenants had moved in, alerted the vice squad. They set a trap for the threesome that very week.

Streng and the two young ladies, who through the policemen's rough handling suddenly realized with frightening clarity what they had become in the course of just a few months, were taken to the police station. Since no charges could be brought against the women, what with the repeal of the regulations, and they would have to walk free, to make up for it Streng was arrested for the exploitation of two whores.

In light of another offence again so soon, in spite of his youth — he was not yet twenty — he was sentenced to two years' unconditional imprisonment, which he started to serve the same month. The prison was located in a small suburb, dominated entirely by the imposing prison building that was visible from every corner of the place and by the stories that made the rounds about the individual prisoners, above all about the murderers.

The correctional institution might have seemed hard and cruel to him just a few months ago, but now he saw it through different eyes, from the perspective of his current abode — a five-square-meter cell with a steel bed, table, and a barred window, through which if he stood on his bed he could see the red bricks of the wall and the top of a tree.

How he longed, in the silence of the second portion of porridge slopped into his tin bowl at Sonnenfeld in exchange for a woven basket, how he longed for a friendly word. Streng stared at the square tiles of the floor and grew melancholic. There was no hope of things getting better.

In his fifth month, one winter morning, Streng was ordered

to get his blanket, clothes, and tin bowl together. Then he was led to a shared cell.

Grown shy through the loneliness that had been drawn like a gray veil over his existence, the young man, not particularly sociable at the best of times, could not look his fellow inmates in the eye when they asked his name and why he had been arrested. Even when he had grown used to the other men and to the sound of his own voice, he remained taciturn and reserved. He got the reputation of being a weirdo, which was a help over the next four months — he was spared the beatings the other inmates dealt out from boredom and living too closely together.

Streng's life changed in the first week of his tenth month in jail, when two older prisoners pinned him down in the showers and, in the presence of a group of onlookers, a third man raped him.

He tried to take his own life afterward by slitting his wrists with his tin bowl broken in two, but the guard discovered him lying in his own blood and saved him.

He was taken to the hospital building and, after two weeks, back to the shared cell. There an inmate ten years his senior, serving his third prison sentence and so respected, bluntly explained to him the general customs of prison life and, when he was convinced that Streng had understood it all, took him into his protection on account of Streng's youth and soft skin.

From now on Streng was no longer molested, and even when his friend had been released — his sentence was completed six months before his own — he was treated with respect. The reason for that was the holy Mother Mary, a silver amulet, a present from the older man to the younger one on the day of his release that hung on Streng's sparsely haired chest as a physical sign of their association.

Shortly after his twenty-second birthday, Streng stepped out onto the soil of freedom, a day covered with a clear layer of shimmering frost. After drinking a beer in a bar and smoking a cigarette lit with respect for him by one of the routine drinkers around at that time of the day — who recognized the former prisoner through his gestures, his way of drinking, and his bent posture, ready to jump up — Streng disappeared.

No one saw him for a long time, and he was only heard of four years later when the criminal investigation department laid an album of criminals in front of a witness who picked out Streng as the man he thought he had seen in the backyard of a restaurant. Streng was suspected of having murdered a prostitute. After a brief uncomplicated search — he was arrested in the bed of a hotel in male company — he was back in jail.

The weight of evidence being crushing, Streng, who now called himself Tony for professional reasons, was sentenced to ten years for murder. Three weeks later he came to a camp, also for professional criminals. Ironically, it was next to the town in which his father had been born and had left to seek his fortune.

2.

Hunger: Streng became acquainted with this gnawing feeling that trumped all other bodily sensations. It alone determined his existence. Although as a "green" — a man of German extraction who had gone off the rails — he was treated better than the other prisoners, he could not fill his stomach properly with the soup and bread allotted him. The growling of his digestive canal and stomach juices accompanied him like penetrating background music to work, and in the latrines, and at the barbed wire. Wistfully he thought back to the prison where Mother Mary had opened the pots of the prison kitchen to him.

Streng grew thinner and thinner, he began to show certain signs of starvation, and he would have certainly died without fuss had a central command from Berlin not drastically changed his life.

Because of his formerly garnered experience Streng, no longer answering to his name in the meantime, was taken to the hospital building, showered, fed, and looked after. After one week in which he could eat to his heart's content, he started to show signs of life. Streng was taken to the commanding officer, who took in his appearance with disgust and gave him orders to set up a site to fight homosexuality, which, in spite of all precautions, had broken out even among Aryans like an epidemic.

Streng understood. Together with the camp doctor, who was taking care of the hygienic aspect, and the commanding officer, who took control of the aesthetics, he picked out twenty girls from the women's camp, who in turn were showered, fed, and sent to Streng for instruction.

Very quickly Streng had set up a brothel in a block provided by the camp management, surrounded by barbed wire for security reasons, one that was hailed as a role model even in Berlin.

Streng made his women, to whom he gave plentiful food, call him Papi, and during lunchtime every day he walked them once around the block, so that they could have a breath of, if not fresh, at least oxygen-enriched air, which was supposed to keep them rosy-cheeked and healthy. He started finding pleasure in life again and all would have worked out for the best for him, after the delay and numerous escapades, had he not, his immediate bodily needs catered for, fallen in love.

It was on a spring evening that Streng saw the cause of his ruin for the first time. As though cut out from dark blue crepe paper with scissors, the crescent moon stood out against the starless sky. Streng was bored and decided to relieve his assistant, a simple-minded political prisoner without ambition who had been admitted for cracking a couple of inopportune jokes when drunk.

After he had taken in twenty vouchers that the kapos and some of the politicals got for good completion of their work and exchanged for scraps of paper with room numbers, racing with them to the first floor so as not to unnecessarily waste any of their allotted twenty minutes, a young man stepped into the hall that Streng used as a reception room and requested to be seen to by none other than the most popular whore, who exclusively served higher officials and had also offered her services in the Reich.

A Pole, thought Streng, identifying the young man as a political one right away. Shaking his head at the stubbornness of youth, he gave him a scrap of paper with the number of a currently free room and took him into the next room, where a previously convicted woman made of pure German fat, by the name of Erna, performed some maneuvers on him that were primarily hygienic. Driven by some inexplicable curiosity, Streng went up to the young man, who had returned indignant, looked into his deep green eyes, and was lost.

Streng spent happy weeks spoiling his charge with delicious nibbles and, besides fresh clothes and shaving implements, gave him a silver chain with a gold-plated amulet. He had his initials engraved on it and it reminded him of the time spent with his friend in prison.

Although he had a privileged position as the manager of the camp brothel, and he could buy the silence of those in the know with the services of his women or with bartered margarine, soon his relationship with the young man known by everyone simply as Pipel was common knowledge. Lying in bed they were taken by surprise one morning and locked up.

He was seized with longing for his father's thrashings, for the beatings in Sonnenfeld Correction Center, the beatings in prison and the hunger in the camp that had then appeared to him as his most difficult and unbearable lot. Streng was afraid. He could not help the young man whose begging cries echoed along the corridor. Forgive me, he thought, and covered his ears.

A week later his Pipel was taken out of the prison cell, put up against the wall, and shot. Streng heard the cries of the boy as they led him past his cell door. Two days later he was taken to the commanding officer and signed a document authorizing his sterilization.

That very day the doctor carried out the operation. Streng felt nothing and saw everything as though through a veil. When the doctor told him it was all over, he fainted, and woke up, trembling with exhaustion, in the hospital building, and waited to be taken to be annihilated.

Especially in the night he believed he could hear the foot-steps of his death angel. However, as he had proved his worth in his post and since the place had not been put in other hands, Streng was allowed to return.

Slowly everything reverted to its normal pace. Streng collected the vouchers, checked the rooms, ordered liquor, and took the whores out daily. They called him eunuch behind his back. He had heard about his new name but was not insulted.

From an always welcome customer, a guard, he learned that his friend had wept as he was shot and that he had written on the wall with his bloody finger, which he had bitten open the night before the shooting.

Often still, when he was sitting alone in the reception room, as the ladies worked above him, Streng was to remember the wording of the sentence his friend had left him as a testament: "Peter Baslewicz reached the age of eighteen years." The guard had wiped it off the same day with a sponge and suds smelling of chlorine and curd soap.

The Ramp

Portraits of Three Normal People

> Fräulein Gigerlette
> Invited me to tea
> Her toilette
> As snowy white as can be
> Just like Pierette
> Was she attired
> Even a monk, I dare to bet,
> By Gigerlette
> Would be afired.

1.

When Johann Paul Kremer was called upon on September 2 to carry out his first "special operation," he wrote in his diary: "Compared to this, Dante's inferno seems almost like a comedy."

He was fifty-nine years old. His hair was thinning, and even his daily exercises could not stave off the toll that time had taken on him.

During the university recess, he took part in fourteen selections on the ramp and the subsequent gassings. Afterward, he returned to Münster, where he had been teaching since 1935. Kremer was an outstanding professor of anatomy and had seen many corpses in his time.

"Corpses," he said in his introductory lecture in the first semester, shocking the new students into embarrassed laughter, "corpses are our field of study."

Kremer was not happy about being ordered to Auschwitz. He had already heard about it in Münster. Nothing good. He had hoped to be sent to France or to some warm country, to Greece, for example, where he would have liked to visit the Acropolis.

In his diary he complained about his lot. It was not nice, but it did offer him chances undreamed of until now.

Indeed, not only could he continue his research, he could also expand upon it in several important areas. Up to now Kremer had been able to experiment only upon the cells of cold-blooded animals. Now he was — as he later reported — to be one of the first, if not the very first, doctor in human history to perform tests on people to see whether the hypotheses he had reached through theoretical deduction alone were founded. Unusual, truly remarkable perspectives were opening up to him.

Above all else Kremer was interested in muscular tissue and how hunger affected it. After the end of the war, in a Polish prison, he said the following about that period of his life:

"If someone interested me because of a well-advanced stage of starvation, then I gave the medical orderly the assignment to reserve the sick person for me and to inform me of the date he would be killed by injection. At that point the sick people I had selected were led to the block and laid on the dissection table still alive. I went to the table and asked the sick person details that were of interest to my research. I asked the weight prior to arrest, what loss of weight there had been during imprisonment, whether he had taken any medicine recently, what he ate daily, and so on. After I had obtained the information of interest to me, the medical orderly came in and killed the patient by injecting him close to the heart. I myself never gave a deadly injection."

Kremer added that he dissected the patients as soon as they were dead.

"I took sections of the liver and pancreas and placed them in jars filled with a preserving liquid and took them home to continue my research."

Five of these jars were confiscated from the cellar of his

house. After Kremer had identified them as his property and handed over the matching documents — he did this voluntarily, without hesitation — they served as incriminating material.

In his diary on this subject he states:

"Today fixated freshest possible material from the human liver and spleen, as well as pancreas."

Similar entries crop up again and again.

Not much is known about Kremer's character. One of his work colleagues described him as a loner. One of the students who was asked emphasized that he had never tried to impose a doctrine and had always rather stayed in the background. Kremer was an inconspicuous, friendly person who did not need much company. He always liked to keep an option open, a guard said.

"More out of principle than caution."

Kremer was one of those few doctors who spoke to the patients with the polite form, "thou." During his trial, former prisoners said he had always been courteous to them, with a distanced arrogance, and that they gathered from the way he dealt with them that he wanted to have as little to do with them as possible.

"He was not coarse like some of the others, but neither was he compassionate. He shut his heart to our suffering. A heart was to him a muscle, and we were a mass of bodies."

During his relatively short stay at the camp, Kremer was able to appropriate, besides the human organs, goods of considerable value, which he sent to Münster either in postal packages or with a guard open to bribery.

The extent of what was stolen from people later determined for selection by him is known down to the last detail. Kremer entered the robbed wares conscientiously in his diary, before entrusting them to a certain Frau König, so that she could look after them until his return. For her services, Kremer rewarded her with perfume and alcohol. Later she claimed repeatedly not to have known where and how Kremer acquired all these things.

Asked about this point in court Kremer said: "The prisoners stuffed my pockets, I could not ward them off." It is well known that new arrivals occasionally tried to buy their life or that of those close to them with valuable objects, an attempt that usually failed. Kremer accepted the things unscrupulously — he was seen doing this by several medical auxiliaries — but then selected afterward as he saw fit medically, and seldom made any exceptions.

"I am not aware," said the auxiliary, "of Kremer ever granting anyone life because he got something from them. He certainly took it, but there it ended. He saw it as a present, crazy though it sounds."

It is to be assumed that this bizarre declaration is true and that Kremer indeed thought that he was legimately entitled to appropriate the things.

When he was informed at the internment prison that his diaries had been found in the apartment and handed over to the judges to read, he replied that at last people would now be convinced of his innocence, as the jottings made it absolutely clear how he had suffered under the regime.

It was only in autumn 1943, during the bombing of Münster, that Kremer wrote the question in his diary of whether there was a God. The mass murder that he participated in never led to such considerations.

Kremer is intelligent and possesses an all-around education, not limited to his area alone. The suppression, which can be called pathological, and his disturbed thinking and memory explain his behavior before the judges and his lacking any sense of guilt.

After completing his sentence, the eighty-eight-year-old Kremer was called before court once again, this time as a witness. The prosecution told him to comment on a diary entry from October 1942, where he claimed that lots of SS men had volunteered for the "special operations," because they got extra rations for it. Kremer replied: "But that is perfectly understandable from a human point of view. It was wartime, and cigarettes and schnapps were scarce."

Johann Paul Kremer was pardoned in a Polish court of law at the end of the war. Some years later he was charged again, this time in Germany, and sentenced to ten years in prison. The judge gave as the reason for this sentence:

"Kremer would still be free of guilt today had he not been placed in that position through circumstances that lay beyond his person, from which these crimes developed."

2.

Dr. Hans Delmotte, who worked at the Hygiene Institute of the Waffen-SS, came from a rich industrial family. Some of his close relatives held high posts in the Party.

Delmotte was sent directly from military school to Auschwitz. At school he had attracted negative attention on several occasions. Among other things, he was observed by a fellow pupil reading a Thomas Mann novel.

Called before the director to justify his reading habits, he explained (and backed up his opinion several times) that Thomas Mann was a good writer and therefore he did not understand the ban. Delmotte was also later called on the carpet for a spectacular deed: he came to the annual carnival ball dressed as a woman, and was therefore sent to Auschwitz as a punishment.

Like all SS doctors he also had to select from the ramp. One knows through his colleague Münch, with whom he shared the house, that after the first "special operation" performed under his direction he had to be carried to his room and threw up noisily. After that he called in sick for a few days.

Delmotte refused to take part in selections after that first "special operation," and requested that the commanding officer, who sent him on to the army doctor, post him to the front.

Delmotte declared repeatedly that the murder of defenseless children and women was beneath his male dignity. He was prepared to serve the Reich, even willing to kill enemies of the Volk in combat; it was just this underhanded way of killing he could not agree to.

In reaction to his qualms, Delmotte was placed under Dr. Mengele, who took over the task of convincing him of the necessity of annihilating world Jewry.

It is not known if Mengele succeeded. It is known, however, that Delmotte, after the short time he spent in Mengele's presence, selected like every other SS doctor: with disgust, as a camp survivor emphasized years later.

He treated the victims gently, she added. He was not one for whipping. Above all, the sight of the children, whom he tried to delude to the very end with the illusion that they were really going to shower, made him agitated. He had admittedly not done this out of mercy, but for his own conscience.

"He just wanted to be able to say that he is different. But he selected nonetheless."

According to the two doctors closest to him and to his fiancée, to whom he wrote every week, his nature was changed for ever after that. Only when the selections had ceased, in the autumn of 1944, did he seem more relaxed.

When the war was over, Delmotte committed suicide. Münch claimed that he had done it out of fear of being arrested.

"He was a coward," said Münch, "he wanted to have his cake and eat it, too. You cannot do that."

His fiancée claimed in an interview in the late forties that it had been an act of despair.

"He could not come to terms with his life. He was just different. Even as a child."

Delmotte did not leave any suicide note. Therefore one can only speculate about his motives.

3.

In the trial against Dr. Johann Marburg, who had to answer to the American military court along with three other SS doctors who had practiced in Auschwitz, three witnesses gave testimony.

The former prisoner Tadeusz Lebowic, camp prefect, who had known almost all the doctors, was first to the witness stand. He claimed that Marburg had often come in slightly drunk to the hospital building and at such times had been sentimental and humanely accessible.

"In that condition I could put the boldest papers in front of him, which he signed freely, without even reading the text," said Lebowic, adding that in this way he had been able to save some people, between fifty and sixty, without Marburg doing anything to stop it. As to the question of whether Marburg's behavior could be interpreted as a sort of passive resistance, Tadeusz Lebowic answered: "It was all the same to him."

Marburg, according to Lebowic, had indeed sometimes made people step down who were meant for selection out of technical considerations — above all young men whom he found to be capable of working — and thus sentenced fewer prisoners to death than the medical orderly Klehr suggested. As for that one, went on Lebowic, he ate Jews for breakfast and tormented all the prisoners with yellow triangles, above all women who were too weak to defend themselves. Marburg had on the other hand sent an entire section of children to the gas chambers he had suspected of having typhus.

"He did not have any proof, only the suspicion," said Lebowic, who now remembered the scene exactly, because even then it had appeared to him to be particularly cynical.

Marburg had given some chocolate to a boy who did not want to go and was clinging to the bedstead and, making promises and petting him, carried him to the truck himself.

"The boy, he must have been around six, smiled at him finally. That smile," said Lebowic, "is branded in my memory."

In answer to the question of why Marburg had acted so overzealously, Lebowic said: "He was afraid of Mengele, who was his direct superior."

Second to take the witness stand was the former political prisoner Willi Gleitze. Gleitze's family, like Marburg's, resided

265

in Luckenwalde. Therefore Marburg often came into the orderly room where Gleitze worked. Out of all the prisoners, Gleitze was the closest to him.

"I did not know Marburg in Luckenwalde. We moved in different circles. He is after all eight years my senior. When you are young, that counts. How can I describe his nature to you? I think most easily through a small, insignificant incident.

"He came once, it must have been after a selection that had really shaken him, into the orderly room and told me it would soon come to an end. Then we will be like two old friends sitting together over a glass of good wine, he said, and clapped me on the shoulder after telling me to be brave.

"He had not gathered what was happening then, or did not want to grasp it. That was the beginning of 1944, and he had still not got it.

"I do not believe that it was fun for him. However, he did carry out his work. I once asked him why he had joined the SS, but I got no clear answer.

"Marburg," said Gleitze, "is a scatterbrain. I could not understand his motives. He could not understand them himself."

The third and most important piece of testimony came from Barbara Feigenbaum, who had reported to him as secretary.

"He was most susceptible to the pleas of women. Every time he had to select from the women's section he drank a lot of the brandy the authorities made available to the doctors to ease their work.

"Once he put a young fifteen-year-old girl to the side. She had typhus and should actually have been taken immediately to the gas chamber. When I asked him what I should write down he only said that she had such beautiful blond hair. He had her taken to the hospital building. I think she was gassed nevertheless, for in Auschwitz that was the usual way of dealing with the plague.

"I also saw him crying, although he tried to hide it from me. That was after a selection on the ramp. He had seen someone there, a woman he seemed to recognize.

"He told me much later that she had been the wife of his university friend Fuchs and kept repeating that it was a crime — I believe he used the word *obscenity* — because the woman was an Aryan. Of German extraction, as he put it. He tried to justify himself in front of me. I do not know why."

She got down from the train with a boy. Marburg spotted her even though she was back at the end of the row. He was very agitated, stood up immediately, and called for a break. Then he went up to her and removed her from the row and led her to the table. He promised he would take care of her.

He then made a long phone call, followed by a detour to the office. When he came back he was perplexed. You could always tell with him. He then told her that he could save only her. Not the child. The woman had wanted to give him a sapphire ring, which she took from her finger. She knew already what it meant to be sent to the left and be disinfected.

Marburg told her the ring could not help either and that it was beyond his power. He took the woman to one side and softly coaxed her. I only overheard the word *half-caste*, could only guess what they were talking about. The woman shook her head and called her boy, whose name was David, over to her.

Marburg tried to restrain her. The woman spat in his face and walked to the left with her child.

Marburg got very drunk afterward, and while dispatching the others, sang a song about a monk. The local doctor came then and told him to pull himself together. Thereafter he always carried the ring with him. It was his "unlucky mascot."

The Jewish Laborer

in memoriam

On June 10, 1943, a fresh transport of ten closed cattle cars arrived at the concentration and extermination camp of Auschwitz-Birkenau. The transport, entered as Convoy Number 17 on the deportation list of the Council for Jewish Affairs, was seen as a particular success of the Gestapo in France.

All the deportees, with the exception of two prisoners, were Jews of German extraction who had thought to escape persecution by fleeing to a neighboring land, a plan that was to prove fruitless due to the minutely performed search operation of the Gestapo and to the cooperation of the French authorities. Thus the Jews who had fled were going to get what their flight alone meant they deserved, only a little postponed.

The transport came from Drancy, a small town near Paris, in which an assembly camp had been set up.

The Jews were interned there for the length of time required to organize their handover to the east that would render them harmless, once and for all, in a concentration camp such as the one they were now entering, with the broad range of possibilities available in the east. The assembly camps did not have such possibilities; they were simply to assemble what was to be later exterminated in the extermination camps.

The train that had made a lengthy stop at the new French-German border to attach two freight wagons with war equipment arrived as planned, in spite of a delay of almost an hour.

The reason for the delay was the side wall of the cars, which — before they could be used to safely deliver Jews to their final destination — had transported animals, lambs, beef cattle, and other four-legged creatures who, like the Jews, ended up dead but whose meat brought in more than the meat of Jews. An eye had to be kept on them, as opposed to Jews, because bruises, cuts, and scrapes reduced the profits.

The reason for the delay was the side wall. To let the air in better, it was made of slats of wood nailed together, through whose fine cracks the muffled cries of a mass of crushed-together Jews penetrated to the outside. They so shocked the railway man that he twice dropped his hammer for checking the wheels, although he was certainly used to yelling at home. What was more, the young helpers commissioned to hook up the cars did not complete their task with their usual speed.

Yet although the Jews knew how to make the most of the cracks between the slats and tried to sabotage the transport with their vocal chords, the train that had set off an hour later than planned arrived at the appointed hour, thanks to the initiative of the Polish engineer — he increased speed once on familiar home turf and made up the lost time — so that a considerable percentage of the passengers of the cattle cars, after their property was registered and their health condition checked, could be exterminated without delay.

But what penetrated the inside from outside? From outside something altogether different penetrated inside, namely the morning air, relatively cool for this time of year, which smelled of linden and chamomile, which did not comfort even one of the Jews in the cars — because only the oral intake of these healing herbs has a soothing effect on the angry organism — but it did prevent them from simply suffocating before their removal, that is to say extermination.

That morning air that impartially also filled the Jewish nostrils gave rise to a longing in the Jews whose mouths and noses were pressed to the slats for something that they had lost along the way.

The air did not know the Nuremberg Racial Laws, which forbade any mixing of Jewish and non-Jewish. Freedom, on the other hand, that it knew.

Since, due to the engineer's initiative, the transport problem played no important role, which is to say was almost completely solved (the way from the railway tracks into the camp could be covered on foot, at a steady trot; the whip was used to urge them on, as it was more reasonable and easier to use than the firearms), Transport Number 17, consisting of 1,006 Jewish men, women, and children, was met at four o'clock in the morning as planned.

The reception committee consisted of some kapos, several SS men, a couple of KZ internees wearing striped suits, three dogs — among them Hasso, who had to be addressed as Herr Human — some heavy leather boots, fifteen whips, and twenty guns, which were used only five times.

No one played music. In spite of the preference of the SS doctor selecting that day for introductory and concluding words, no speech was held. Instead there was shouting.

For this the vocal chords of the kapos were used, who, in contrast to the SS men, were replaceable if not as superfluous as the KZ internees.

With a "faster, faster, make it snappy" or "make it quick," the prisoners were driven out and sorted into groups of five. Oh, what quick progress.

He to whom it was not yet clear, now knows that he has reached the final destination of his life. And what that sickly-sweet-smelling smoke signifies, he will soon learn to understand, when he himself, or his mother, or his father, or his younger brother who is under fourteen — whether four or ten does not play any role for the statistics — wander up the chimney.

What cannot be used as a full-value labor Jew will be struck off the camp list. Who is no longer profitable will be burned. For the camp commander has received orders from Berlin. They read:

> Maximum profit is the aim of every undertaking. The decrease in value or the demise of Jews is not to be viewed as loss, but rather as success. One has managed to collect a large store of this raw material. But one does not know what to do with it.
>
> The Jews should be driven on to work and to wear themselves out working. They should be used until they are worn out morally and physically, and then away with them.
>
> For guarding and looking after Jews is too costly. In these difficult times even bread and nettle soup are expensive foodstuffs and nothing must be wasted, especially not on a defective, that is to say, too young, or too old, labor Jew.

And when he cannot go on? Simply cannot get up anymore? Then he has a shower and swallows gas, to sing hallelujah with the angels that are black in Auschwitz because of the soot, or gray because of the human ashes.

The regular controls only serve the cream of the crop. Only the best are allowed to help build the Thousand Year Reich and its enrichment. That is a beautiful privilege. A reward that makes all the torment worthwhile.

The Jews are put into groups of five and selected. An SS man goes past and orders the old Jews, whose age is apparent, and the young men, whose youth one can see, to sit down in the truck, for they are to be sent sitting, not walking, to their hereafter. Auschwitz is a well-mannered place.

"Do not climb up," a striped KZ internee whispers in the ear of a new arrival and makes a motion of the hand expressing the cutting of a throat and thereby death: a gesture that the green kapo sees and he whips the KZ internee immediately for betraying a secret of Reich business to the new arrival, who should come upon it himself as soon as possible. The new arrival does not register because he is seeing everything through a veil and understands nothing of what he sees.

For the new arrival is under confrontational shock, heightened further by the camp management by attacking the multitude without reason or letting a dog rush at them in the hope of a tasty morsel. Intimidated arrivals are particularly apathetic, and therefore easier to polish off.

"Thank you, thank you," says the man over sixty who was once a professor, and sits down waving to his daughter, whom he will see soon again when the formalities have been straightened out, next to his wife, who is already sitting, or rather crouching, her legs wide apart: confrontational shock has made her forget her manners, quite unlike the SS man who helps a mother up with an infant in her arms, for the woman is certainly still weak from the birth.

On the plank serving as a desk, a man dictates his name: *k* like Karl, *a* like Adalbert, *h* like Holger, *n* like Norbert. Kahn, that is, Richard Kahn from Richard Kahn, Inc. Not Kohn. Herr Kahn is a Jew of German origin, as the *a* proves. Indeed, he is from Bukovina, but he lived in Berlin. Knows that beautiful city and even managed the former arts and crafts school once, now the Gestapo headquarters — such are the twists of life.

The Kahn family were all seized, that is to say Frau Kahn, Herr Kahn, and the two Kahn children, already seated. A one hundred percent success for the Gestapo.

A one hundred percent profit for the hotel proprietress, whose little pension was so small and cozy, even breakfast — baguette, café au lait, and jam — included in the nightly rate, and who was allowed to keep the suitcases for providing the information and the silver wristwatch that father Kahn had left on the bedside table by mistake.

He was a stupid idiot, the scribe retorted, and next to his name noted the number that the prisoner would wear from now on. A nice number, not too high, and not too low. A middle-class KZ internee, who went to the right.

His two boys, Dani and Benjamin, already had their numbers written on their chests with ink, for it makes no sense to tattoo in such cases. They are driven away with the first truck-load, and have the honor of being first to enter the bathing and inhaling rooms, in front of which they are now standing naked because, as everyone knows, one cannot be disinfected with clothes on.

Only they do not know that they are the lice that are to be exterminated.

Only they do not know that out of the showerheads in the twenty-five-square-meter large room that can hold between seven and eight hundred Jews, no water and no soapy water and also no rosewater, but pure expensive Zyklon B will come streaming out, which will slowly choke them, paid for by their parents through their labor and confiscated valuables, over-looked by the hotel proprietress, because here in Auschwitz one pays for everything, above all for the death of children.

Only the parents do not know that they will not see each other again, and that they will not see their children again, because that relatively slow choking to death, which can last between five and fifteen minutes, for children, however — because they are smaller than adults and therefore closer to the ground and closer to death, as the gas is so heavy it sinks — lasts nearer five minutes, which for Auschwitz is a really quick death.

Be glad, children Kahn. You had it easier with the thirty other children than the other 736 prisoners, the men and women who came with Transport 17 at four o'clock in the morning and at five-fifty were gassed with you. They took five minutes longer to choke to death. They stretched and strained to gulp the last remnant of air that was still fresh up there by the crumbling ceiling.

For at Wannsee they had found the final solution to the Jewish problem. They had opted after some consideration for the final extermination of the Jews. Because the Jew was mis-fortune. Because the Jew was the root of all evil. If Mother died, the Jew was to blame. If the girlfriend left, if the children had chickenpox, if the cake burned, if one had not got one's raise, if a fingernail split: all the fault of the Jew. Penned up in the ghetto as plague carrier, running around free in the town as representative of illicit trade, in his home with others of his sort as conspirator, and in contact with others as seducer, the Jew posed a threat, so that an end had to be made of him, once and for all an end. And afterward there was beer and dancing, toasts were given, and swaying to music, because it was relaxed and there was even singing at Wannsee, but not "Rose on the Common"; coarser stuff, although Goethe belonged up there with the great Schiller in German culture, as the whip belonged in the German man's hand.

Be glad, children Kahn. Your parents did not have it as good as you. Your mother, labor Jew number 468752, had to undress and run with the other ninety-nine female work animals naked through the gates and because she was shy and did not want to get undressed in front of the pair of guards, the kapos, the commanding officer of the preventative detention camp, the block prefect, and some of those from the political section who had positioned themselves to see the fresh supplies, she was whipped through to the hairdressing salon, where her brown locks fell to the floor. They would not stay there long since they could be used in the homeland.

"My children, hairdresser, sir, my children have certainly already been with you."

"How old are they then?"

"The big one is eight and the small one is five. They look very much alike. They are both wearing blue pants and light-colored shirts. And have curly hair like me. You would not forget such beautiful waves."

"Next one, quickly, quickly."

"Hairdresser, sir, you have seen them, haven't you?"

The barracks are in darkness. There is no light. One has to save where one can. Number 468752 has a bunk, a straw sack filled with wood shavings and a blanket. Those are her possessions.

She must take good care of them, for one can freeze in winter without a blanket.

If she had paced the room with a measuring stick, she would know that it is twenty-five meters long and ten meters wide. But number 468752 does not have any time for that because she is busy tearing out her remaining bristles of hair.

She does not even notice the blood that runs down her face and neck and turns to crust on her shirt, while number 468752 batters her head raw against the planks of her bunk because a fellow internee has explained the fate of her children to her.

Exit Kahn children. They have already perished, ashes beneath ashes in the crematorium oven, for as God himself said, dust to dust.

Welcome to Auschwitz, number 468752, if you do not stop your nonsense soon, you will not survive the week.

How many women fit into a barrack twenty-five meters long, ten meters wide, and three meters high?

If one rather than laying a floor — the bottom layer of concrete and the cement covering takes up twenty centimeters too much space, for stone flagging one also needs a bed of sand, therefore ten centimeters too much, not to mention an attic floor with beams, insulation boards, rafters, and mortar, because that adds on a good twenty-five precious centimeters — if one then stamps the earth flat instead of laying a floor, and covers it with bricks, remaining intact through the trampling of women, and if, to save space at the top, you forget about a ceiling and simply bang on a roof, you can easily have three levels. Then all you have to do is divide the length and breadth into bunks using wooden timbers, each one two meters wide and two meters long, and that on three tiers. It is well constructed and well planned, because it saves so much room.

Eight women have to sleep in each.

Do seven to eight, let us call it seven and a half, women fit in a two-meter-wide and two-meter-long bunk?

They will simply squash each other a little, they will grow thinner by the day anyway and take up less space.

For one thousand women have to fit in a barrack and get out of it when it is time for work or for the selection. Even in the gas chamber, you are squeezed up to your neighbor, only on the gallows do you have sweet isolation.

Labor Jew 468752 takes up a bit more space because she is a fresh arrival and is therefore rounder than the old inmates, who are on familiar terms with death and can smell like tracker dogs that 468752 is one of those who will soon wander up the chimney, one whose number will easily make it onto the death list, because she now has a defect.

Something has broken in her, so she cannot be used to her full capacity and therefore is not profitable according to the hard rules of market economics: a female working machine that does not function at full power is to be removed from the effective ones in the camp and therefore run through the kidneys.

She should certainly not think that she can be granted five centimeters more space so that she can rock from side to side because her soul is momentarily in torment. Because her two children, little Dani who occasionally, fairly often recently, wets his bed, and darling Beni who paints such beautiful pictures with a sun and a house and a tree, pictures that they gave as presents to Granny, who hung the framed picture of the tree with the red apples up in her living room — in which someone else was now sitting. Because Beni, her oldest, and Dani, little Dani with the curly hair, are now ashes in a crematorium oven. Because the children, whom she had painfully brought into the world and brought up and at whose beds she had sat on so many evenings to sing them songs and tell them stories or simply to wait until the witch had flown away on her broomstick and had smoothed their foreheads; because the children she had taught to walk and how to say the alphabet, and to add and subtract; because the children, who were her joy and her sorrow, when Beni had that high fever, and Dani had broken his arm, are not there anymore.

Because they died before her, because she has outlived her little boys, because her children have asphyxiated, because they are dead, because quite simply they are no longer alive. And she could do nothing, and she was not there to hold their hands and to silence their cries with a last kiss, and to hold them to her, and to ease the act of dying, and she was not there, no, she was not there.

Oh, Frau Kahn, Frau Kahn, if your husband could see you now, qualified real estate agent, underpaid plumber on the run, now number 547811, who is thirsty because he has not drunk anything for three days, and for three hours has been lugging sacks of coal — because he not only has to pay for the death of the children and the imminent (everyone is agreed on that) demise of his wife, but also for that of Herr Kahn: if he could see you like this now, what would he say?

The Coral Necklace

ONE OF THE WOMEN STRENG HAD IN HIS PROTECTION for a short time was the German Jew Vera Lipmann. When she was committed she had just completed her twenty-first year of life. A few days after her arrival at the camp, during a selection, she was ordered neither to walk to the left nor to the right, but, as an object possibly worth channeling further, to march straight on toward the chimney, from which the thick gray smoke belched day and night, whose sickly-sweet smell spread over the heads of the prisoners and guards and settled on their clothes.

Vera drew the attention of the doctor, who had shown his predilection several times for skillfully crafted objects of art and for that reason had granted some women a week or even a month, when she came up to him during a break with an already crossed-off prisoner and a coral necklace. In contrast to the stroma just chipped off the reef, it was deep red in color and perfect in form.

"Where did you get it then?" asked the doctor, who recognized its worth immediately, and was surprised by her specialized knowledge when Vera replied that it was an Italian piece from the last century, named after the first woman to wear it, the fair Beatrice.

"It belonged to my grandmother on my father's side," said Vera.

Encouraged by the doctor's interest, she told him of her request. Immediately upon her arrival in the barracks she had discovered her cousin, ten years her senior. She was to be killed as she had grown too weak to work. She hoped to buy her free with this family heirloom she had smuggled into the camp.

"She is already struck off the camp lists," said the doctor, putting the necklace into his pocket, pointing to Else Kahn, who followed the discussion dumbly, "but I want to save you."

Vera collapsed weeping and after being separated from her cousin, was assigned with another woman, a Hungarian with high cheekbones and hair that gleamed red in the morning sun, to the brothel. On arrival, she was given a meal of soup, two potatoes, and bread, and after eating her fill was taken to be tattooed. Then she saw Karl Streng.

As he immediately noticed the value of the young woman in spite of her soiled clothing — she had a delicate, almost childlike body, particularly highly estimated by some customers — he entered Vera in the square notebook in which he listed his stock, but left her in peace because new supplies were treated considerately by him.

When after the first week Vera had still not declared herself ready to begin, Streng, who made it a general rule not to use force to persuade any of his women to practice their profession, lost his patience, and energetically tapped the as yet unwritten page of his book in which next to the name, age, and number of his protégée, he entered her weekly intake.

"Yes, yes," said Vera, "I know what you want," and began to cry.

"There is no point," replied Streng, who had more life- and camp-experience than the young lady, "You have to do it anyway." He patted her shoulder soothingly, told her to be brave, and, after asking a woman to prepare Vera, paved the way for the first rendezvous.

That very afternoon Streng found a suitable client. He

would have been handsome if it had not been for his hard glinting eyes like raw emeralds in his emaciated face, which lent him something uncanny.

It had to be. He accepted the voucher and led him to the first floor. There Vera lay, merry as could be and almost unconscious with a half empty bottle of Polish vodka, waiting in a dressing gown for her client.

Three weeks later as Streng was looking through the peephole to make sure all was well, he noticed the first red blotches on the white back of his whore. When he called her to him and ordered her to undress, Vera collapsed in tears at his feet and begged that he keep her; a referral to the infirmary meant death.

Streng regarded the woman, whom he did not want to touch and — as she had desired just a few weeks earlier — who would never be touched again by any man, with compassion in his eyes.

"My poor child," he said, "my poor, little child," wrapped the shaking body in a blanket, and sent Vera upstairs. Then he reported the typhus-ridden whore and thus signed her sentence.

Although he no longer feared death, and though he had grown unfeeling — albeit not harsh — with his women and seldom listened to their complaints of brutal clients and insufficient food, he was really hard hit by Vera's handover.

"She is so sweet," he said, and had to think of his boyfriend who had been so young and pretty. All the years of life Vera and Peter could have had. It was a crying shame. He shook his head and found comfort only in the thought that what she and he and all the other camp internees had of life could not necessarily be considered worth living.

Vera was taken to Block 25. Her appearance quickly altered. Her face grew thin. The cheekbones stuck out, her eyes were sunken hollows. She still fought it, and chewed long on the slice of bread she held in both hands to prevent a stronger person wrestling it from her, and drank the soup to muffle her hunger in small slurping mouthfuls.

Often Vera's thoughts turned to her mother, to her throaty laugh, to the holidays in the mountains, to the spicy smell of the earth and the heavy hands of her father stroking her head as she fell asleep. These memories comforted her. One week later, when she was spared from the selection, she believed everything could still work out fine. That was the start of her rapid and painful decline.

From now on, as superfluous human material whose life would anyway be extinguished soon, Vera was marked for death by starvation and only got a small part of the ration apportioned to the prisoners.

She wept. Since after a few days she did not have any strength left, even the tears stopped. Within the course of just two weeks, through constant diarrhea, she lost a third of her body weight. On her eyelids, feet, thighs, bottom, and arms blisters broke out, which subsided if the auxiliary pressed them. Although only twenty-one, she developed the wrinkled appearance of an old lady.

"Please," she begged, whenever anyone approached her bed, "please, a little bread." But she continued to get only the ration meant for those chosen for starvation.

She started to have strange visions. She saw the faces of auxiliaries and doctors who bent over her critically and followed her condition with interest, with a red halo of light around them.

Vera tried to quell the constant emptying of her body by drinking, but she couldn't keep anything in her stomach and shook with cold. In a state of half-sleep came comfort-bringing dreams.

On a Saturday — Vera had now been in the infirmary for almost three weeks — she tried to get up and collapsed next to the wooden bed. An auxiliary put her back up. She learned from him that she was to be selected the next day.

That night Vera did not sleep. With the help of a new arrival who still had some strength she made it to the window and, since she could no longer stand, sat down on the stove.

There she stayed until dawn, looking at the starless sky that offered her no answers.

In the morning, during the course of a selection, she was chosen for extermination by the same doctor who had sent her to the brothel a few weeks earlier but now did not recognize her.

Vera looked out of the window. A fine morning mist lay over the barracks. Everything was still. Only a guard stood smoking outside. She listened to the doctor discussing the technical details of her death with the auxiliary. She turned around. A light had been lit over the table. The doctor arranged the syringe and scalpel on the medical trolley, then stepped back into the shadow. Vera trembled all over and saw the auxiliary coming toward her. She was lifted up and felt a light pressure on her hip.

Vera thought about her father, who carried her up to bed when she had been overcome by darkness. Softly he had hummed tunes to her and rocked her to sleep. She felt the cold tabletop. The light was glaring. Vera turned her head to the side and looked at the doctor standing in the corner, waiting. Then she closed her eyes.

The Final Balance

But what were the others doing that day?

Fräulein Barbara Dahl stretched, turned to her side, and reached for a slice of whole-grain bread spread with cheese and topped with radishes. Her friend had prepared it for her before going off with the children to her family, and it was now next to a glass of milk on her bedside table. She pulled the covers up, took the magazine that had awarded her first prize — she had saved the magazine for the weekend — and after skipping past the fourth installment of "Brown Soil" turned to the column dedicated to beauty.

Otto Wagner was asleep.

His sister set the breakfast table and after putting on the water for coffee went down to the cellar, returning a few minutes later with a jar of plum compote.

The divorced Frau Wagner drew back the heavy curtains, opened the window, and looked out at the meadow that stretched as far as the adjacent pine forest, gleaming in the first light of day, breathed in the country air with its smell of rain and fresh grass and damp rich earth, and contemplated what she should wear to the party Paul Raeder the real estate agent was hosting.

Her former bedfellow, the dramaturge Johannes Schellenberg, was dreaming of Italy.

Paul Raeder was standing with a stopwatch in front of the delivery entrance of his newly acquired department store, which was no longer called O.B. but instead Raeder's Shopping Arcade, and checked how much time the apprentices needed to unload the goods.

The gymnast Gerta Berg was helping Harald Hartmund take down the tent. He had gotten up before her, even beating dawn. Now she was holding the rope tight while he pulled the last peg out of the ground with a jerk. She was yawning loudly and at length after staying up late into the night celebrating the fiftieth birthday of a clown.

The former numismatist Blumenfeld was standing in front of the Australian embassy with his cousin Alfred, because it was no longer safe on the French Riviera. He wanted to emigrate with Pierrette, the housekeeper, his cousin Alfred, his wife, Eva, and Eva's little niece Andrea, who cried every night because Daddy and Mommy Feigenbaum had landed in a concentration camp.

Since he would have to wait for some time, he unpacked his rye sandwiches filled with tuna fish, tomato, salt, and egg over which Pierrette, who had been sharing his bed for a year, had trickled olive oil as was her habit, and she could not change.

After handing over a sandwich to his cousin he took out his chessboard.

Meanwhile Pierrette was placing a fresh bouquet of anemones on the living-room table and then waking up the child.

Blumenfeld's acquaintance, the numismatist Dr. Heillein, who had purchased a considerable part of Blumenfeld's collection, has become propaganda leader of his district. He is lying back propped up by an extra cushion behind his back and preparing the lecture he is to hold at the primary school the next day. "Bleeding Frontiers, the Enslavement of Germany: The Jew Is Capitalizing on the German Plight." That is to be the subject matter, to be continued a week later with "Adolf Hitler and the German Uprising."

Oswald Blatt, son of the village teacher, made off just before the graduating exam. He did not want to be beaten up anymore for pedagogical reasons and has now become, among other things, a messenger in a ministry, which he keeps quiet, however.

Frau Pfeifer was cursing. Her sons had not even bothered to put the dirty dishes in the sink, presenting an appealing sight first thing in the morning when she entered the kitchen still half asleep in her dressing gown.

Her eldest son had fallen in the war for the sake of the Fatherland and final victory.

Her second son had also suffered a tragic death: he had fallen from a tank during an exercise and broken his neck. Not even a hero's death that could have filled the members of the family with pride.

The second youngest was still in bed, having a wet dream. No one took offense. Little Karl was to be called up soon, too.

The youngest was waiting for all to grow still in the bed next to him, for he did not want to disturb anyone although he desperately needed to go to the bathroom.

Werner Eckstein was reading a novel, *Hero in the Thick of Night*.

Shame, he thought, for the Wehrmacht soldier had managed to rescue the woman from the clutches of the Jewish debaucher so she could faint calmly before he could rape her.

Werner's former classmate Uhland had told too many jokes and had been sent to a concentration camp, where he had just exchanged a silver fountain pen for a fat slice of sausage.

Werner's mother was cooking cabbage.

His father was drinking a beer. Too early, many would say. Too early, Herr Eckstein.

The former baker Uhland was sleeping off his intoxication in the police station. His poor mother had died shortly after his enforced sterilization. Now there was no one to prohibit his drinking. That he had not been done away with was a mystery to everyone.

Herr Mehler, arrested because of his homosexual activities, was working in Buchenwald in the shoe workshop and stretching the boots of the camp commander. He no longer thought about his wife, but instead thought of his children very often.

The union leader Ulrich Tilling was back in prison. High treason. Four years this time.

His brother Volker sought to comfort his mother and prepared some sandwiches. They were planning a trip to the country to distract his mother from her brooding.

Police constable Erich Hagel was still in bed. His uniform was hanging on the door. He had been clever enough upon his release not to go to the SA but to go straight to the SS. He was now first officer and was sure to make it to staff officer by next year — eliminating Ella Feigenbaum had opened many doors to him.

Ernst Fuchs stood up straight and hoped that the SS man would pass over him this time, too, without looking at him. He was hungry and scared.

Peter was also hungry, and put his new model airplane up on the shelf, although he had not started painting it yet. Then he went into the kitchen and let his mother, the pussycat, pour the still-warm ersatz coffee into his cup.

His father was in the bathroom. After the story with stupid Anna he had stopped smoking and was generally not as communicative as before.

Herr Rößler, three months after he had been informed, with the heartfelt sympathy of the doctors and the employees of the institute, of the loss of his daughter and told to find consolation in the knowledge that the death of his daughter had released her from her severe, incurable sufferings — her death was brought about by an phenol injection directly in the heart — swallowed two bottles of sleeping pills. For he had not found any consolation and had to think of Anna continually and therefore, at the time at which we have to conclude, he was already dead.

Dead, too, were:

Klara Fuchs and her son David.

Käthe Simon, formerly Fuchs, and Ernst Simon, her husband.

Otta Fuchs and her mother.

Reinhard, Dora, and Hermann Lipmann, last residents in Buchenwald.

Reinhard's Aunt Helene and her husband Leo, who in spite of his numerous brochures, written in his free time, never managed to convince the German citizens of Christian belief that he and his fellow German citizens of Jewish belief were not subhumans to be exterminated.

His brother Ernst — in spite of his fleeing to a neighboring country he ended up where he had to end up.

Richard Kahn of Richard Kahn, Inc., qualified real estate agent, plumber on the run, lastly number 547811, and his wife, Else. (While Herr Kahn survived the death of his sons, Dani and Benjamin, by several months, Frau Kahn was struck off the camp lists shortly thereafter.)

The opera singer Werner Kurzig — he died a natural death in a small guesthouse in Switzerland.

Seven hundred sixty-six men, women, and children of Transport Number 17 from Drancy — they arrived at four in the morning and at 5:50 A.M. were skillfully eliminated.

Professor Dr. Justus Bernstein, chief editor of a cultural magazine — he had seen the synagogues burn — his wife, and their daughter, Cilly.

Karl Schneider, former owner of the former O.B. department store.

Max, Felice, and Leo Lewinter. Adieu.

Thirty-five of the forty male residents of the fishing village.

Herr Bernhard and a further twenty men, seized in the operation that was to contribute to the stamping out of homosexuality in Germany.

All the men, women, and children of the transport from Wilna — before evening fell they had all been shot in front of the ditch. It had been done hurriedly because there were not any searchlights.

The married couple the Recktenwalds. They refused to respond to the "German greeting," came to Dachau, and then, as Herr and Frau Recktenwald were closely connected to the Jehovah's Witnesses, sent to the East.

The young Pole Peter Baslewicz. *Do widzenia.*

The communist Karl Kowalsky. *Salut*!

Little Löwy, his father, his mother, and his sister.

Stupid Anna.

Karl Streng is scolding a whore who will not keep her room clean.

The whore listens passively, staring down at her shoes that arrived with a transport from Greece, already disinfected, and thinks, the old eunuch.

Corporal Zink was sitting with Vogt at the dinner table. After seeing the transport from Wilna being shot to death he had taken sick leave and had now come back to the front, strengthened and with fresh courage after two weeks with Berti in the barn.

"All interventions must be well calculated," said Vogt, well known for his opinions, "and we have to strike quickly. A special operation has to be prepared and well thought through. The Jews are a crafty race."

"Yes," replied the accountant, whom everybody just called Accountant because his name sounded so Slavic, and looked over to Zink's plate. He was buttering two slices of bread thickly with butter. "Our boys will certainly master that."

The waitress Berti has let the milk boil over and gets a slap in the face, for these days nothing must be burnt. She takes it without a fight. She wants to marry the proprietor's son, the darling Zink, and will not be so easily shaken off. On his next home leave she will try to get pregnant by him.

Marianne Brackmann threw up. She was pregnant. After it was ascertained in the interests of the healthy body of the Volk that Marianne was suitable for marriage — Father Brackmann may be a friend of the Jews and a music lover but that is not, thank God, despoiling — she has married at last. She has also received a loan for her marital status, because now she is a future wife, and a housewife should not work.

Everyone is happy about it. Marianne, who was not partial to her work as a secretary. Father, and Mother Brackmann. And even Erna was happy, although Ecki did not want to marry her and she had every reason to be jealous, since she did not possess anything, and Marianne possessed so much.

The local group leader, Dieter Walter, has also married again. This time a nice girl, however, a brown sister who is already in the kitchen as he sleeps.

His divorced wife, Vicki, went down a slippery path after the story with the compact. She had an affair with the Jew Blumenfeld and with a Frenchman. Now she is sitting on a wooden bunk in a camp, scratching her head. Her romances have made her guilty.

Detective Mehring has his day off and throws the stick with an impatient movement for the dog to bring back. He did not get the raise in salary and is annoyed. From now on he will not work quite so conscientiously.

Frau Liselotte Schneider, formerly Oppenheimer, is scolding her maid, Fatima, whom she suspects of theft. Her two sons are sitting sweating on the verandah playing scat.

The social democrat Neumann was hanged. He was caught at the same time as Ulrich Tilling, but unlike Tilling was polished off right away.

The publisher Siegfried Scholem has emigrated to Palestine and is unsuccessfully trying his hand at a translation of *Cabal and Love*.

Herr Neunzlinger is sitting in the front room. He has just arrived and is terribly tired but wants to eat something before going to bed. Mommy is already standing proudly at the oven in her pearl necklace. Home leave, home leave, she cried from the stairs because nothing better came to her with the surge of feelings, and thus woke up little Nette and Thomas, who raced to their father with joy because he had most certainly brought something nice for them from the east.

His brother-in-law, the furrier Heinz Schröder, is drinking a glass of French tap water. He is in the Wehrmacht now. After the shop of his employer Alfred Blumenfeld was smashed up, he could not find another job. So it was very good timing with his call-up.

The secretary Marianne Flinker is getting out of the bus. Oswald has disappeared, along with the inventory, without a trace. Marianne is furious. She cannot help thinking of him in the night, though.

Dr. Johann Marburg is sleeping. The ring, his unlucky mascot, is lying on the bedside table next to him. He does not have a shift today, nor does he have to select at the infirmary.

His colleague Delmotte is snoring. He does not have the earlier shift either.

The camp prefect Tadeusz Lebowic steals a slice of bread. He is about to get orders to strike through Vera's number, among others, with a ruler. He swallows the bread on the way to the hospital building. The KZ guard is well-disposed today and looks the other way.

Bettina Feigenbaum is standing up straight. She, too, is a scribe today. Although a Jew, she speaks such a beautiful high German that the doctor likes her and has her keep the lists of the dead. She is crying now, standing up straight, and crying. How is her daughter Andrea getting along?

And Dr. Johann Paul Kremer is writing, after extracting muscle tissue, spleen, and liver: "Today fixated freshest material from the human liver, spleen, and pancreas."

For everyone was doing something that day on which the world crawled into the furthest-off hole of the dirty milky pathway, because God was playing hide-and-seek with Mars, Jupiter, Luna, and Earth. And God found Mars, Jupiter, and Luna, but not little Earth, who had run so far away. She held in her breath in joyful excitement and waited to be discovered, while God forgot all about her and played war with Mars. Forgot about her and did not see what was being done to his chosen people, to the people of Abraham, Isaac, Jacob, and Sara, who received a visitation from God when Abraham was one hundred, and bore him laughter.

Epilogue

After her parents had been taken away, Erika went back to the apartment immediately and packed the suitcases. There was no time to be lost. Going through the papers eventually they would realize that they had left one family member behind and would return. But she would not wait for them. She would not serve the child up to them on a silver platter. If they wanted the child, they would have to come looking for her.

They drove out to her brothers' in the country. Where else could they go? At first he did not want to take them in. He was up to his neck in trouble as it was without them. They wanted to draft him even though he was the only man on the farm.

They called her Käthe. It took a few days for the child to realize she had to change her name. She did not know the danger she was in and that they would all be in if she had been called by her real name. They stayed there for six years, although the agreement had been they would leave the farm again in a few weeks' time. Six years of fear. Above all at night.

After the war, Erika started making inquiries. Max's, Felice's, and Leo's whereabouts were unknown. Through the Red Cross she learned that the unknown residence of the Lewinter family at the end had been Buchenwald, and that Herr Lewinter had by a year outlived his wife and son, who were murdered immediately.

She waited until Lea had come of age before telling her.

They moved to Zurich. The Jewish World Association paid for Lea's education after some hesitation, for she, Erika, was not Jewish.

She had battled for custody of the girl. It was not easy. She was German, there were doubts. But finally victory was hers. She adopted Lea when she was fourteen, two years after her Bat Mitzvah.

She invested the reparation sum — Lea's father, before his fall from grace due to his descent, had been a respected sociologist — in a Swiss bank for her. More than anything she wanted to spit in the face of the official who had at that point calculated how much Lea would be paid monthly, how much the skin of a Jew was worth. She did not do it, did not once complain, for she felt she should not deprive the child of the little capital she was entitled to.

In 1957, Lea married an American Jew, who was in Zurich on business, and moved back with him to New York. On Lea's and her husband's insistence, Erika went with them. They moved into an apartment, just a block away from the Friedmanns' house, and she fulfilled an old dream of hers. She learned stenography.

Lea's children do not speak any German. Samuel, thirty-three today, has become a sociologist like his grandfather. He teaches at the university and has a three-year-old son.

Roberta, two years younger, works at a bank. Last year she went traveling in Europe again with the boyfriend she will be marrying next year, to Italy and Switzerland, where they went skiing. She has yet to set foot on German soil.

For a long time Lea could not speak about the war years, not even to Erika. About five years ago, at a seminar, she met Ernst Fuchs, a man who like her had lost all his family. With his help she learned how to come to terms with her past.

She realized as an almost sixty-year-old woman that she had still not forgiven her parents for leaving her behind and that her life had been determined by her fear of being left alone again. She understood that she felt guilty because she was the only one to survive, and that it was not her fault that she was alive.

Lea often thinks of her family, of her father and her mother, who remains in her memory a young woman — much younger than she herself today — because she was shot when she was twenty-eight.

From her parents' home she still had her parents' wedding photo and a silver cigarette case engraved with her father's initials, which Erika had packed as it was on the chest of drawers in the hallway.

Lea gave it to her son on his eighteenth birthday, since she thought it would be important to him to possess something from his family — as a sort of proof.

He lost the case after a week.

To begin with Lea was depressed, but then she felt a kind of inexplicable and liberating lightness spreading through her, as if after all the stormy years at sea she had finally thrown the ballast over the side of the tossing boat, to save herself from drowning.